D0535470

New York London Toronto Sydney Tokyo Singapore

SCRIBNER

BY THE SAME AUTHOR

SCREENPLAYS AND PLAYS

   My Beautiful Laundrette &
the Rainbow Sign

   Sammy and Rosie Get Laid

   London Kills Me

   Outskirts and Other Plays

FICTION

   The Buddha of Suburbia

NONFICTION

   The Faber Book of Pop
(edited with Jon Savage)

by

HANIF KUREISHI

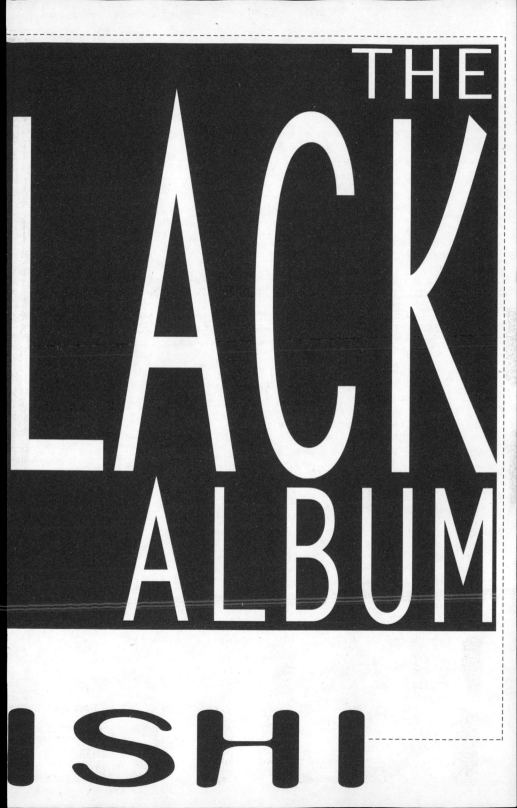

Scribner
1230 Avenue of the Americas
New York, NY 10020

This book is a work of fiction. Names, characters,
places, and incidents either are products of the author's imagination or are used fictitiously. Any re-
semblance to actual events or locales or persons,
living or dead, is entirely coincidental.

Copyright © 1995 by Hanif Kureishi

All rights reserved,
including the right of reproduction
in whole or in part in any form.

First Scribner edition 1995
First published in Great Britain by Faber & Faber
Limited

SCRIBNER and design are
trademarks of Simon & Schuster Inc.

Designed by Hyun Joo Kim

Manufactured in the United States of America

10 9 8 7 6 5 4 3 2 1

Library of Congress Cataloging in Publication Data
Kureishi, Hanif.
The black album/Hanif Kureishi.—1st ed.
p.   cm.
PR 6061.U68B77 1995   95-18668
823'.914—dc20   CIP

ISBN 0-684-81342-4

For Sachin and Carlo

C H A P T E R

1

One evening, as Shahid Hasan came out of the communal hall toilet, resecured the door with a piece of looped string, and stood buttoning himself under a dim bulb, the door of the room next to his opened and a man emerged, carrying a briefcase. He was slight, wearing an open-necked shirt, brown shoes, and a suit that was not fawn or much of any color—it wasn't that kind of suit.

Shahid was surprised. The college had allocated him a bed-sitting-room in a house beside a Chinese restaurant in Kilburn, northwest London. The many rooms in the six-floor building were filled with Africans, Irish people, Pakistanis, and even a group of English students. The various tenants played music, smoked dope, and filled the dingy corridors with the smell of bargain aftershave and boiled goat, which odor, amongst others, caused the wallpaper to droop from the walls like ancient scrolls. At all hours, though favoring the night, the occupants disputed in several languages, castigated their dogs, praised their birds, and practiced the trumpet. But until that moment Shahid hadn't heard a sound from next door. Presuming the room wasn't let, he had, he was afraid, made uninhibited noises, of which he was now embarrassed.

The lightbulb gave out: each flight of stairs was illuminated by a push-button light sweetly timed to switch off before you reached your destination, however swiftly you moved. The man blinked at Shahid through the gloom and seemed to bar his way. Shahid was about to apologize when his neighbor said a word in Urdu. Shahid replied, and the man, as if having an idea confirmed, took another step forward, offered his hand, and introduced himself as Riaz Al-Hussain.

Shahid's initial impression had been that Riaz was in his forties, but when the sallow, balding man spoke, he could see that Riaz was at most ten years older than he was, with a fastidious manner and weak, bookwormy eyes.

But this gentle way was surely deceptive. The man had to have something formidable in him, for as they shared friendly exchanges and confirmed they were both studying at the local college, he observed Shahid intently, as if he'd look right into him, which made Shahid feel both pleased that someone was taking an interest and also a little exposed and tense.

The man decided something. "Let's go."

"Where?"

He placed his hand on Shahid's arm. "Come."

Shahid was led willingly, but for reasons he didn't understand, down two flights of stairs, past the bicycles and piles of unclaimed mail in the hall, and out into the street. Sniffing the air, Riaz turned and instructed him, kindly, to fetch a jacket and scarf, if he had one. They seemed to be embarking on a journey.

When Shahid had wrapped himself up and they began walking, Riaz spoke to him as if it had been some time since he liked someone so much or understood anyone so well.

"Have you eaten? When I am thinking and writing I forget for hours to eat and then I remember suddenly that I am ravenous. Are you like this?"

Shahid, who had barely received or been able to give an amica-

ble smile in the weeks since he'd started at college, was warming.
He said, "In the past few days my mouth has been watering for
good Indian food, but I'm not certain where to go."

"Naturally you miss such food. You are my fellow countryman."

"Well . . . not quite."

"Oh yes you are. I have observed you before."

"Have you? What was I doing?"

Riaz didn't reply, but walked rapidly in a straight line. To keep
up, and to avoid charging into the Irishmen who gathered outside
the pubs, Shahid had to jig on and off the pavement. This was a
road he was becoming familiar with; so far most of his notions
about London were based on it. During the day it was well known
for its secondhand shops and lined with rotten furniture. Miserable
proprietors would sit out in armchairs with damp, blistered tables
in front of them, reading the racing papers beneath the tasseled
shades of 1940s standard lamps; stained mattresses with puddles on
their plastic covers would be piled up around them, like sandbags.

Riaz appeared to take no interest in the life around him. Shahid
wondered if he was trying to solve a philosophical problem or was,
perhaps, hurrying to an appointment and merely required company for the journey.

Before Shahid came to the city, sat in the Kent countryside
dreaming of how rough and mixed London would be, his brother
Chili had loaned him *Mean Streets* and *Taxi Driver* as preparation.
But they were eventful films which hadn't steadied him for such
mundane poverty. On his first day he had seen a poor woman,
wearing only plastic sandals on her feet, drag three children across
the street and, there on the other side, remove her shoes and beat
them across the arms.

He wondered, too, whether a nearby asylum had been recently
closed down, since day and night on the High Road, dozens of ex-
hibitionists, gabblers, and maniacs yelled into the air. One man with
a shaved head stood all day in a doorway with his fists clenched,
mumbling. Derelict young men—Shahid had at first presumed they
were students—clutched beer cans like hand grenades; later, he'd see

them crashed out in doorways, with fluids seeping from them, as if they'd been pissed on by dogs. There was a girl who spent the day collecting firewood from building sites and skips.

All the same, the different odors of Indian, Chinese, Italian, and Greek food wafting from open doorways gladdened Shahid, as they had done the first time he passed them, full of anticipation and expectation, humping his suitcases. Between the restaurants, though, many of the shops had been closed down and boarded over; or they'd been converted to thrift or charity shops. Shahid had considered Londoners particularly munificent, until his Pakistani landlord explained, laughing, that the origin of such shops was bankruptcy rather than virtue.

When Riaz spoke again, he didn't look at Shahid but said, "Naturally you are hardworking. We all are who come here. But you are also dedicated to something serious."

"Am I?"

"I am without a doubt over your earnestness."

Shahid wasn't ready to question Riaz's understanding. What surprised him was the intimacy of the remark. Perhaps Shahid had been among too many undemonstrative English people lately.

"Yes, I have made up my mind to work very hard at college, because I—"

"This restaurant is excellent. The food is simple. Ordinary people eat here."

"I will remember it," said Shahid.

"Without a doubt."

Situated between a Caribbean wig center and a Romanian restaurant—behind filthy net curtains sat rows of plain white chairs and stark tables—was an Indian café, into which Shahid followed his new companion.

"You will really feel at home."

How did Riaz know he would feel at home in a place with five Formica tables and screwed-down red bucket seats, all as brightly lit under white neon as a police cell?

Each dish was displayed in rectangular steel pans beneath a glass counter, and on each was taped a sign indicating whether it was "korjet" or "oberjean." The food was heated in two microwaves which sat on a shelf. On the wall was a brass plate inscribed with Koranic verses. A boy, whom Shahid guessed to be the owner's son, sat at a table doing his homework.

Possibly Riaz feared he had been a little peremptory with his new friend, for as Shahid examined the food he said more softly, "Even if you've already eaten, perhaps you would sit with me. Or is it bothering you too much to keep me company?"

"Not in the least."

"You see, it is not just your college work I was referring to here. You are searching for something."

"I'm not sure," Shahid said pensively. "But you could be right."

Shahid sat down while Riaz went to the counter and ordered from the owner, whose teeth were scarlet from betel chewing. He ladled the food onto plastic plates and placed them inside the microwave. Shahid overheard Riaz asking the owner about his other son, Farhat.

Blood-teeth then had his youngest boy interrupt his homework to carry the food to the customers.

"Where's your brother now?" Riaz whispered to the boy, sitting down.

The boy glanced at his father, as if to ensure he wasn't listening. "Hat studying. Upstairs. Not allowed out tonight. Dadda very annoyed."

Riaz gave a little nod. "Tell him I'll see him tomorrow."

"OK."

After this odd business Riaz and Shahid tore with scorching fingers into the hot chapattis, soaking them in dhal and oily keema. When Shahid looked up and saw Riaz eating in this way—and he had rarely seen anyone eating so quickly, as if he were fueling a machine—he thought, what a stroke of luck! So far, waiting for college life to really start—he had wanted to be challenged intellectually, and in every other way—all he'd done was read and write, attend lectures, and wander around. He went to the cinema or obtained the cheapest theater seats, and one night he had attended a socialist political meeting. He went to Piccadilly and sat for an hour on the steps of Eros, hoping to meet a woman; wandered around Leicester Square and Covent Garden; entered an "erotic" bar where a woman sat beside him for ten minutes and a man tried to charge him 100 pounds for a bottle of fizzy water, and punched him when he walked out. He had never felt more invisible; somehow this wasn't the "real" London.

"Did you know," Riaz said with his mouth full, "that the chili was discovered in South America? It was an Aztec word, and it came only to India during medieval times."

"I had no idea. But we call my brother Chili. Suits him."

"In what way?"

"It just does. Tell me what you're studying, Riaz."

"The law. For a long time I gave general and legal advice to the many poor and uneducated people in my district who came to me. As an informed amateur I did all I could to help them. Now I am taking up serious study."

"And where are you from?"

"Lahore. Originally."

"That 'originally' is a quite a big thing," Shahid said.

"The very biggest thing of all. You recognize that, eh? I was brought away to this country at fourteen."

Shahid established that Riaz had lived and worked "with the people, showing them their rights," in a Muslim community near Leeds. His accent was certainly a compound of both places, which explained why he sounded like a cross between J. B. Priestley and Zia Al Haq. But his English was precise and without slang; Shahid could feel the punctuation hanging in the air like netting.

Shahid was reminded of his uncle Asif, a journalist in Pakistan (imprisoned once by Zia for writing against his Islamization policies), who liked to assert that the only people who spoke good English now were subcontinentals. "They gave us the language but it is only we who know how to use it."

Mind you, uncle Asif, in whose house he and Chili used to stay every winter, lying in hammocks beneath the mango trees in the courtyard and discussing which parties to attend, liked to entertain his nephews with his satirical views. He'd say that the Pakistanis in

England now had to do everything, win the sports, present the news, and run the shops and businesses, as well as having to fuck the women. "Your country's gone to the wogs!" He labeled this "the brown man's burden."

Shahid's elder brother Chili had adopted this idea in his late teens, before he married the glamorous Zulma and their wedding video, longer than *The Godfather* (both parts), became essential viewing all over Karachi and even in Peshawar. Swaggering into the kitchen at breakfast after another conquest, he'd say, "We are having to do everything here now, yaar! It's our burden—but I can personally take it on!"

Now Shahid warned himself to keep quiet about his personal life. But Riaz didn't volunteer much more about himself and Shahid wondered whether there was something specific that Riaz wanted to put to him. He suspected that Riaz was going to ask him a favor. But he rejected his misgivings; he was determined not to be a closed person.

And so, minutes later, Shahid was explaining to Riaz that his parents and brother were travel agents. Twenty-five years ago Shahid's mother was a secretary and his father a clerk in a tiny agency. Now, although Papa was recently dead, the family owned two shops in Sevenoaks, Kent.

Riaz listened. "And did they lose themselves when they came here?" he said.

"Lose themselves?"

"That's what I asked."

It was a strange question. But wasn't this, after all, why he had come to college, to distance himself from the family and also to think about their lives and why they had come to England?

"You could be right. Maybe that is what has happened. My family's work has always been to transport others around the world. They never go anywhere themselves, apart from Karachi once a year. They can't do anything but work. My brother Chili has a . . . a looser attitude. But then he is a different generation."

"Is he one of these dissipaters?"

"A dissipater?" Shahid almost choked on the evocative word.

"What gives you the right to say that?"

For a moment passion flared beneath Riaz's cool persistence, and he slapped his hand on the table. "What right?"

"Yes," Shahid asked.

"I'm suggesting, what do these people—our people—really have in their lives?"

"They have security and purpose, at least."

"They have lost themselves, then."

"How?"

"Surely, if that is all they have. It makes sense!"

Shahid looked at his fingers, which the food had turned the color of nicotine. Riaz was trying to provoke him. He regretted being so candid. But he was enjoying the discussion, too. He would say just this one thing.

"They have certainly lost something," he admitted. "They can't love the arts, for instance. And at the same time they despise their own work and laugh at their customers for boiling their ugly bodies on foreign beaches and going off to karaoke bars."

"Yes, they are precisely right! No Pakistani would dream of being such an idiot by the seaside—as yet. But soon—don't you think?—we will be parading about everywhere in these bikinis."

"That is what my mother and Chili are waiting for. Asian people to start taking package tours."

"Excuse me, can I ask you—I know you won't mind—but your family has some distinction, I can see."

"To me they have, yes."

"How, then, did they let you come to be at such a derelict college?"

With his shy air and none of the whiskey-drinking braggadocio of Shahid's uncle, for instance, Riaz seemed polite. But all the same, he wondered if he wasn't being slightly coerced by Riaz, as if he were trying to find out about him for some ulterior purpose. But what purpose could that be? Who was this man who could ask such questions?

"Because of a woman called Deedee Osgood. Do you know her?"

"Oh yes, she has a reputation at the college."

"Deservedly. And because I did badly at school."

"You?" Riaz said with concern. "But why?"

"At the time I had, you know, other things on my mind. My girlfriend was pregnant. She—er—had to have—"

"What?"

"A late abortion. It was a shabby business." He was apprehensive that this would make Riaz think badly of him, probably because he felt badly about it himself; and because he had, in the end, fled. Riaz did, indeed, sigh. Shahid went on, "After that, my parents forced me to work for them."

"And you respected them?"

"Not as much as I should. Because, instead of sending people to Ibiza I sat in the office reading Malcolm X and Maya Angelou and *The Souls of Black Folk*. I read about the Mutiny and Partition and Mountbatten. And one morning I started reading *Midnight's Children* in bed. Have you read that one?"

"I found it accurate about Bombay. But this time he has gone too far."

"Yes? I found the first book difficult initially. Its rhythms aren't Western. It dashes all over the place. Then I saw the author on television attacking racism, informing the people how it all arose. I tell you, I wanted to cheer. But it made me feel worse, because I was finally recognizing something. I began to get terrible feelings in my head. This is the truth now, Riaz—"

"Anything less is worthless."

"Yes." Shahid's heart began to beat hard. "I thought I was going mad."

"In what way?"

"Riaz, I—"

Just then a man rushed into the restaurant with such velocity that Shahid wondered if he might not dash out the back door followed by the police. He was able to halt himself, though, and vibrate beside them. Before he could speak he was hushed by Riaz with an authoritatively raised finger. Immediately he obeyed Riaz and sat down, quivering.

Riaz said, looking at Shahid, "Continue."

"I began to feel—"

"Yes, yes?"

"—in that part of the country, more of a freak than I did normally. I had been kicked around and chased a lot, you know. It made me terrifyingly sensitive. I kept thinking there was something I lacked."

Shahid's attention was now awkwardly divided between the man beside him, whom he'd barely taken in and who was now hearing of his deepest life, and the man opposite, who was waiting to know everything.

"Everywhere I went I was the only dark-skinned person. How did this make people see me? I began to be scared of going into certain places. I didn't know what they were thinking. I was convinced they were full of sneering and disgust and hatred. And if they were pleasant, I imagined they were hypocrites. I became paranoid. I couldn't go out. I knew I was confused and . . . fucked-up. But I didn't know what to do."

Shahid turned to the recent arrival, who was listening intently, nodding as if to a beat, his fingers tending to dance.

"I am hearing every moment of your soul cry," the man said. "Call me Chad."

"Shahid."

"He is my neighbor," Riaz explained to Chad.

They shook hands. Chad was a room-filler, a large, big-faced man who looked like an adolescent attempting to be an adult. He appeared to be bursting with appetite.

"There's a much worse thing." Shahid's mouth was dry and his hands had become unsteady. He attempted to lift his glass but spilled water on the table. "I don't think I can talk about it. But perhaps I should."

"You must," said Riaz.

"Yep," said Chad.

They leaned toward him, ignoring the water soaking into their sleeves.

Shahid said, "I wanted to be a racist."

Chad's seriousness became very serious indeed. With a glance at Riaz, he rose and went to the counter to fetch his food. Shahid waited for him to return. Riaz seemed to be humming to himself.

Shahid was trembling. "My mind was invaded by killing-nigger fantasies."

"What kind of thing are we talking about here?" Chad asked.

"What kind of thing? Of going around abusing Pakis, niggers, Chinks, Irish, any foreign scum. I slagged them under my breath whenever I saw them. I wanted to kick them up the arse. The thought of sleeping with Asian girls made me sick. I'm being very honest with you now—"

"Open your heart," Chad murmured. He didn't touch his food.

"Even when they came on to me, I couldn't bear it. I thought, you know, wink at an Asian girl and she'll want to marry you up. I wouldn't touch brown flesh, except with a branding iron. I hated all foreign bastards."

Riaz cried softly, "Oh, how is this done?"

"I argued . . . why can't I be a racist like everyone else? Why do I have to miss out on that privilege? Why is it only me who has to be good? Why can't I swagger around pissing on others for being inferior? I began to turn into one of them. I was becoming a monster."

"You didn't want to be a racist," Chad said. "I'm tellin' you that here and now for definite. And I'm informing you that it's all right now."

Chad looked at Riaz, who, with a compassionate incline of his head, confirmed that it was indeed all right now.

"Don't take it too personal." Chad indicated himself and Riaz. "Because we two are the ones who know. And we're not thinking of you in that racist way at all."

"I am a racist."

Chad smacked the table. "I already said you only a vessel!"

"I have wanted to join the British National Party."

"You have?"

"I would have filled in the forms—if they have forms." Shahid turned to Riaz. "How does one apply to such an organization?"

"Would the brother know?" Chad's temper was fraying. He referred to Riaz, who was now looking through his briefcase: he had given his definitive nod.

With strained patience Chad went on. "Listen. It been the longest, hardest century of racism in the history of everything. How can you not have picked up the vibe in this distorted way? There's a bit of Hitler in all white people—they've given that to you. It's all they ever done for us."

"Only those who purify themselves can escape it," Riaz said.

He got up and made for the door.

"The brother need fresh air," Chad said. "We all do. Phew."

Chad and Shahid followed Riaz back to the house. Shahid was in a turmoil, concerned that he had disturbed his new companions so much they wouldn't want his friendship. He liked Chad. Laughter took place over all his body—shoulders, stomach, chest—and his hands quivered like fans, as if someone had activated a motor in his stomach. Yet he had also chosen the arduous task of policing this excess laughter: Chad seemed ashamed of finding so much mirthful.

Outside Riaz's door, Shahid took Riaz's hand apprehensively and with some implicit deference. "I'm pleased to have met you this evening."

"Thank you." Riaz said. "I too have learned."

"Good-bye."

"No good-byes."

"Sorry?"

"We are pleased to have you with us." And Riaz smiled at Shahid as if he had passed some kind of test.

CHAPTER

2

M oments later, when Shahid unlocked the door to his own room, he found Chad behind him, wanting to shuffle in.

"Come," Shahid said unnecessarily.

Chad shut the door behind them and stood close to Shahid. He kept his voice low. "How is he?"

"Not bad," Shahid said, grasping that Chad was referring to Riaz and wondering if perhaps poor Riaz had some illness. He certainly didn't look in the full flower of health. "Want something to drink?"

"I'll have some water, later. Honestly, you are lucky enough to be living here beside him, and you are saying he seems not bad to you?"

"Why not?"

Chad studied Shahid's face as though he thought Shahid shared Riaz's secrets. "Good, good," he said, relieved. "I've been keeping away these last few days because there's some project special to his heart he has to complete. I know he'll offer me first look soon—it nearing the end. But he's not working too hard?"

"He's at it all the time," Shahid said confidently.

"There's a lot to get done."

"Absolutely." Emboldened, Shahid felt ready to ask a question. "You know exactly what he's working on?"

"Pardon?"

"I mean . . . is there anything more specific than normal?"

"But he won't talk about it, Shahid."

"I know, I know. But—"

"Yeah, it something special. As well there is the usual—letters to MPs, the Home Office, and the immigration authorities. Articles for the newspapers. He trying as well to pump money from business to start a paper. He also up to something with the Iranians. He don' like to talk about that. 'Pect you know. Anyhow . . ."

Shahid noticed how sorrowful Chad's eyes were, as if there were some deep hurt there.

"What you said in the café—it touch my heart right through." He and Shahid knocked fists. "Good for saying it. A man who speaks is like a lion. You a lion." Chad held the door open. "Let's go."

"Where?"

"Come."

Shahid followed Chad as he had followed Riaz earlier.

Chad gave a coded rap on the door of the room that Shahid had thought was vacant. At a word from within they entered.

Riaz sat an overflowing desk with his back to the door, working under a lamp, with a view of the bingo hall opposite.

Chad put his finger to his lips. "Shh . . ."

Shahid appreciated seeing Riaz like this: he associated scholarship, study, and the thirst for knowledge with goodness.

Riaz's room was larger than Shahid's, with the same curling wallpaper. But it was infinitely more cluttered with books, papers, files, and letters. They were piled up on the floor and overflowed from filing cabinets and were somehow pasted to the windowsill, perhaps by mango chutney or Lucknow pickle. Shahid was sure that some of the crispy-looking files were made of nan and dried chapattis, contained old poppadoms, and were secured by cobwebs.

Upstairs, someone was playing a Donna Summer record and

male squeals could be heard. Shahid was about to smirk, but intuited quickly that neither of his new friends would share his amusement. Shahid wondered if Riaz was aware that their lodgings were inhabited by, besides everyone else, several gay men. Above Shahid was a queenie speed-freak, who incessantly cleaned the hallways. "You could breakfast off this linoleum," he'd say as anyone passed.

Behind Riaz's back Chad began to lug papers from one unstable stack to another. He glanced assuredly at the spines of disheveled tomes before carrying them from a chair to an inconvenient spot on the floor where, tiptoeing backward, he tripped over them. When Chad dropped some papers in his arms, Shahid, getting into the spirit of the thing, attempted to shift them to the windowsill—but without having to breathe in.

A shelf collapsed, delivering a score of Arabic books onto the floor; Chad plucked from beneath them a loofah, several shirts, a pair of underpants, and numerous brown socks. For a moment he held them up, looking as though he thought the photocopier was the most satisfactory location for soiled clothes. But he passed them to Shahid. Then he peeled open a plastic bag while Shahid bundled the washing in.

"Someone might as well take it to the laundrette."

"Needs it." Shahid sniffed.

Chad was looking at him in an inquiring way. "Laundrette stays open all night."

"What a great city this is."

"With many temptations for young men."

"Oh yes!" Shahid agreed. "Thank God."

"But laundrette is useful."

"Very."

Shahid grasped from Chad's look that he meant him to take Riaz's washing to the laundrette! It was outrageous. He was about to decline but instead hesitated. Wouldn't it be churlish to refuse? Shahid had been seeking interesting Asian companions. Why did he have to start getting proud when things were looking up? Did he want to spend every evening alone?

When Shahid left the room, he saw that Chad was smiling to himself. Even Shahid chortled as he swung down the street with the bag over his shoulder.

It was late and the laundrette was deserted. He stuck the stink in the machine, inserted coins on the silver shelf, pressed it in, and got out.

He turned off the main road and walked toward a vast dark housing project. Exhilarated by the relief of what he'd confessed in the restaurant, he moved quickly, hardly caring where he was. He found himself going down a flight of stairs and climbing through the underground parking area, devoid of cars and only containing partially burned rubbish. It was filthy, and some thug might easily have sprung out with a knife. But he wasn't apprehensive. Rather the spooky shadows of the city than the thin sunlight of the countryside.

He laid out his jacket and sat down under a muddy light. He would note down whatever took his interest, as if making a record could keep at bay the excesses of reality, like a talisman.

Papa had been ill. Finally, nine months ago, he died of a heart attack. Without him the family had seemed to fly apart. Shahid had left his girlfriend acrimoniously. Zulma and Chili had been fighting. His mother had been unhappy and without purpose. It had been a rotten time. Shahid wanted a new start with new people in a new place. The city would feel like his; he wouldn't be excluded; there had to be ways in which he could belong.

He put away his pen and returned to the laundrette. The washing had gone; even the bag had disappeared. He dashed to the other machines but none of them revealed Riaz's colorless items. He charged out into the street but there was no legging suspect.

There was only broken glass beneath his feet and a black kid crashing across the pavement on a bicycle, pitching it down, and running into a burger bar; a man with his head over a rubbish bag, stuffing half a pie into his mouth, and a woman screaming from a window, "Go away, cunt, or I'll sort you!" Two people lay end to end in a rain-swept doorway under a mound of newspapers and cardboard; empty cider bottles stood at their head like skittles. The streets of deserted burger bars, kebab houses, and shuttered shop fronts mocked him, as they did, he realized, anyone who'd contrived no escape.

Shahid kicked and thumped the washing machine, but it had been built for abuse. Outside, he stomped around in the cold, fearful of returning to Riaz's room. He certainly didn't feel like describing this area of thieves, hundred-carat cunts, and ruthless detritus.

Riaz was in the same position and just as concentrated, despite Chad stroking his ink pots with a feather duster. It was a scene of silent, late-night contentment. Would Shahid be allowed in here again? He wanted to begin his explanation but was forced to wait until Chad had moved away from Riaz.

"Chad, this is terrible, but it's not my fault. I've—I've—er—lost the clothes."

"Sorry?"

"You know the clothes you gave me to wash?"

"Riaz's clothes?"

"They've been stolen."

Chad glanced over at Riaz but he was writing hard. He whispered, "You've lost the brother's kit?"

"I'm afraid so."

"I don't believe you could have done that."

"Chad, listen, tell me this. He's not, you know, particularly proud of his clothes, is he?"

"He's not proud full stop."

"No, no, I'm not saying that, it's just—"

"What is your point?"

Shahid faltered and choked back a sob. "I'm truly sorry."

"What use is that?"

"I've made a big mistake."

There was a brisk rap at the door.

Chad nodded toward Riaz. "Didn't you stand guard on the brother's clothes?"

"I didn't think anyone would steal a load of—"

Chad glared at him and went to the door.

Shahid continued: "I didn't, Chad. I want to learn, but I'm hurled into London, it's gigantic, and everything's anonymous! Lunatics are everywhere but most of them look normal! Chad—will he forgive me?"

"That we will have to see. Are you saying you want me to sort it for you?"

"Can you?"

"I'll try to see what I can do. But this is serious."

"I know, I know."

"Wait a minute," Chad said.

A man with a crew cut and a full black beard stood at the door carrying a green holdall. Riaz turned to acknowledge him and the man greeted him from where he stood, unbuttoning his long overcoat to reveal a butcher's overall smeared with blood.

"You asked for this equipment," he said.

"Yes."

He passed the clanking holdall to Chad, who peered into it, stuck his hand inside, and pulled out a butcher's knife. He touched the blade.

"Wicked. Ta very much, Zia. I'll return them—when we've finished."

The man nodded, bowed at Shahid and went away. Chad pushed the bag under a chair and resumed their business.

"So you just threw everything away?"

"It was stolen, Chad!"

Chad thought for a moment. "Immorality is rife outside. Thing is, we got to do something before the brother need a change of clothes."

"How long could that be?"

"Who knows? Could be in five weeks. Or in five minutes. He

might just jump up and decide to wear that stuff." Shahid suspected
it wouldn't be in five minutes. "What have you got in your room?"

"Bed, table, a bunch of Prince records, and a ton of books."

Chad looked interested. "Did you say Prince?"

"Yeah."

"Let me have a look."

"What for?"

"I'd better check them out."

"Why?"

"Don't ask so many questions, that's the first thing, if you want me
to save your skin. Now get out of my way. This is an extra-urgent
emergency!"

Chad strode into Shahid's room and began rooting through a
cardboard box on the floor which contained Shahid's Prince
records. Chad was riveted, but surely this was irrelevant to the matter of Riaz's clothes?

"What is it—you got a thing about Prince?"

"Me?" Chad shook his head emphatically and closed the box.
"Pop music is not good for me. Nor for anyone. Why are you making me think about that now?"

"Am I doing that?"

"Things are looking real bad at the moment. Now. Let me
check to see you got The Black Album." He peered interestedly
into the box again. "Not many people have. Hey, you got the bootleg CD, too," he added with a sneer. "Where d'you get that?"

"Camden market."

"Right. It good for bootlegs."

"Want to hear it?"

"Never!"

Chad tore himself away from Prince, stood up, and took in the
contents of the room.

In his bedroom at home Shahid would take art books out from
the library and prop them open so that while he was shaving, or
just pacing about lamenting his life, he would look at a Rembrandt
or Picasso or Vermeer, and try to understand them.

Here he had covered large areas of the brown-and-yellow strobing wallpaper with his favorite postcards. There were many Matisses—he liked to think that Matisse was the one artist about whom nothing bad could be said; Blu-tacked up were Liotard's portrait of Mary Gunning, Peter Blake's *Venice Beach* meeting of himself, Hockney, and Howard Hodgkin, several Picassos, Millais's strange *Isabella*, a photograph of Allen Ginsberg, William Burroughs, and Jean Genet, Jane Birkin lying on a bed, and dozens of others which he had torn from his bedroom and brought to London.

Chad said, "An' you got a ton of books here."

"Yeah, and many more at home."

"How come?"

Shahid explained that his satirical uncle Asif had returned to Pakistan leaving his books in Papa's house. Shahid had picked up Joad, Laski, and Popper, and studies of Freud, along with fiction by Maupassant, Henry Miller, and the Russians. He had also gone to the library almost every day; desultory reading was his greatest pleasure, with interruptions for pop records. He had moved from book to book as on steppingstones, both for fun and out of fear of being with people who had knowledge which might exclude him.

Shahid said, "Mostly I prefer novels and stories now. I usually got five at least going on."

"Why do you read 'em?"

"Why?"

"Yeah. What's the point?"

Chad looked hostile. It wasn't an objective inquiry. So inexplicable to Shahid was this opposition that he forgot about Riaz's clothes and became intrigued. He didn't think anyone had asked him such a question before. He certainly hadn't expected it of Chad. But it was exactly to discuss such subjects—the meaning and purpose of the novel, for example, its place in society—that he had come so keenly to college.

He looked ardently at the books piled on the desk. Open one and out would soar, as if trapped within, once-upon-a-times, opensesames, marriages like those of Swann and Odette or Levin and Kitty, even Sheherazade and King Shahriya. The most fantastic characters, Raskolnikov, Joseph K., Boule De Suif, Ali Baba, made of ink but living always, were entrapped in the profoundest dilemmas of living. How would he begin to answer Chad?

He began, "I've always loved stories."

Chad interrupted: "How old are you—eight? Aren't there millions of serious things to be done?" Chad pointed toward the window. "Out there . . . it's genocide. Rape. Oppression. Murder. The history of this world is—slaughter. And you reading stories like some old grandma."

"You make it sound as though I were injecting myself with heroin."

"Good comparison. Nice one."

"But don't writers try to explain genocide and that kind of thing? Novels are like a picture of life. Just now I'm reading this one by Dostoevsky, *The Possessed*—"

"You can't impress me. What about the dispossessed? Eh? Go out on the street now and ask people what they read lately. The *Sun*; maybe, or the *Daily Express*."

"That's right. Sometimes I see certain people and I want to grab them and say, read this story by Maupassant or Faulkner, this mustn't be ignored, a man made it, it's better than television!"

"It's true, people in the West, they think they're so civilized an' educated an' superior, and ninety percent of them read stuff you wouldn't wipe your arse on. But Shahid, I learned something a little while ago."

"What?"

"There's more to life than entertaining ourselves!"

"Literature is more than entertainment." Aware of his earnest excitement, Shahid tried to curb it. He picked up a book, flipped through it, and declared nonchalantly, "Books are not as difficult as they look."

Chad flushed at his patronizing tone. "Yeah—it how intellectual people elevate themselves above ordinary ones!"

"But Chad, surely intellectual people think more than ordinary people? That must be good."

Shahid's contrived gentleness seemed to be making things worse.

"Good? What do intellectuals know about good?" Chad was becoming incensed by Shahid's naïveté. Then he made a show of calming himself. "Brother, you got a lot to learn. But let's waste no more time discussing frippery. We got many real things to accomplish. You made a heavy error tonight."

"I'm so sorry, Chad."

"Stop that apologizing before you give me a pain." Chad rubbed his forehead. "Maybe we can repair it."

"How?"

Chad went to the cupboard, yanked out a drawer, and held up Shahid's underpants and Gap jeans as if considering them for purchase. Then, laying them on the bed, he opened the wardrobe with such force the door broke from its hinges. He flung it across the room as if it were a matchbox. After a brief but critical inspection he began stuffing Shahid's clothes into the bag he dragged from the bottom of the wardrobe, including his pure cotton ruby socks, a green Fred Perry shirt, and some white Italian T-shirts that had belonged to Chili.

"What are you doing?"

"These are for brother Riaz."

"But Chad—"

"What now?"

"Are you sure they'll suit him?"

"You think they won't?"

"I can't see him in the Fred."

"No?"

"Let me put it back. And this purple number, might make him look a bit effeminate."

"What?"

"Like a poof. Here."

"No, no," Chad, pulled it away. "What choice do we have? Do

you want the brother to go up and down the street naked and catching pneumonia due to your foolish stupidity?"

"No," moaned Shahid, groping to salvage one of Chili's shirts before Chad sacked his closets. "I wouldn't want that."

"Hey, where d'you get this red Paul Smith shirt?"

"Paul Smith. He got a shop in Brighton."

"Riaz'll be thrilled," Chad said, holding it against his chest. "He look best in plain colors."

"Oh, good."

"Give us a hand, then. You are with us, aren't you?"

"Yes," Shahid replied. "Yes.

ext morning, on his way to Deedee Osgood's lecture—
and he looked forward to her lectures more than to
anyone else's—Shahid pressed his ear against Riaz's
door. As usual he heard no sound. Maybe the unusual
events of the previous evening—the strangers to whom
he'd sung of his soul, the stolen clothes and danger of
naked pneumonia, the butcher's visit plus machete, the
literature debate and ruby socks—had been a hallucina-
tion. Or maybe Riaz had gone to the mosque.

The college was a cramped Victorian building, an old
secondary school, twenty minutes' walk away. It was
sixty percent black and Asian, with an ineffective library
and no sports facilities. Its reputation was less in the aca-
demic area but more for gang rivalries, drugs, thieving,
and political violence. It was said that college reunions
were held in Wandsworth Prison.

In the early morning rush, as he shoved through the
turnstiles, past the two security guards who occasionally frisked students for weapons, and into the lightless
basement canteen for coffee, Shahid felt more spirited
than he had since starting the course. He had breakfast
with two people in his class, an Asian woman in salwar

kamiz and blue-jean jacket, and her friend, a young black woman
in baggy white dungarees, trainers, and round gold spectacles.
He couldn't wait to see Deedee Osgood.

He had first met her because of
a club on the Brighton seafront called the Zap. It was so cool kids
from London used to bomb down to it on the last Saturday night
train. They'd dance all night, fuck and frolic on the beach at dawn,
and haul themselves home at lunch time. It was Shahid's first time.
He'd wanted to start going out again after splitting up with his girlfriend, so one evening a friend said he'd drive him down to the
most vigorous place he knew.

Shahid had never heard music so fast; the electronic beats went
like a jackhammer. Everyone wore Lycra cycling shorts and white
T-shirts imprinted with yellow smiley faces. They hugged and
kissed and stroked one another with an Elysian innocence. Early in
the morning he fell into conversation with a black London kid
who reckoned he'd been taught by a great woman.

Knowing it was time to take the initiative, he went to find her in
London. After knocking on her door, in the moment before she introduced herself, he thought she was a student. Her office was only
three times the size of a telephone booth. Pinned above the desk
were pictures of Prince, Madonna, and Oscar Wilde, with a quote
beneath them, "All limitations are prisons."

Deedee interrogated him about his life in Sevenoaks and his
reading. Despite her difficult questions about Wright and Ellison,
Alice Walker and Toni Morrison, she was willing him to do well, he
could feel that.

Noticing him looking at the Prince photograph, she said, "You
like Prince?"

He nodded.

"Why?"

Idly he said, "Well, the sound."

"Anything else?"

Grasping that this was not chatter but part of the interview, he strained to order his words into sense, but for months he'd barely spoken to anyone with half a brain. She coaxed him. "He's half black and half white, half man, half woman, half size, feminine but macho, too. His work contains and extends the history of black American music, Little Richard, James Brown, Sly Stone, Hendrix . . ."

"He's a river of talent. He can play soul and funk and rock and rap—"

Off he went, being exemplary, until, that is, she crossed her legs and tugged her skirt down. He had, so far, successfully kept his eyes averted from her breasts and legs. But the whole eloquent movement—what amounted in that room to an erotic landslide of rustling and hissing—was so sensational and almost provided the total effect of a Prince concert that his mind took off into a scenario about how he might be able to tape-record the whisper of her legs, copy it, add a backbeat, and play it through his headphones.

"Why don't you write a paper on him?"

"For the course?"

Shahid couldn't think of anything he'd like more.

He hated saying good-bye that day, and taking the tube to Victoria Station. The city turned into suburbs; the suburbs into the English countryside. The train returned him to the house where his father no longer was. Not that Papa's death had decreased the number of people living there. But his absence at the center of things had made the place more cruelly anarchic, particularly since Chili's wife, Zulma, had returned and she made Shahid the special target of her teasing. But at least Shahid had a task; for ages he'd listened only to Prince.

Yet he was discomfited by the freedom of instruction Deedee offered. She and other postmodern types encouraged their students to study anything that took their interest, from Madonna's hair to a history of the leather jacket. Was it really learning or only diversion dressed up in the latest words? Were students in better colleges studying stuff to give them the advantage in life? Could this place be like those youth clubs that merely kept bad kids out of trouble? He didn't know. But he would get away at last, and read and write and find intelligent people to discuss with. Maybe even Deedee Osgood herself would have time for him. She was pleased by how much he'd read. At home he still had a few school friends, but in the past three years had lost interest in most of them; some he had come to despise for their lack of hope. Almost all were unemployed. And their parents, usually patriotic people and proud of the Union Jack, knew nothing of their own culture. Few of them even had books in their houses—not purchased, opened books, but only gardening guides, atlases, *Reader's Digests*.

The summer had passed slowly. In August he was packing for college; every day he wished he were already there.

"Listen."

She looked particularly keen and mischievous this morning. Shahid hurried into his usual seat, the place he called "the stalls," in the middle of the front row. From here none of her gestures would escape him.

As the other students sat down in the "circle" and "the gods" she put on a tape he recognized. Chili had long ago passed Hendrix's "Star-Spangled Banner" on to Shahid, preferring George Clinton. Two kids stuck their fingers in their ears and Sadiq—a cool Asian boy with whom Shahid had chatted—rolled his eyes. For a moment their lecturer looked confused. Shahid could have whacked them. What other teacher would kick off the morning with Hendrix?

"What's that stand for?" she asked.

Shahid's hand shot up. He couldn't sit still.

"Yes, Shahid?"

"America."

"America, indeed. Our subject today."

To his relief, she was not discouraged. Without notes, and as if she were addressing each student individually, she described how, around the time of Presley, Negroes couldn't even see a film in downtown Washington, their own capital. Miscegenation was illegal in half the country. Fifteen-year-old Emmett Till was lynched in 1955 for whistling at a white woman. Her voice modulated with emotion as she spoke of King, Malcolm, Cleaver, Davis, and the freedom riders.

Shahid listened exultantly and scribbled continuously. The living, breathing history of struggle: how had he lived so long without this knowledge? Where had they kept it? Who else were they concealing it from?

She concluded by playing Marvin Gaye's "What's Going on?"

Because he wanted to hear her talk for the rest of the morning as well as the afternoon, and, for that matter, the whole weekend, he asked a question and pursued it with a hypothesis, followed by a query and a factual inquiry. He could have continued but the churlish class were restless for their mid-morning crisps.

He was the first to leave, heading for the library to write up his notes. But as he walked from the lecture room—a dilapidated outbuilding at the rear of the school—he heard his name softly called, and turned. She was behind him, books, newspapers, and student essays tumbling, as usual, from her arms.

"I liked your questions."

"Thank you, Miss."

She winced. "For God's sake, don't call me that."

He hurried to keep up as they walked through the college. Two women in his class crossed ahead of them, one hissing at him, "Blackboard monitor!" Optimism made him reckless; sycophancy was the least of his fears; he had to push himself forward, this was his life! With as little concern as he could muster, he asked, "What are you doing now?"

"Why, is there something you would like to do?"

"Have coffee."

She looked at him. "But why not?"

He didn't think to ask if they might try a place outside the college. So they queued for their drinks, before sitting rather self-consciously in the center of the canteen. Other students kept glancing their way. She was popular, but it was unusual to see a student and staff member sitting together. There were giggles and remarks.

Perhaps because of this, she and Shahid didn't, at first, have much to say. She seemed a little uncomfortable and reserved, as if now she didn't know what they were doing there. Perhaps she expected him to whine on about how the college wasn't suiting him so far.

He said, "D'you like your students?"

She said pointedly, "I believe in giving my students my full attention—but only when they deserve it."

Was she talking about him, he wondered. But no; she went on to say, she was too often tempted to mother them, especially the Asian girls. Two had even come to live in her house. "That was heavy."

"In what way?"

She was about to say but checked herself and grimaced. "We'll save that discussion. I think it'll interest you."

Responsibility. Heaviness. She took things on; she wasn't afraid.

She asked him how he was coping. He'd been lonely, he said, and sometimes didn't know what to do with himself, in the evenings particularly. Fortunately, in the past few days, he'd run into people who'd excited him. With her fist under her chin she leaned toward him. "Who excites you here, then? What kind of people? The girls or the boys?"

"Just new friends."

"OK, I'm sorry."

She had blushed.

"It's all right," he said, also feeling flustered. "Have you read anything interesting lately?"

"Oh yes."

She was attentive and liked talking about books, especially if they were written by women. There was, too, an unruly edge to her, as if she didn't always feel the need to bother about good manners; there were more urgent things. He wondered if she'd been a hippie—they'd been quite romantic, hadn't they, and neglected social convention?—for she smoked and laughed at herself; and she would suddenly stretch, stick her arms in the air, and yawn; she was tired beyond belief; he was boring her. Her desires were strong and mixed, things could get out of hand with her; this college was too small. She wanted him to know this, he imagined, except it was difficult: she was a teacher and with students she continually had to remember herself, she could be misunderstood; if they spoke, much had to be implied.

This is a woman, he wanted to say; and there was everything to know. The others, such as they were, had lacked such pressure. He felt he needed to walk round the building a couple of times, to get some fresh air and remember who he was, before returning to her less distractedly. But he didn't want to part from her now, didn't want to be the one to say, "See you next time."

He said her lecture made him want to spend the day in the library.

She gathered her numerous things. "I'll walk with you."

The library was also in the basement and it was one long room, cramped and hot, like a submarine. The desks had been churned up by knives and many of the books had been stolen. But few students went there and he could be alone and contented.

"You're a good student." She laughed. "Unlike most people here."

"Why are the students not good?"

"Because they know there's no work. They're not being educated, just kept off the dole. I've never known such a lack of inner belief."

She looked at him as if about to say something more, but turned and left him to work.

He read for the course on colonialism and literature, determined to write an immense paper, riddled with quotes, weighed down by footnotes, brilliantly argued, which would require detailed discussion in her office.

When he had to take a break, leaving his desk in a fog of inchoate anger and illumination late in the afternoon, he had been concentrating so hard that he was surprised to find the college functioning as usual and the students still joshing each other on the narrow stairs which wound through the center of the building.

Across the canteen he spotted Chad and Riaz, who were sitting with a student Shahid recognized but didn't know, and with Sadiq. Their attention was taken by a middle-aged white man who wore wire-rimmed glasses, and a herringbone sports jacket and tie.

Shahid went and stood by their table. "Anyone want coffee?"

The white man was trying to speak but appeared to have something caught in his throat. He kept giving a kind of abrupt laugh, and his Adam's apple bobbed like a Ping-Pong ball on a drinking fountain. There was spittle on his chin. Shahid was afraid he was having a minor fit.

Taking advantage of the distraction, he quickly bent down to check Riaz's lower half under the table. He was wearing the same suit and socks as the day before. Shahid sat down and attempted to smile. Riaz ignored him. What if he had taken the theft of his belongings so badly that he was not only refusing to wear Shahid's donated clothes but had cut him off altogether? Shahid panicked. He didn't want to lose his new friends through such stupidity. Could it have already happened?

He didn't know, for these friends were still compelled by the man who, being collectively willed, was working his mouth, and thumping himself on the side of the head as if to repair a connection. Then the man smashed his fist into the table, shook hands with everyone, and strode away, waving to other smirking students as he thrashed out of the place.

"How very sad I am for him," said Riaz.

"You know Dr. Andrew Brownlow, Shahid?" said the other student. "I am Hat, by the way."

"The Mad Hatter," said Chad.

"His father owns the restaurant we went to," Riaz explained.

"Hi, Hat," said Shahid. "Good food."

"Any time. Sorry I missed you in there the other night. I hear you had plenty to say."

"Yeah," said Shahid.

"It's OK."

"Yeah," said Chad protectively. "This boy OK."

Hat had a soft voice and his face was as smooth as a young woman's. Shahid remembered seeing him in a class with his elbows on the desk, head in his hand, writing furiously. He'd noted then how enthusiastic and genial he was and liable to giggle at the wrong moment.

"I think I've seen Dr. Andrew around," Shahid said. "But I don't know who he is."

"Teaches history here. A couple of decades back he was at the Cambridge University—"

"The top student of his year," Chad interrupted.

"Yeah, I'm telling you," Hat said. "He come from the upper-middle-classes. He could have done any fine thing. They wanted him at Harvard. Or was it Yale, Chad?"

"He refused them places down."

"Yeah, he tol' them to get lost. He hated them all, his own class, his parents—everything. He come to this college to help us, the underprivileged niggers and wogs an' margin people. He's not a bad guy—for a Marxist-Communist."

"Leninist," said Sadiq.

"Yeah, a Marxist-Communist-Leninist type," Hat said. "He always strong on anti-racism. He hate imperialist fascism and white domination, yeah, Riaz?"

They looked at him and waited. After a pause Riaz murmured, "Andrew Brownlow has some personal integrity."

Chad nodded. "Problem is—"

"Yeah, problem is—" Hat made a miserable face but was suppressing a yelp. "He been developing this s-s-s-stutter."

"It's a new thing, then, is it?" Shahid asked.

"Yeah, it come on since the Communist states of Eastern Europe began collapsing. As each one goes over he get another syllable on his impediment, you know. In a lecture, it took him twenty minutes to get the first word out. He was going h . . . h . . . h . . . he

... he ... he ... We didn't know if he was trying to say Helsinki, hear this, help, or what."

"What was it, then?" Shahid asked.

"Hello."

"Hello?"

"Yeah, you idiot, the greeting. By the time Cuba goes he won't even manage that, I reckon."

"Maybe he should try good-bye," Shahid suggested.

Hat knocked fists with him. "Yeah!"

"Still, it make him the best listener," Chad said. "I put to him my entire theory about the evolution of society and he heard from top to bottom."

"He the first to do that, then," Hat said.

Sadiq guffawed. Chad went to cuff him. "Watch out."

"Communism. What a good idea, don't you think?" Riaz said. They looked at him, neither agreeing nor disagreeing. Not that Shahid imagined that Riaz had recently put his name down for the CP. He went on, "But in the end atheism doesn't really suit humanity."

"Nope," Hat said. "Atheism only a tiny minority thing anyway."

"Atheism won't last," Riaz explained. "Without religion society is impossible. And without God people think they can sin with impunity. There's no morality."

"There's only extremity and ingratitude and hard-heartedness, like beneath this Thatcherism," Chad said.

He was about to continue but Riaz said, "That's a lesson well learned. Gluttony, nihilism, hedonism—capitalism in a nutshell. Along with it, we are witnessing the twilight of Communism. Those revolutionaries weren't even able to achieve socialism in one room. Altogether we are seeing the shriveling of atheism."

"It over," Chad confirmed. "They been saying God dead. But it being the other way round. Without the creator no one knows where they are or what they doin'."

"Dr. Andrew certainly don't know what he doin'," Hat said. "Shahid, surely his wife you've met. Deedee Osgood?"

"Ms. Osgood? She's his wife?"

"She his wife."

"Surely she can't be!"

"Why not?"

"She's not like him."

"You got a thing about her?" inquired Sadiq. "I noticed your tongue hanging."

"You know," Chad said firmly, "without God-consciousness you can get away with everything. And when that happens you're lost. Now I know God is watching me. With him seeing every single damn thing, I have to be pretty careful about what I'm up to."

"Like living in a glass room?" Shahid said. "Or a greenhouse."

"That's it," said Riaz, smiling. "Exactly the correct idea. Everything you do and think is witnessed."

Shahid returned to the library. He had planned on working on, riding the inspiration of the morning. But the moment had not only gone, he was starting to feel badness coming down over him like a tarpaulin.

He didn't even know if he should sit down to gather his papers or stand and do it; or leave everything and walk out into the cold rain with the other lunatics and have a Big Mac, a milkshake, and a wank in his room. He could read and learn, but to what end? He knew he wanted to be a journalist of some sort, in the arts area, either on a paper or in television. In his spare time he would write stories and, eventually, a novel. But it was all too far in the future to satisfy him now.

Moving his notes, Shahid discovered a piece of paper he hadn't placed there.

The librarian opened the door of his office and announced across his empty domain, "We're closing now."

Shahid tore open the stapled note. He didn't look up but read it three times. "I'm not stopping you," he said. "Because I'm in a hurry myself." He began to pack his things into his bag. A woman had written to him, giving her address and inviting him to see her—that night.

He had reason, now, to return to his room. He would have to get ready.

He got out of the library, walked through the college and into the late rush-hour traffic. For the first time he didn't notice anything on the street.

The drain of the communal shower was blocked. Water was pouring down the side of the building. Shahid had to wash in the cracked yellow sink in his room, first one foot, then the other, followed, awkwardly, by armpits, balls, cock. To distract himself from the freezing water which dribbled through the vibrating taps, and the unusual positions he was forced to adopt in order to splash himself, he strapped on his Walkman—he was mindful of Riaz now. He snapped on the coolest white female voice. Chrissie Hynde did "Stop Your Sobbing" to chill and enchant him for the evening ahead. But she was hardly into "I Go to Sleep" when he was obliged to turn off the tape because of the voices.

He was hearing arguments, murmurings, conversations in Punjabi, Urdu, Hindi, English, and cacophonies of all babbling away outside. The house was a universe of insistent voices, but these sounds didn't hush behind a slammed door. He dressed quickly and opened the door.

Hat was holding two cups of tea, and issuing instructions to a queue of Asians that started outside Riaz's room and stretched along the hall and down the stairs.

While the tenants of the house passed, grumbling, into their rooms there were whining babies, impatient children, and men and women in ill-fitting overcoats expecting to be tended to, as if the hallway had become a doctor's waiting room. A young woman wearing the hijab, with skin the color of melon, was assisting Hat.

"Please, come here, over there, sit down, sit down," she was saying to an old man.

Hat noticed Shahid. "'Bout time you stopped doing that," he said. "It drop off."

"What's going on?"

"We need a chair," said the woman.

"This wonderful woman is Tahira," said Hat, adjusting the red baseball cap that he was wearing backward.

"Are you helping or getting in the way?" she said, in a northern accent. He guessed she was from Leeds or Bradford. Maybe she had followed Riaz down to London.

Hat indicated a stooped, bearded man in baggy salwar kamiz. "First off, get a chair."

Shahid fetched him the only chair from his room. The elderly man, who was ill-looking with breathing trouble, sat down gratefully.

Hat leaned toward Shahid. "Chad downstairs lookin' out for landlord. The community hall got vandalized, you hear?"

"By the police," the man said without smiling.

"What?" Shahid said, surprised to hear an old man say such a thing.

Hat said, "So Riaz havin' to hold his weekly advice surgery here instead." Hat then took the old man's hand. "His boy was going to school when he is jus' arrested, charged with assault, and sentenced to fifteen months. They got him confused."

"No, really?"

"Yes! We gonna be running big campaign for release. Headquarters in your room. All these people especially love our brother Riaz. They come from miles. They know when he say sometin'—he gonna write to the MP or recommend a solicitor—he mean it."

"Who's he got in there now?" Shahid asked.

"You keen to learn, yeah?" Hat handed him the two mugs of tea. "Take these in. Then you understand something about how nice your little England is."

Shahid stepped quietly into Riaz's room. The man sitting opposite Riaz was weeping and talking so intently he didn't notice Shahid.

"These boys, please, sir, are coming to my flat and threatening my whole family every day and night. As I told you, they have punched me in my guts. For five years I have lived there, but it is getting worse. Also my sister and my brother and his wife are writing to me saying, have you forgotten us, you are living in luxury there, why don't you send the money we need for the medicine, the money for the wedding, the money for our beloved parents . . ."

Riaz was looking into his eyes, making a low humming sound as a sign of unobtrusive comfort.

"Sir, I am already having two jobs, one in the office during the day, and the restaurant until two in the night. I am flaked fully out, and the entire world is leaning on my head—"

Riaz glanced up, his face as impassive as always; but pity had made him flush. Shahid put down the tea.

"I see," Shahid said to Hat outside.

Now Chad was standing there.

"Hey, Shahid, you all dressed up, yaar. Got somewhere to go?"

"Nah, just a function, you know, student thing."

"Yeah, function, right, eh, Hat?" Chad flapped his right hand as if it had caught fire. "'Fraid we need you to help us."

"Yeah," Hat said, "Riaz working too hard. He need some letters typed an' I see you got an Amstrad in there."

Shahid looked at both of them. "Now?" He took off his jacket and extracted the key to his room.

"He a serious boy. His attitude I like," Hat said. "Don't you, Chad?"

"I don't mind."

Hat relented: "But later."

"Later," Shahid agreed. "I'll be back in a couple of hours." He pointed to the queue. "This is incredible."

Hat smiled but Chad said with a sardonic attitude, "You all busy, but there's someone downstairs looking for you."

"For me?"

"That's what I said."

"Who?"

Chad shrugged. "I don't know those kinda people—no more. He wearing a slick gray suit. And crocodile shoes."

"Probably a relative," Hat said, smiling at Chad.

"Yeah," Shahid said uncertainly.

"Well, he gone to get cigarettes."

Shahid started suddenly. "Hat, say I had to go out, and I'm doing nicely, very nicely thanks, good bye."

"Hat don't tell no lies," Chad said.

"Sorry?"

"No," Hat confirmed. "I'm training to be an accountant."

Chad looked up. "Anyway, too late. Looks like *Saturday Night Fever* rollin' right along here."

Shahid looked up to see the man Riaz had called "the dissipater" shouldering through the queue with the assurance of someone used to line-jumping and with the fastidiousness of someone who didn't enjoy crowds. He did indeed have on the iridescent gray suit, with, today, the Bass Weejuns. Chili would never wear crocodile shoes.

"How you doing, baby brother?"

In Chili's hand were his car keys, Ray-Bans, and Marlboros, without which he wouldn't leave his bathroom. Chili drank only black coffee and neat Jack Daniel's; his suits were Boss, his underwear Calvin Klein, his actor Pacino. His barber shook his hand, his accountant took him to dinner, his drug dealer would come to him at all hours, and accept his checks. At least he wasn't smoking a joint.

"Chili."

"What's this?" Chili opened his arms. "Hug me, babe."

Shahid was pulled into Chili's chest and clapped on the back, hating his own stiff reluctance. This recent friendliness still made him wonder.

Shahid got free. "Want to look at my digs?"

"Why d'you think I'm here, babe? I want to see everything, toot sweet."

But before he could lead Chili away Shahid had to introduce him to Chad and Hat, who were refusing to find something better to do despite the coughs and groans of the queue. While Shahid held the door for his brother Hat said, "Hi," and looked Chili over. Chad nodded sardonically.

Shahid told his brother, "Make yourself at home. Try not to look at the wallpaper."

"Better get my Rays on."

Chili rubbed the lenses of his shades with his handkerchief. At that moment Shahid saw that Chad, after shaking hands with the invariably fragrant Chili, was sniffing his fingers and making a face at Hat. Shahid hoped to God that Chili didn't notice.

Shahid shut the door behind them.

"It's not like home."

"Must be why you're here," said Chili.

Their family house was an immaculate 1960s mansion, just outside the town, a caravanserai, as filled with people as a busy hotel. Papa had constantly redecorated it, the furniture was replaced every five years and new rooms were necessarily added. The kitchen always seemed to be in the front drive, awaiting disposal, though it appeared to Shahid no less "innovative" than the new one. Papa hated anything "old-fashioned," unless it charmed tourists. He wanted to tear down the old; he liked "progress." "I only want the best," he'd say, meaning the newest, the latest, and, somehow, the most ostentatious.

"Where the hell to sit?"

"Anywhere."

In illustration Shahid threw himself on the bed, shoving his books and clothes on to the floor.

But Chili wasn't the type to sit on foul beds. He snorted derisively and walked up and down, negligently picking up notebooks, tapes, letters. He glanced over them as if they were a matter of due family knowledge. All the same, Shahid could tell he was containing his excessive condescension. For once Chili didn't seem about to mention something he liked to call "the real world." As he rapped a pile of books with his keys, there even appeared to be a shade of respect.

"Why are you being in a hurry with me, brother?"

"I'm not, am I?"

"I don't give a shit if you tap your foot like with other people. But never pull that hurry-up shit with Mr. Chili."

"Sorry."

Chili pouted.

Until recently Chili had always deemed Shahid a hopeless little shit. In their teens Chili had frequently taunted and beaten him. Once, in front of his drunken friends, Chili made Shahid leave the room—by jumping out of a second-floor window. Shahid broke his arm. Later Chili had done his best, when he wasn't out, to keep a sneering distance from Shahid.

At twenty Chili married their cousin Zulma and moved away, in the Western fashion, to a flat in Brighton. There they attempted to continue the fashionable life she led in Karachi. But such glamour was only possible with help. Zulma wasn't used to housework. She had many specialties, including, it was said, fellatio; but washing up wasn't among them. Nor was it among Chili's.

Last year, after Papa died, Chili took Zulma and their little girl, Safire, back to live in the family house. Since then Shahid doubted whether Chili had seen much of her. He claimed to be obsessed with developing a business plan. He was certainly bored with being a travel agent and had stuck to his business duties only to please Papa and to draw a big salary. Now Chili claimed that the family business had to expand—to London. This was how he justified never being at home.

"You being a ruffian because you're studying tonight?"

"I got an appointment, Chili. But it's not till later."

"Pussy?"

"Pardon?"

HANIF KUREISHI

50

"You heard."

"No. A tutor from the college."

"Aha. Class pussy. How old is she?"

Shahid thought for a moment. "Above the age of consent."

"And she's invited you to her house?"

Shahid nodded.

Chili whistled. "Wow. No worries. I'll drive you to the exact spot, wherever it is. Just think, she's slipping into her most favorite lacy underwear right as we speak."

"Don't be stupid, she's a teacher."

"Excited, eh? Just don't introduce her to me."

"I won't."

"You're starting to pull. What babe is powdering her cunt for me tonight, apart from . . . I can't even remember the bitch's name. No, the family is delighted. By the way, cool trousers. Tartan suits you. They're not mine, are they?"

"No."

Chili fingered the remaining clothes in the doorless wardrobe. "Where's my red shirt?"

"What? I'll give it to you later."

Chili's relentless passion had always been for clothes, girls, cars, girls, and the money that bought them. When the brothers were young he made it clear that he found Shahid's bookishness effeminate. He was influenced in this by the practical and aggressive Papa, who originated the idea that Shahid's studiousness was not only unproductive but an affliction for the family, especially after the incident with Shahid's short story. But since Shahid had been at college, Chili's attitude had softened.

Papa's dying had done that. On his deathbed Papa, dragging away the oxygen mask, had kissed Chili and gasped, "Don't let the boy go down. Don't let me say cheerio thinking Shahid will be alone."

Chili had begun to ring Shahid. He took him to tenebrous clubs in South Kensington basements, where, at their table, acquaintances paid their respects. These included German drug dealers who wore black leather gloves indoors and carried handguns in their jackets, and were accompanied by teenage Italian girls; bent English solicitors taking crooked policemen out on the town; Bulgarian fencing champions; French croupiers with gigolo looks who peeled twenty-pound notes from rolls the size of a runner's baton; and millionaire Bermudan barristers. Between urgent, whispered conversations Chili bought Shahid margaritas and introduced him to burnished girls who would turn away the moment Chili left them together. He also tried to ask him what he wanted to do, but Shahid was too sensible to say anything on this topic. Shahid gained the impression that his elder brother had appointed himself a reality guide, pointing out pitfalls before the boy made a serious error due to credulity, sensitivity, and lack of cunning.

Shahid would have been angrier if he hadn't felt that Chili also wanted to open himself up, but didn't know how to. Chili didn't have friends; he had pals, mates, and those he called "personal" friends, who were, usually, criminals. He gave his girlfriends too much grief and respect to be able to speak to them.

As Shahid stood before the pitted mirror Chili said, "You're starting to look good, more healthy. Getting rid of the glasses, the contact lenses and all . . . that shorter haircut . . . you've become less womanish. You look quite determined. You were always such a crybaby. I s'pose you're nearly a man now. Papa would be pleased."

"Would he?"

"Don't be surprised. He always admired your brains."

"Papa?"

"Course, he'd have wanted you to put them to good use. You're not still doin' that scribbling, are you?"

"What d'you mean?"

"I'll give you a slap if you waste your time like that." He caressed Shahid's cheek with his open palm, pleased with his brother's instant recoil. "Let's go. You're getting nervous."

Shahid imagined that the queue to see Riaz would have dwindled, but now the downcast supplicants were even waiting in the street.

Normally Chili would have made smart-arsed remarks but he took it all in amusedly, with a sly glance at Tahira. Except that on the way to the car, glancing at Shahid with curiosity, he said, "That big boy, is he a new friend of yours?"

"Chad? Yes."

"Tell him if he sniffs his hands at me again, his children's children will feel the pain. OK?"

"OK."

Shahid settled down in the sumptuous seat of Chili's BMW. On the dashboard was his copy of *One Hundred Years of Solitude*. Flicking through the book, he said, "Can I take this back?"

"Leave it. I've started."

"I should hope so. I'm already sketching out the questions."

A couple of months ago Shahid was carrying some books and Chili, who boasted of never having read anything—"literature's a closed book to me"—said he might give one a turn to see what the tingle was. Shahid contended that Chili wouldn't be able do it; and it would be a mistake, on the first time out, to go up against Márquez. "Plus," he added, for flavor, "you're functionally illiterate."

"Eat shit, you little fucker," Chili had giggled. He would cruise through the pages in six months and soar through any verbal test Shahid could devise. If he failed the examination, he'd hand his brother a grand—cash.

"I go for a challenge," Chili said now. "But it's a steep one. *One Hundred Years*. Ten would have been enough. Or even six months. Tell me, how come this writer gives all his characters the same name? Does that other writer, the one who slags the religion, do that kinda thing?"

"No."

"Books are OK, but apart from Ray Charles's voice, there's nothing better in life than a beautiful woman. And that, little brother, is where we're headed!"

She lived in Camden. While Chili negotiated the one-way systems, cursing until he hit a clear patch of road to speed across, Shahid studied the *A to Z* street guide. When they found the street, Shahid stuck his head out of the window, trying to make out the numbers of the houses. Suddenly he pointed.

"Stop! That must be the place."

Chili reversed the car. They looked the house over.

"Your honey's got a little money," Chili mused. "Nearly fashionable neighborhood. On a clear day she can see the niggers and workers without having them on her doorstep, or ripping off her microwave. Ain't too house-proud, but likes a bit of gardening. She a feminist?"

"They all are now."

"Right. Difficult to avoid. Make a virtue of necessity, I say."

"How?"

"There's a lie going around about the feminists. People say they're all hairy legs and won't cooperate with the dick. But I'm telling you, sexually they can be filthy dirty—once they agree to fuck you—because they ain't ashamed. The other thing they do, though, is tell you your prick's too small."

"They don't, do they?"

"Don't get agitated." Chili patted his brother's head. "That won't happen tonight, I'm almost certain of it. Thing is, they're scared their cunts are too wide. If you get any trouble just mention that, but wittily."

"What d'you mean, wittily?"

"Eh?"

"Give me a witty example."

"Now?"

"Yeah, just in case."

"Right." Chili thought for a moment. "Say, 'Fucking you, babe, was like throwing a banana up Oxford Street—I'd have preferred to touch the sides now and again.' "

"Is that it?"

"Yeah."

"That's never happened to you, has it?"

"One time, not long ago, I was fucking this woman. She said, 'Fill me up, give me your big chopper.' " Chili chortled. "And I was right inside. So I said, 'It's all in, babe, that's tonight's helping.' She was OK about it. They always are, if you explain. Now, this teacher woman, d'you want her?"

"Chili, how can you ask that? I hardly know her."

"People know within two minutes if they want to fuck some-one. Within an hour they know if they want to be with them. You want her—then take her."

"I can't do that."

"Why not? Christ, your teeth are practically chattering. What would Papa say?"

Chili put the car in gear and grasped the wheel as if he were in the cockpit of a dive bomber. They shot up the road.

"Where are we going?" Shahid cried.

"You're too early."

Shahid almost grabbed the wheel. "We're right on time!"

"She'll want you more if you make her wait."

Interminably, Shahid thought, Chili sped up and down Camden High Street like a joyrider, past the tube station, cinema, and pubs, playing the Pakistani qawali singer Nasrut Fatah Ali Khan loud. Shahid began to wonder if something was wrong with his brother. Chili usually always had somewhere better to go and far more important things to do than be with him.

"Now—" Outside the house Chili hauled his wallet from his back pocket. It was the size of half a loaf of bread. "Take this in case you're forced to get a taxi back." The Reality Guide gave Shahid some money. "And don't forget, they're always more scared than you are."

"Chili."

"What the fuck now?"

It had occurred to Shahid that his brother hadn't mentioned his wife.

"How's Zulma?"

"Zulma? Don't be a bloody fool. Zulma will always be Zulma. What the hell are you saying?"

"Nothing."

"You trying to start me up?"

"No, Chili, I promise."

"Sure?"

"It was a family inquiry."

Chili kissed him. "Don't forget my red shirt."

"Course not."

"Good boy."

Shahid went up the drive, stopped and hesitated. He didn't feel like going in now. But turning back, he saw that Chili was still sitting there, revving the engine and hissing, "Puss, puss, puss."

Shahid rang the bell. As Deedee opened the door Chili honked his horn and laughed.

He stood there anxiously, hands in pockets.

"Where d'you want to sit?" she said. He had no idea. "Oh, just make yourself comfortable."

It was a large family house. The doors had panels of stained glass and the hall floor was resplendently tiled. But it was unkempt and even untidier than Shahid's room, with bare floorboards, crumpled rugs, torn Billie Holiday and Malcolm X posters, and three old bicycles leaning against a wall. On chairs and the floor were piled dusty, yellowing newspapers, some of them cut up, as if for filing. It was like a student place, and Deedee told him that three kids from the college occupied the spare rooms.

There was an open fire, too, with the sofa in front of it. On the floor was a wooden board accommodating a piece of Gruyère. She went to fetch some wine. He sat on the sofa before realizing that when she joined him she would have to sit beside him. He had had such bizarre and hopeful thoughts on the way over, partly inspired by Chili, that now he felt apprehensive and bashful.

He jumped up, went to the window and checked the street.

Chili's car hadn't moved. The music was off; Chili was staring into space. Shahid wondered when he'd ever seen him sitting still before. As if sensing him, Chili turned suddenly, grinned, and gave the thumbs up. Shahid shuddered. What would happen if Chili suddenly decided he wanted to meet Deedee? It was just the kind of stunt he would pull. Then Shahid would have to explain why she shouldn't open the door.

There was a sound from the kitchen. He quickly spread himself out across the sofa with his feet hanging over the end and occupied himself looking at the small TV, which was across the room on a shelf, though not turned on.

"Great to see someone who can make themselves comfortable anywhere." She was carrying a bottle and two glasses. She put them down and pushed a cassette into the video. It was an early Prince tape. "While you watch that I'll heat up some pumpkin and co-conut soup, with ginger. It's delicious. Would you like that?"

"It sounds great, thanks, if it's not too much trouble. And by the way," he said as she went to the door, "thanks for inviting me over to look at this stuff. I wouldn't be able to write my Prince paper without it."

"We'll discuss it later."

"Sure."

Discuss it later?

He settled down to watch the tape but it ended before he could take it in. He couldn't find the changer so he had to get up, rewind it, and watch it again. Then he watched another video which he ran twice more, all the while straining to think of a comment to make. The word "seamless" kept entering his head. That was the level to aim at. But he couldn't think of any words to escort it. What would she think if he just said, "It was really seamless"— twice?

He was changing the video when she came in with the soup on a tray, along with French bread and a Greek salad. She was about to sit down on the sofa. He couldn't race back now, push her over, and take up his old position.

She indicated the videos. "D'you find them sexy?"

He was sitting beside her. The soup was hot and almost ignited his tongue as he tried to dispose of it. He couldn't help wondering where her husband was.

"Quite. But they're a bit like a pantomime, too." He hesitated and then went ahead. "Do you find them seamless . . . seamless and not a little cathartic?"

"I hate this house."

"Pardon?"

She was looking around the room. "We're trying to sell it. Sorry, what did you say?"

"The videos. Seamless."

She stared into her soup. The fire was warming him, he would have to remove his jacket if he wasn't going to break out in a sweat.

He was down to his shirt and beginning to unbutton it, when he was aware, from the hallway, of a pair of eyes on him. Brownlow hurried into his overcoat. Then he tried to smile and wave. Shahid did the same, all the while attempting to move away from Deedee. But he feared he had transgressed because Andrew came into the room, stood beside him, and looked down.

Brownlow was about to say something but, as he opened his mouth, recalled that he lacked the power of speech. Instead, he stuck out his adhesive hand and Shahid shook it as genially as he could, trying to ignore the fact he almost had the man's wife on his knee.

As Brownlow turned to leave, and Shahid, relieved, could resume nibbling at his soup, he saw Brownlow and Deedee looking one another over with objective curiosity, as if searching for clarification, like strangers trying to recall where they'd seen each other before.

The front door closed. "Quiet man, isn't he?"

Deedee put down her spoon to laugh. "He is my husband! Can you imagine it?"

"I find it difficult, I must say."

"One time you are passionately in love and then another time, not that long after, you can't believe how you could feel so much.

Has that happened to you? Once, years ago, Andrew came home from a party and described kissing a woman. In those days couples were trying to be as honest and open as they could, you know."

"Why was that?"

"I can't quite remember. For political reasons, I think. Anyhow, for two nights I didn't sleep. I had never felt so let down. Now I can't even understand how I felt that way." She sighed. "One would hope, as well, that intimacy would leave more of a mark, that more of it would remain. But it doesn't. You just end up thinking, who is this person?"

They finished their soup.

Deedee asked if he fancied looking at the videos once more, but although he knew he'd remember little of them when it came to writing his paper—other than that Prince clearly enjoyed wearing women's underwear—he knew he wouldn't be able to sit so still again. The trouble was, he didn't know if it was what she wanted or whether it would bore her. She removed the bowls.

On returning, she stood there with a finger twisting her hair and said, "I'm sorry, I need to go out. I get tense if I'm here too long. And I don't want my lodgers to talk. There's nothing—" she indicated them both—"nothing going on. But—" She shrugged. He shook his head in agreement. "But nothing will be all round the college by tomorrow morning."

He jumped up and yawned in illustration. "Anyway, I'm tired."

"No, no. You're coming with me."

"Am I?"

"Unless you're too tired, I'd like you to, Shahid."

"No, I'm not tired." He was so impressed by her will and so off balance that he added, "I'll . . . I'll go anywhere with you. So—yes."

"That's nice. I love 'yes.' It's practically the most interesting word of all, don't you think? Like a hinge opening a door outward. Yes, yes, yes."

He took a step toward her.

The corners of her eyes were wrinkled with pleasure. "Can I get ready?"

She disappeared for longer this time.

He went, experimentally, to the window. Chili was lying back in his seat smoking, not looking at the house but staring into the distance, his music rumbling sluggishly.

What would Virgil in the Bass Weejuns do now? Surely, so far, Shahid hadn't made a false move? But Chili, with his car and knife, would have been more in charge. Except that Deedee wouldn't have gone near him.

No, Chili was the last person Shahid wanted to be like. There was much he hated in his brother. If Chili believed Shahid had problems, they were nothing to the problems Shahid believed his brother had.

Chili's basic understanding was that people were weak and lazy. He didn't think they were stupid; he wasn't going to make that mistake. He saw, though, that people resisted change, even if it would improve their lives; they were afraid, complacent, lacking courage. This gave the advantage to someone of initiative and will.

Chili thought, for instance, that men were scared of making fools of themselves with women, so they held back when they should have been going forward. Chili called himself a predator. When a woman offered herself—it was the most satisfying moment. Often, it wasn't even necessary to sleep with her. A look in her eyes, of eagerness, gladness, acquiescence, was sufficient.

At home Chili used to settle on Shahid's bed in the morning and tell of the previous night's exploits: Chili slipping down someone's shorts behind the tennis club; Chili in the dormitory of a girls' school, escaping through a window; Chili's penchant for threesomes, him and two girls—"King's Road sandwiches" they were dubbed; Chili being picked up in a club and fucking the woman while the husband, an old man, watched.

Papa, also, delighted in his boy's adventures. Not that Chili would recount the most salacious, for fear Papa would denounce them as "too shady by far." But, "Keep me informed," he would cry across the house, when Chili went out on another "burdensome" expedition. Papa's interest was meeting the women. "I'm sure they like going out with you," he'd tell Chili. "But it is me they would rather talk to. Bring them!"

Chili would take them in to witness Papa lying on his bed in the center of the room, wearing a shimmering maroon dressing gown (under which he always wore blue silk pajamas). A Glenn Miller record played while he swigged whiskey in a long glass, half Bushmills, half carbonated water. This bed Papa took to whenever he was not at work. He lay there like a pasha, with a pile of comics on his bedside table. The "center of operations" he called it. Meanwhile Shahid's mother kept to herself with her own friends, her sisters, and their children, in another part of the house; it was as if they were living in Karachi.

Like Papa, though more maliciously, Shahid delighted in Chili's adventures as tales of appetite and folly, particularly when they involved Chili looking foolish. Like the time he picked up a particularly bewitching woman at a club and woke, after an unblemished night, to discover the house was laden with National Front posters and magazines, and her two cropped-haired brothers were twanging their braces in the lounge. Chili had adopted a Spanish accent, pretended he had little English, and raced out of the front door.

The problem was, Papa wanted Shahid to emulate Chili.

When Shahid was fifteen, Papa persuaded him to take out a local girl. They drifted around the countryside, and Shahid read Shelley to her in a haystack. On his return Papa insisted that Tipoo—his youngest brother, who was schizophrenic and worked around the house—bring Shahid to the "center of operations."

"Did you touch her?" Papa stabbed at his own wheezing chest. "Or further down," he continued, slapping his legs, as thin as a medieval Christ's. Chili was smirking in the doorway.

"No."

"What have you been doing?"

"Reading poetry."

"Speak up, you bloody eunuch fool!"

"Reading Keats and Shelley to her."

"To the girl?"

"Yes."

"Did she laugh at you?"

"I don't think so."

"Of course she did!"

Papa and Chili couldn't stop laughing at him.

Despite Papa's penchant for carousing, there was much that was upright and respectable about him. A small man, just over five feet, with a toothbrush mustache, he wore, at the office, suits or blazers, ties and gray trousers. During the war he'd flown RAF bombers from East Anglia, for which he'd been named a member of the Order of the British Empire. There was always plenty that Papa had wanted to achieve. He had illimitable pride, gallantry even.

Papa took his boys personally to the shops, ensuring that both he and they had the finest clothes. Even as his sons made faces at each other in the mirrors of Burtons the Tailors, he and the manager turned the fat books of cloth squares, patterned and plain, like scholars peering into manuscripts. Papa would return, several times, for adjustments—always the trousers were too long—before deciding, after interminable consideration, which tie and vest were slightly wrong for the suit. At home, he took Shahid and Chili into the bathroom to demonstrate the only correct way to shave, the loading of the brush and angle of the razor, soaping, rubbing, scraping, and pinching the flesh. Then Papa stripped naked for the bathing demonstration, which was followed by an illustration of how to powder the balls, armpits, and between the toes. Papa would rather have laid down in the street than walk through a door before a woman. He taught his boys such courtesies, and how to shake hands firmly while saying, "How d'you do?" He wanted people to say how smart his sons were. But had they benefited?

Deedee still hadn't returned. Shahid was getting spooked by her absence. What was she doing?

Their parents had come to England to make an affluent and stable life in a country not run by tyrants. Once this was done, their remaining ambition rested with their sons, particularly the elder. Papa loved Chili, but would he have approved of him now? His

most recent ambition was to make it in America, though it wasn't
so much the voice of liberty that called Chili, as the violent intensity. Time and again he watched *Once Upon a Time in America, Scar-
face,* and *The Godfather*—as career documentaries. He had even
cursed Papa—out of earshot—for coming to old England rather
than standing in line on Ellis Island with the Jews, Poles, Irish, and
Armenians. England was small-time, unbending; real glory was impossible in a country where the policemen wore helmets shaped
like sawn-off squashes. Chili thought he could be someone in
America, but he wasn't going to go there poor. He'd get himself
more established in London and then hit New York with a high
"rep," or reputation.

The problem was, as their uncle Asif once stated, money had
come too easily to Chili in the 1980s. He didn't respect where it
came from. "It's easy for people, especially if they're young," he said,
"to forget that we've barely arrived over in England. It takes several
generations to become accustomed to a place. We think we're settled down, but we're like brides who've just crossed the threshold.
We have to watch ourselves, otherwise we will wake up one day to
find we have made a calamitous marriage."

This was laced with bitterness, of course. Their uncle had the
impossible task of living in a country which couldn't accommodate
intelligence, initiative, imagination, and in which most endeavor
bogged down into hopelessness. But Shahid recognized what he
said.

He got up. There was still no sign of Deedee. Something might
have happened.

He ventured out into the hall to try to find her. He started to
climb the stairs. Somewhere upstairs she was singing along to music. He recognized the tune; it was a song Chili often played while
he was dressing in the evening, the first track of *Beggars' Banquet.*
He turned back.

He heard a voice from the top of the stairs.

"Shahid. Is that you down there?"

"Yes."

"Would you mind coming up and telling me something?"

"What is it you want to know?"

"I'm not sure what to wear. Can you tell me if I look all right?"

He mounted the stairs, wondering what she and the night promised.

6

N ot long afterward they left the house. Chili spotted
them, started the car, and drove off, for which Shahid
silently thanked him.

They were walking up the road. A bus stopped. The
conductor looked at them and when Deedee shook her
head, pushed his bell.

By the Camden Plaza she didn't so much hail a taxi
as motion into the traffic. Directly a cab halted beside
them. Deedee got in, and leaned forward to instruct the
driver. Shahid lingered a moment, thinking how brilliant she looked in her short skirt and wide-lapelled
jacket, under which she wore a black bra.

In the cab they sat close together. "We're trying to
sell the house now Andrew and I have split up," she said.
"I can't wait to get a place of my own."

She smelled of flowers. Her earrings quivered like
two drops of water about to fall.

He said, "Why'd you split up?" and cursed himself for
asking such a clumsy question.

She didn't reply but kept plunging her hand into her
bag as if trying to extract a prize.

He sat there; at least he was in a London taxi.

She told him, "That man is only interested in one thing, politics. For years I was involved, too. I couldn't admit to myself how much it restricted me. It all makes you feel guilty."

"What d'you like now?"

"I'm trying to find out. Other things. Culture. When I can, I do a lot of nothing. And I make stabs at pleasure. Yes." Again she stuffed her hand in her bag. "Andrew has got a new girlfriend so he's at her place most of the time. We've got one rule—we don't bring our lovers to the house."

Shahid found the word "lover" as applied to Andrew comical and he briefly entertained himself imagining Dr. Brownlow without any trousers on; except that then he saw Andrew kissing Deedee and wondered how she could have such a man.

He couldn't help thinking Deedee was probably more complicated than he could comprehend, when she pulled a small wooden box with copper corners from her bag. She took from it two white grooved pills. They sat in her proffered open hand like tiny bombs.

"I don't know why I'm exposing myself to you in this way— maybe I've got a feeling about you," she said.

"Is that why you invited me over tonight?"

"Yes. And because you're lonely and I liked the way you looked at me."

"D'you get a lot of offers from men?"

"What?"

"I just wondered. I'm sorry, I didn't really mean to say that."

She looked intently out of the window. "I want to take something. Will you join me?"

"What is it?"

He could feel her body against his. "It'll make you laugh. And dance."

She told him what it was; the pharmaceutical terms she used and the professorial way she put it ("You will experience . . .") made her sound like a reckless doctor. He relished listening, she knew so much. Yet he found it unsettling, how she talked about what his mother called "wrong things," pop music and drugs, in the way adults discussed wine or literature.

"Yeah," he said. "We used to smoke draw but I only had that pill once before, in Brighton."

"Did you enjoy it?"

"I swallowed half and the person who gave it to me said I should come and see you. That's the effect it had."

"I'm glad you took it. These are quite mellow. They make me feel. What d'you say?"

The cab progressed smoothly, there wasn't much traffic. Shahid had no idea where they were going. You could drive for two or three hours through this limitless city which had no shape, and not come out the other side; and after a certain point, where tourists never went, people's clothes became more ragged, the cars older, the housing more neglected.

She dropped a bomb onto her tongue and threw back her head, pulling on the plastic bottle of water she had brought along.

"I think I'm all right, actually," he said.

"Sure?"

He wiggled on the seat. "The Prince videos already perked me up no end."

Deedee didn't speak or look at him. She was annoyed with him, or maybe with herself, he couldn't tell. Some misunderstanding was definitely going on.

He would ask her to stop the cab. It wouldn't take long to get back on the bus or tube. Riaz labored late, there was so much to do—he needed help with the typing; his work couldn't be more worthwhile or essential. Riaz and Hat and Chad were the first people he'd met who were like him, he didn't have to explain anything. Chad trusted him. Hat had called him brother. He was closer to this gang than he was to his own family. But this woman who had invited him out—he had to be careful not to call her Miss—seemed tense. She seemed to be the type who imagined they had a lot of problems, which they would discuss constantly with their friends and therapists; whereas, compared to most people, it was obvious that she led an agreeable life and was probably quite frivolous. Hadn't she admitted that, saying she longed for pleasure? Anyway, she was making him nervous. What did she want to do with him?

"Where are we, Deedee?"

In reply she pointed. The lip of the bridge was slipping them into the mouth of south London. He could have worked that out for himself. He didn't like her pointing at rivers.

The cab's heater was functioning and the warmth was working its way through his clothes to his skin, dampening it. He needed to strip off or get out into the air. He figured it would be easier to get out, out of this whole thing, whatever it was, and disappear into the city.

They stopped at traffic lights. He leaned forward to grab the door handle. He thought, though, before he killed himself, that this required reflection. He would open the window. But it wouldn't budge, and, after dragging up and down and sideways on it and even scratching on the metal, he couldn't release the thing. He couldn't keep on scrabbling away like a cat out in the rain. Looking away from him, she tipped water into her hand, splashed it over her forehead, and rubbed it into the back of her neck. Burning, he sat back.

She leaned across him and freed the window with one stroke. A fumy river breeze swept through the cab; it was welcome. The cabby reached up and switched on the radio. There was a crackling snatch of something about the weather in the Orkneys, which was the only thing they had to think about up there, before the driver hit a pop station and turned it up.

Suddenly Shahid was hearing something that made his knees bob. Was it the Doors? No, crazy, it was something new, the Stone Roses or Inspiral Carpets, one of those Manchester guitar groups. Whoever it was lifted him. Music could act like an adrenaline injection on him, and he wanted to go woo-woo-whoa for being here with his lecturer who was taking him out. (If only he'd been able to ask where.) When he stopped trying to hold himself together, he realized he was liking this. He was certain now that he wanted to be here. Yes, this wasn't too bad; Chili wasn't doing it.

"OK," he said.

"Sorry?"

"I want it."

"Sure?"

"Yes."

He shut his eyes, dropped the pill into his mouth, and swigged from the bottle. Then he stuck his arm out and bent it around her. Instantly she cradled her head into his chest. He wanted to kiss her now, he was gathering his courage, but he was scared of making a blunder; Chili said, it's all in the voice not the body language, that was the mistake people made. But this was his teacher, for God's sake, he could be expelled.

They turned into a narrow cul-de-sac designed for murders, past workshops, lock-up garages, and miserable-looking trees. They took a sharp corner into a lane. The building at the end, subtly vibrating, was the White Room.

It was a silver warehouse.

In front of it was a forecourt along the center of which had been laid a pathway of rolled barbed wire. The whole area was circled by a high fence and was washed in harsh yellow light, making it resemble a prison yard. Three pillbox entrances were manned by sentries mumbling into radios. Crowds surrounded them in the freezing night. Some kids, not admitted, clung shivering to the fence. Others attempted to climb it like refugees, yelling through at the building, before being yanked back to earth and pushed away.

Deedee gave her name and they were admitted. Filmed by security cameras, they swung through the floodlit walkway while being watched enviously. It was like being pop stars at a premiere. They entered a dark bar area of tables and chairs, where people sat drinking water and juice beneath billowing parachutes. Alcohol was not for sale.

"This way."

He followed her through mazelike tunnels of undulating canvas. Eventually they were released into a cavernous room containing at least five hundred people, where shifting colored slides were projected onto the walls. There was a relentless whirlwind of interplanetary noises. Jets of kaleidoscopic light sprayed the air. Many of the men were bare-chested and wore only thongs; some of the women were topless or in just shorts and net tops. One woman was naked except for high heels and a large plastic penis strapped to her thighs with which she duetted. Others were garbed in rubber, or masks, or were dressed as babies. The dancing was frenzied and individual. People blew whistles, others screamed with pleasure.

Deedee put her lips to his ear. The potent intimacy of her hair and skin scent carried a shocking charge.

She cried into the inferno, "We'll just check it out and then move on."

"Am I going to start thinking I can fly?"

"Why, are you buzzing?"

"I can't tell."

She said, "You know, I feel I forced you into this."

"You did, but I'm grateful. You could say it's an education, right?"

She began pumping her arms and legs. Then she moved more sensually, like a rope uncoiling. He stood in front of her, keeping his feet on the floor for fear of starting to float.

With his eyes half closed, he peered into the incandescent ultraviolet haze. He noticed, through the golden mist, that no one appeared to have any great interest in anyone else, though people would fall into staring at one another. Then he was doing it; everyone was looking so beautiful. But before he could think why this might be, or why he was enjoying himself so much, an undertow of satisfaction rippled through him, as if some creature were sighing in his body. He felt he was going to be lifted off his feet.

The feeling left him and he felt deserted. He wanted it back. It came and came. In a pounding trance he started writhing joyously, feeling he was part of a waving sea. He could have danced forever, but not long after she said, "We should go."

Electric waves of light flickered in the air. Fronds of fingers with flames spurting from them waved at the DJs, flown in from New York, sitting in their glass booths.

"But why?"

"There's a much better place that one of my most reliable students told me about. It's an end-of-decade party."

"The decade hasn't ended yet."

"No, but it'll feel as if it had."

"Deedee, it's not possible there's anywhere better."

She nodded confidently. She knew everything. "Let's have a cigarette and get on our way."

He followed her.

The cold air froze the sweat on their foreheads and seized his mind temporarily into lucidity even as he gawked at the resplendent street, lit like a stage set for a musical. He and Deedee didn't talk much but they couldn't stop looking at one another.

They were in another taxi, he knew that, but he had no idea how they got into it, and he had lost his sense of time. They were heading even further south and he wondered if they were riding through a park; it was a lush, open, suburban area without shops. The frosty roads were silent, there was no traffic or pedestrians. The unlit mansions, behind tree-lined high walls and iron gates, sat far back from the road. He wondered where Chili was now. He thought of his mother sleeping in her bed; this was where his family would have loved to have lived.

They arrived at the ominous iron fence of a white mansion, the sort of place an English Gatsby would have chosen, he imagined. Trucks were parked in the driveway. Big men stood in the gloom. They searched Shahid, putting their hands down his trousers; he had to remove his socks and shake them while standing on one foot in the mud.

They went into the marble hall and found themselves staring up at a grand staircase. Then they passed the efficient cloakroom, the bar, and the stuffed polar bear on its hind legs with a light in its mouth, traversed the deep white carpet, through doors, wide passageways, and a conservatory where trees touched the roof, until they came to a Jacuzzi in which everyone was naked. Beyond was an illuminated indoor swimming pool. On its shadowy surface floated dozens of lemon- and lime-colored balloons.

Beyond that the garden stretched away into the distance, lit by gassy blue flames.

It was the perfect venue for a house party. Deedee took his arm as they looked on and said into his ear, "A savage place! as holy and enchanted/As e'er beneath a waning moon was haunted/By woman wailing for her demon lover!"

The house had been squatted the previous evening after being claimed by the drummer of the Pennies from Hell, a window cleaner who'd spotted it on his rounds.

Tonight it was overrun by hordes of boys and girls from south London. They had pageboy haircuts, skateboard tops, baseball caps, hoods, bright ponchos, and twenty-inch denim flares. Deedee said that most had probably never been inside such a house before, unless they were delivering the groceries. Now they were having the time of their lives. By the end of the weekend the house would be ashes. "The kids, too," she added.

Deedee and Shahid started up the stairs, but dozens of people were coming down. Others danced where they stood with their hands in the air, crying, "Everybody's free to feel good, everybody's freee . . ." Some just sat nodding their heads with their eyes closed. Then Shahid lost Deedee.

On the landing a runty little wiry kid had taken up a pitch and was jigging about and shouting, "Want anything, want anything . . . Eeeee . . . E for the people! Up the working class!"

"How much?" Shahid said to him.

It was an outrageous price.

"How many d'you want?" the kid said.

"Three."

The kid laid three of the bombs in his palm; Shahid popped two.

"What d'you call these?" Shahid asked.

"These white ones? Leg-openers. I've got other sorts."

"No, these'll be fine."

"Have a good time, yeah," said the kid. "See you."

"What are you doing?" Deedee said.

She was behind him, arms around his chest.

"Here."

He placed a grooved one on her out-thrust tongue. Then she was lost again, in the multitude. Alone, he climbed onward.

Upstairs in the chillin' space no one was vertical; kids were lying on the floor not moving—except to kiss or stroke one another—as if they'd been massacred. Shahid needed to join them, and he lay down, slotting into a space between the bodies. The moment he shut his eyes his mind, which in the past he had visualized as ancient and layered like a section through the earth's crust, became a blazing oblong of light in which colored shapes were dancing.

Someone was nudging him and when he opened his eyes he saw a girl watching him.

"How are you?"

Surprised, he said, "What are you doing?"

"Feelin' good, like you."

"And what about the rest of the time?"

"The rest of what time?"

"Any time."

"I do this," she said.

"Not all day?"

"Every weekend. Friday, Saturday, and Sunday. The rest of the week . . ."

"What?"

"I have to stay in bed—you need to. Tomorrow, you'll see."

He was high and accelerating—liquid, as if the furnace in his stomach was simmering his bone and muscle into lava. But what the girl said grated. Somewhere in his mind there lurked desolation: the things he normally liked had been drained off and not only could he not locate them, he couldn't remember what they were. He needed to find a pen and list the reasons for living. But what on the list could be comparable to the feeling of this drug? He had been let into a dangerous secret; once it had been revealed, much of life, regarded from this high vantage point, could seem quite small.

He and the girl next to him were kissing, drawing on one another's tongues until they felt their heads would fuse.

Someone was lying down beside him and tugging at his shoulder. Shahid ignored them. The room had become one nameless body, one mouth and kiss. Then he was being dragged round; it was Deedee and she was coming at him with a ferocious look, before pushing away the other girl and falling into his mouth.

She took his hand and led him away; they were the first in the pool.

They clambered into the silence of the taxi and discovered their ears were yearning for music much as one's stomach complains for food, but there was none available. Deedee put her head on his shoulder. "Tell me a story."

"What sort?"

"Oh, something romantic and dirty." She shut her eyes. "I will visualize it as you tell. Tonight I can see around corners."

At first, out of fear and shame, he made his story deliberately childish, but since she tugged his lapel and lapped his ear as he stumbled on, he had, by audience demand, to discover a story with sufficient bendy dirtiness in it, a story to turn her on.

When he could invent no more, she said, "Please, you won't tell anyone about this night?"

"Course not." He could see it still bothered her. "I promise, baby."

"Yes, call me baby." She was kissing his face. "Baby, baby, baby." Yet she was still worried. "I wish I wasn't always the oldest woman at that kind of thing."

"I wish it wouldn't worry you."

"It makes me think that all my friends are married or they live with people. Most of them have at least one child now. They wouldn't dream of doing this kind of thing. I couldn't begin to tell them about it."

He recognized the street but all the doors looked identical. She was laughing as she helped him try several buildings with his key. At last one of them worked and they stepped into the cat-piss odor of the hall. The cab waited. They fell kissing against the wall.

"Again?"

She replied, "Again and again."

He climbed up to his room, repeating "again and again" until the words lost all sense.

He could have slept but knew when he woke up life would be banal. Why did Deedee have to go? Why wasn't she with him now? Why hadn't he been able to ask his teacher to spend the night with him after such a high time in the swimming pool of dreams?

As he let himself into his room, threw his clothes down, and fell into bed, he realized that she would be on her way over. Surely she'd get out of the taxi and find the solitude unbearable? She'd come to him through the streets of burning polar bears, knowing he would be waiting. After all, she had whispered in the taxi—and this was what he'd wanted to hear since his teens—"Would you let me suck you? I would love to have your cock in my mouth." She had said it, hadn't she?

But now that happiness was happening at last, his teeth were chattering. Would he be able to satisfy her? He couldn't even feel his balls. Surely, finding him in this state, she would slip her Katharine Hamnett jacket back on and skip down the stairs past Riaz's open-mouthed queue. She would take a taxi to a club in the West End; he saw her running through the door and into the arms of a tall man in evening dress who had been waiting for her.

At least Shahid didn't have to be tucked up in bed in his pajamas when she rang the bell. He could be up—doing what? Preparing an omelette. He put on his trousers and Walkman, turned on the three gas jets and lay down on the dusty floor by the stove, determined to remain alert until it was time to crack the eggs—if he could find some eggs. Maybe she would bring some with her. Yeah, she would know to.

What else had she said, he pondered, extracting his dick and trying to stroke it into shape. (Soon she would be there; he would lift her clothes up and lie next to her; in the morning they would go to college: lovers.) As they parted she had apologized for taking him to places where there were only white people. "The White Room's very, well, you know, white."

What was that sound? She was knocking. She had arrived! He had to let her in. But he couldn't move; the room was swirling so much he couldn't even grip the floor with his hand. Of course she would know that. Anyway, he'd left the door unlocked. She was coming toward him, light as an angel.

She was waking him! He stirred as she pulled him into her arms, warm as mother, where he dissolved.

CHAPTER 7

You're definitely the lucky type," Chad said to Shahid, not without sarcasm. "Hey, Shahid, I'm asking why you so privileged!"

Riaz stood by his desk sorting through a pile of papers. As he finished with the sheets Tahira handed them to Chad, who was arranging them in a file for Shahid.

Brother Shahid was sitting on Riaz's bed with, at this moment, one hand over his eyes and the other hovering near his mouth—which felt as if it were full of Parmesan—in order to catch any deplorable projection.

He made himself say, "Why am I lucky?"

"To be of such use. The brother asked for you particularly."

Half an hour before Chad had pulled Shahid out of bed, had stood there with Shahid's clothes while Shahid held on to him, stumbling into shorts, trousers, and shirt. At the time, transfixed by a brown roll of fat on the back of Chad's neck, he'd laughed at the absurdity of it. But now he was getting irritable.

"And there is this," Riaz said. "Shahid."

"Shahid!" Chad said.

Shahid noticed that Riaz was standing over him with

the sheaf of papers. Riaz waited until Shahid opened his eyes before offering them to him, and then he did it reluctantly, as if under
irresistible pressure.

"What is it, Riaz?" Shahid asked gently.

"Please." Riaz invited him to hold the papers.

With clammy fingers Shahid turned the pages, marking a damp
print on each one. The manuscript was about fifty pages long. The
handwritten title was "The Martyr's Imagination."

Chad was looking from Shahid to Riaz in amazement. Tahira
was beaming at Shahid.

"Yes, it's my . . . It's my little book," Riaz said.

"No!" Tahira exclaimed. "It's finished?"

"Pen-written only until now. Please," Riaz said to Shahid.
"Would you do one thing for me?"

"Anything, Riaz."

"Will you convert it to print?"

"Of course. No problem."

"Chad here tells me you have some literary airs."

"Yes, I'm working on a novel."

"About?" interjected Chad.

"My parents. Growing up. A typical first novel."

"Not an insulting one, like some other people have been writing, I hope?" Tahira said.

"He is not that type," Riaz said.

"No," she agreed.

Riaz said, "Now, some others have volunteered but I have been
thinking a few days that you are the right person for this task."

Intrigued, Shahid opened it on the first page. The writing didn't
fill the page. It was poetry. Riaz had written a book of poems. He
was a writer, too.

Riaz smiled shyly at Shahid. "You know, I am from a small village in Pakistan. They are basically . . . songs of memory, adoles-
cence, and twilight. But perhaps they will change the world a little,
too."

"I didn't know you—" Shahid began, turning the pages. He

could see that Riaz liked adjectives but figured the verbs would be in there somewhere.

"Oh, yes," Chad said. "Riaz a poet."

Riaz smiled modestly. "It's God's work."

"With your name on the title page," Shahid said.

"Yes," Riaz beamed. "I am entirely to blame."

Tahira gave Shahid a glass of water and two painkillers. "Perhaps this will help you with the work." She turned to Riaz. "What message does the book have, brother?"

"The message—and all art, to speak to us truly, must have a message—is of love and compassion."

"Beautiful," Chad murmured. He pointed at Shahid. "Now we gotta leave the brother to think."

Shahid's eyes shone with tears as, backward, he moved to the door. "Brother Riaz, thank you, thank you for . . . everything!"

"No, no," said Riaz.

Chad pursued Shahid into his room, hardly able to contain himself.

"Wow, that's incredible, he's given you his book to type. It's a privilege, it really is."

"You didn't want to do it, did you, Chad?"

"What? I will offer you one warning—you must be strictly confidential about this."

"What do you think I am?" Shahid said. He was getting annoyed. Papa and Chili had taught Shahid the uses of a temper: it had been something he wanted to cultivate, but as yet didn't come easily to him. "Are you saying I'm not trustworthy?"

"No, no, brother." Chad tried to soothe him. "But Riaz is dangerous, too radical. To us he is a friend but many important people in the community wouldn't like him being creative. It's too frivolous, too merry for them. Some of those guys go into a supermarket and if music playing, they run out again."

"Yes?"

"They say the emotions shouldn't be discussed. He should be doing more serious things with his time." Chad put his hand on

Shahid's shoulder. "Sorry, brother. How you feeling?"

"A little weak."

Chad slid Riaz's book from Shahid's hands. "Why don't you enjoy some rest before you begin such important work?"

Shahid lay down on his bed. Meanwhile Chad sat down at Shahid's desk and studied the book, even though Riaz didn't appear to have given him permission.

At about six o'clock that morning Shahid had awoken on the floor of his room freezing cold, with aching temples. A finger was skewering into one of his eyes; water gurgled in his ears. Worse, he felt sealed, as if someone had dragged a plastic bag down over his skull. He couldn't breathe. His mouth, throat, and nose were blocked. Even as he struggled like a drowning man, he couldn't make out the obstruction or the source of the thick wetness soaking the front of his body. He feared his brain had melted and was seeping through his nose and mouth. To make things worse, Deedee was striking him on the back and his dick was hanging out.

It was Riaz, not Deedee, who had heard him come home; alerted by the smell of gas, and wondering if he would type some letters to the Labour leader George Rugman Rudder, he had come into his room.

It was Riaz who had clapped the clogging vomit from his throat; Riaz who grappled him to the sink to flush out his nose and mouth. Finally Shahid, prostrate on his bed, had beheld, behind a range of undulating purple pyramids, his spiritual brother scrubbing vomit from the walls, the floorboards, and several Penguin Classics with the flannel Shahid's mother had bought him. Then Riaz rinsed the flannel, laid it on the edge of the sink, checked his neighbor was still vital, and tiptoed away.

Now Shahid wanted to sleep. He needed to sleep and he wanted to dream about Deedee, what she wore, what she had said, what they could do together, where they could go. More: he wanted to

see her again, maybe that night; as soon as she wanted, as soon as he
could get there. How could he go back to being without her! What
a coup, too, people would be impressed no end—if he knew any
people. But there was no one he could boast to about this lover,
least of all his new friends.

Now, as he drifted off and discovered that he could reanimate
the hallucinations of the previous night, they merged with Chad's
voice from across the room. "Magnificent," he was purring. " 'Pure
beauty in my hands . . . How fragrant is the shadow of the sword.' "

Shahid sat up and reached for the bowl beside the bed.

" 'Your body was wet and your captivating tongue told a fairy
tale, you bitch woman.' " At Shahid's whimper, Chad turned to
him. "Sorry, not talking to you. You know, Shahid brother, here's
something else Riaz wants you to do. He was shy of asking you, I
know."

"What is it?"

"He needs you to help him get the book published."

Shahid retched into the bowl and wiped his mouth on the duvet, before saying, "You know, I was pretty sick in the night. But
Riaz came into my room—"

"He intuitive—"

"He saved my life."

Chad grunted with satisfaction. "You owe him the lot."

"Yes," Shahid agreed. "I've promised to do everything I can to
repay him."

"You'll help him find a publisher for the book?"

"Sure."

"I thank you on his behalf."

For the rest of the day Shahid was unable to sleep, possessed alternately by fear and happiness, as if he were being plunged into
cold water and then into hot.

But at least he was in bed. At home he rarely got the chance to
laze around. Papa, who would have gone to work hours before,
would send Uncle Tipoo—who did all the gardening, cleaning, and
washing—to wake him up. But Tipoo, too nervous to confront

Shahid, would vacuum the hall outside; then he'd do under Shahid's
bed even while he slept, before sucking the sheets from Shahid's bed
and fleeing.

When Shahid wasn't working with his parents, he rarely saw
them. They ate out several evenings a week with business clients,
there were parties, or they worked late, or Papa was in his room
with his cronies. Shahid knew them more by their bathroom
noises. Lying in bed he heard the Niagaras of water his father used,
doing what, Shahid didn't know, but the taps ran and ran. His
mother constantly dropped things, eye-pencils in the sink, earrings;
her various bags snapped, her heels clicked on the floor.

Then the front door would shut and the car would start. Shahid
would get up to remind himself of which relative was living in the
house; and if Zulma was there, he'd stay in his room as much of the
day as he could, or think of ways to avoid her.

Those days of stifling, self-sodden uselessness wouldn't return.
He was going to do something.

By early evening he was able to pull himself from bed and sit at
his word processor. He opened Riaz's manuscript; his fingers
dropped into their familiar places on the keys. He began to type
Riaz's words but, staring at the screen, couldn't avoid falling into a
dreamlike state.

When Shahid was fifteen, his father, provoked by Chili, com-
mandeered Shahid to work in the agency. It wasn't an easy job, because Shahid had to make himself appear busy. Fortunately, in the
back office there were two abandoned typewriters and a *How to
Type* book from which Shahid started teaching himself. He loved
the squat, gray machine with its black-and-red ribbon, and the
sound of the keys peppering the page like rain on a tin roof, and
the bell tinging at the end of each line, signaling him to smack the
carriage arm. To increase his speed, he copied passages from his favorite writers: Chandler, Dostoevsky, Hunter S. Thompson. When
he grew weary of keeping the place, he altered their words and had
their characters do what he required. On Papa's headed notepaper
he began writing stories.

The first effort he copied—he created a sandwich of flimsy carbon paper which resulted in two smeared reproductions—was called "Paki Wog Fuck Off Home." It featured the six boys who comprised the back row of his class at school, who, one day when the teacher had left the room in despair, chanted at Shahid, "Paki, Paki, Paki, Out, Out, Out!" He banged the scene into his machine as he relived it, recording the dismal fear and fury in a jagged, cunt-fuck-kill prose that expressed him, like a soul singer screaming into a microphone.

One evening he returned to his bedroom to discover his mother, still in her raincoat, reading the piece. She flapped the sheets at him, as if she had discovered a letter in which he had written intolerable things about her.

"I always know when you're playing some trick. I hope you're not trying to publish this!"

"I haven't thought about it," he lied. "It doesn't depend on me, does it?"

"What does it depend on?"

"Whether anyone's interested."

"Not one person is interested! Who would want to read this? People don't want this hate in their lives." She began to rip up what she'd read. "Good-bye to filth, good-bye to filth—and don't you spread it!"

It was not physically easy for his mother to obliterate the fifteen pages, a copy of which he had posted to the literary magazine *Stand* along with a stamped self-addressed envelope—every morning he hurried downstairs to see if the envelope had returned. She even glanced toward her son, but he would not assist her, oh, no, especially as she was so intent on doing it that she leaned forward to lay more of her weight into the assault.

For days she gave him severe looks.

More than anything she hated any talk of race or racism. Probably she had suffered some abuse and contempt. But her father had been a doctor; everyone—politicians, generals, journalists, police chiefs—came to their house in Karachi. The idea that anyone might treat her with disrespect was insupportable. Even when Shahid vomited and defecated with fear before going to school, or when he returned with cuts, bruises, and his bag slashed with knives, she behaved as if so appalling an insult couldn't exist. And so she turned away from him. What she knew was too much for her.

Nevertheless, her attitude toward his writing particularly shocked him. Two years previously they had been to see *The House of Bernarda Alba* at the Kent University theater.

From the first moment—a servant scrubbing the stone floor, the peeling church bells, the chilling entrance of the black-garbed, inquisitorial matriarch shouting, "Silence!"—to the final blackout, Lorca's burning, confined world compelled them. Shahid hadn't known the theater could have this effect. To his joy, he could feel his mother beside him, as gripped, excited, disturbed.

At the end he couldn't bear to break the spell by speaking, and he wanted to avoid the comments of anyone else in the auditorium. His mother seemed to sense this, and as they drove home through the rain they were complicitly silent, though Shahid did ask if the play reminded her of life in Pakistani families. She thought for a time before dipping her head.

"This is it, this is it!" Shahid had said to himself, jigging around his bedroom later. Literature hadn't been like this at school, where books were stuck down their throats like medicinal biscuits, until they spat them out. He was filled with the play; he relived the claustrophobic and tragic passions the actors had evoked; he repeated aloud the blazing language. Something in him felt triumphantly justified. He was discovering new emotions and new possibilities. More than anything he wanted to achieve such an effect with a piece of writing.

But who was he to presume he could be so subtle and profound? Every third person thought they could write and should tell their story. Yet the play Lorca wrote two months before his murder didn't intimidate him. Something in its gentle greatness inspired him to think that, in his own way, he would have experience, imagination, and dedication. Why did he have to diminish himself? There were plenty ready to do that. Anyhow, writing had been a compulsion for a couple of years. Of course, it wasn't as if he didn't have to force himself to do it, and wouldn't, often, rather do almost anything else. It was work and never entirely pleasant; there would be a moment's satisfaction compared to a week's discouragement. The rewards weren't instant, as with childish things, and they were never unalloyed. Whenever anything was achieved, there was always something harder to be attempted. There would be no end to it, fortunately.

The feelings animated in him by his "Lorca night" made him yearn for other experiences as affecting. He taped opera, jazz, and pop records from the library. He listened repeatedly to composers he had learned weren't as bad as they sounded, like Bartók, Wagner, and Stravinsky. He searched out good movies. His wish was granted. He extended the Lorca experience again and again, each time being brought to think and feel in new ways. He never lost his appetite for the compelling exhilaration.

He had assumed that the Lorca evening had been an enduring ravishment for his mother. But the next time Shahid found himself in his father's car, Papa asked why he had started writing "such damn bloody things." Papa, always conscious of his own failings, didn't like to lecture his sons, but clearly felt the necessity now. "You're not the type to do this. Can't you stick to your studies? My nephews are lawyers, bankers, and doctors. Ahmed has gone into the hat trade and built a sauna in his house! These artist types are always poor—how will you look relatives in the face?"

It began to dawn on Shahid that there were a multitude of true things that couldn't be said because they led to uneasy thoughts. Disruption of life, even, could follow; the truth could have serious consequences. Clearly the unsaid was where it all happened.

Papa said, "Your type can never do this booky stuff."

"But why not?"

Heartbreakingly, Papa didn't hesitate, "Because these writers—"

"Who?"

"Howard Spring, Erskine Caldwell, and Monsaratt, for instance, they are concerned with flowers and trees and love and all. And that's not your area. We must," said his father with tenderness, "live in the real world."

Not his area. Flowers and trees and love and all. The real world.

"I'll break your bloody fingers if you try anything like that* again," was Chili's aside, later, as he sat there with his arms around Zulma. "I've never seen Mum so brokenhearted. And Papa, he came to me. Already he's had one thrombosis—the pressure you are putting on his heart. I can't even think about when you will bring on the next one."

Shahid adored and venerated his father; both he and Chili, in their different ways, wanted to be like him. (Shahid remembered copying the authoritative way Papa walked.) But this was different; Shahid had to admit that Papa was wrong and find his own direction, whatever that was.

Now, he sat at his desk and began typing Riaz's manuscript into the lighted box. Shahid had become a secretary—and a stoned one at that—as he found himself squinting into the corrugated handwriting.

Soon he was halfway down the first page of "A Heretical Artist." His typing fingers, sensing Deedee's body beneath them, danced on the keys too euphorically for the subject matter. He told himself that concentration was the cornerstone of creativity. He pulled himself together, but got an erection which just wouldn't go away.

CHAPTER
8

To make things easier later, Shahid stripped the seal from a new packet of condoms. He had spent the afternoon in the library rewriting his essay before returning home to type the first draft. Now it was early evening and already dark. The street outside was noisy. He pulled the curtains and turned up the gas fire. Having exerted himself and cleared his conscience, he could savor this part of the day, lower the lights, and play "Dancing in the Dark" while deciding whether to wear the black, blue, or red jeans. The promise of love and the night— the whole night—was ahead of him.

He was going to see Deedee. Since their last meeting they'd phoned one another several times and met in her room at college, where they had kissed. This time he's the one who'd said, "Can I take you out?" though she was making the arrangements. She knew London and would enjoy showing it to him. Wasn't she an educator?

She'd booked an Indian place where she went constantly, The Standard in Westbourne Grove, which had neither flock wallpaper nor sitar music. The menu never changed, the waiters were quick and professional, not students or actors. The hot mutter paneer was tangy; in all of London you could get no better chickpeas, though you might need to open the windows later.

They could wash it all down in a Maida Vale pub overlooking the canal and boats. The patrons drank European beers in dark bottles, and dressed up, as only London kids could, in peculiar combinations of designer labels, junk shop, and American sports clothes; some people behaved as though they were on a photo shoot. There were more ponytails than at Ascot. You could sit there until closing time, observing and passing comment. She had obtained some hallucinogenic grass, too. Or they could take in a movie. There was a weird cult film on at the Gate that people were arguing about.

She said, and he could hear the tension in her voice, "There's a flat. In Islington. It belongs to a friend, Hyacinth, who's away. We can go there later, if you want. Spend the night. OK?"

"Yes," he said.

"Excellent. See you later, then."

Someone was knocking at the door. Shahid opened it hesitantly, dreading the arrival of Chili. It was Chad's round and incessantly perturbed face. He charged into the room and, without a word, snapped off the music.

"Hey, listen."

Shahid pulled up his trousers, concealing the condoms in his hand and slipping them into his back pocket. "To what—nothing?"

"Sometimes silence makes the most beautiful music."

Chad suddenly pretended to be all dreamy. But he had interrupted at the wrong moment.

"Don't you find all this music too . . . noisy?"

"Not noisy enough right now."

Shahid was afraid of Chad's bulk and suppressed violence, but he pushed him aside and turned up the music, with added bass, until the furniture vibrated. At this Chad banged his palms over his ears while simultaneously, Shahid observed, bouncing his foot.

"Riaz sent me. I'm on brother business."

"I've been meaning to ask, Chad, why were you looking through my cassettes the other day?"

"Shahid, I tell you, man—I mean, brother, I used to be a music addict. Sit right down and hear me!"

"Not now, Chad."

"But I was like you, I listened to it day and night! It was over-taking my soul!"

"You were being controlled by the music?"

"Give me a few minutes!"

It was getting late but Shahid had no choice. Chad grabbed him by the shoulders and forced him down on the bed, holding his face, hot as a fire with conviction, only inches from him. To Shahid he looked crazy, as if he were reacting to remembered hallucinations.

"Not like some mad schizophrenic! But by the music and fashion industries. They tell us what to wear, where to go, what to listen to. Ain't we their slaves? I was doing everything else, too. To get the day begun I'd do any coke I had left. When that stressed me I'd have a spliff and a bottle of cider. To swing I'd pop two Es, or drop acid. Into the night, when I got dazed and thought the police were watching me through the television, I'd shoot gear. Look at these arms."

"Christ, Chad."

"Yeah, I'll present you me legs in a minute."

"Pass."

"I went to the coolest clubs. I never saw daylight unless it was the dawn. I rejected whole shoals of people because of their clothes or their music! I took my motto from Aleister Crowley: 'Do what thou wilt shall be the whole of the Law.' Crazy slavery, eh?"

"I'm no junkie."

"No? But what direction you going in, then?"

"Tonight I'm going out with a friend."

"The same friend as before?"

Shahid said, "I'm not living without music. Tell me the truth— you miss it, too."

"I'm stronger without those drugs." Chad squeezed Shahid's arm, and, looking at him with mad kindness, as if he were handing him truth on a plate, said, "Don't you want to swim in a clean sea and see by a clear light?"

"Isn't that what art helps us do? Life would be a desert otherwise. Wouldn't it, Chad?"

Chad made quick breaststroke motions. "Imagine the warm water holding you up!"

Shahid tried to shrug Chad off. He wasn't going to be pulled about by this man, to whom reality was clearly a lost kingdom, especially when he had a date to prepare for.

But Chad held on to him as if he had to save him.

"Take me seriously! We are not dancing monkeys. We have minds and sense. Why do we want to reduce ourselves to the level of animals? I am not descended from an ape but from something noble! You'll find yourself looking deeper into things. Aren't you with us?"

"Yes."

"Yes, you say. But I am not sure you're a real brother. Get clean! Gimme those Prince records!"

"Don't touch those—some of them are imports!"

Shahid found himself struggling with Chad.

"We are slaves to Allah," Chad cried. "He is the only one we must submit to! He put our noses on our face—"

"As opposed to where?"

"Our stomach, for instance. How can you deny his skill and power and authority?"

"I don't, Chad, you know I don't. And you know I respect you as a brother, too, that's why I'm asking you to stop!"

"We think we cool but we break our trust with Allah. Listen to Riaz. You've come with us to the mosque to hear him. Were you impressed?"

Shahid had to say he was. Twice he'd visited the large, cool building with the posse, to watch Riaz's Sunday talks. They were well attended by a growing audience of young people, mostly local cockney Asians. Not being an aged obscurantist, Riaz was becoming the most popular speaker. He must have tasted the atmosphere of his time without drinking it in, for he entitled his talks "Rave to the Grave?," "Adam and Eve not Adam and Steve," "Islam: A Blast from the Past or a Force for the Future?," and "Democracy is a Hypocrisy."

Sitting barefoot and cross-legged on a low podium in gray salwar, with a bowl of flowers in front of him, Riaz didn't use notes and he never hesitated. The momentum of his conviction made him fluent, amusing, passionately coruscating. He appeared more comfortable addressing a crowd than being with one person. He never ran short of words or appeared uneasy. No subject could hold him. He may have begun his talk under the guise of discussing Islamic identity, for instance, but soon he would be expatiating on the creation of the universe, the persecution of Muslims worldwide, the state of Israel, gays and lesbians, Islam in Spain, face-lifts, nudity, the dumping of nuclear waste in the Third World, perfume, the collapse of the West, and Urdu poetry.

Even if he'd opened by wryly saying, "Today I'm not going to blast anything," he would start to rage, fist in the air, throwing down his pen, creating a frisson of humorous agreement in his audience. Then, pretending to be contrite, he'd beg the brothers to apologize to anyone they might have argued with, and to love those of other religions.

At the end, when he was empty, brothers like Hat and Chad would have to usher him away, putting a jacket around his shoulders, before he was smothered by the praise he was due.

Chad said, "Don't he say we becoming Western, European, socialist? And the socialists are all talk. They are paralyzed now for good! Look at that slug Brownlow, for instance! Or his wife, that Osgood woman!"

"What about her?"

"They are existing at the lowest level! And we think we want to integrate here! But we must not assimilate, that way we lose our souls. We are proud and we are obedient. What is wrong with that? It's not we who must change, but the world!" Chad was looking at Shahid. "It's hellfire for disbelievers, you know that."

"And heaven for the rest?"

"Yes. What d'you say, brother? What do you say?"

At that moment Riaz came into the room. He was dressed in a large, thick overcoat and gloves.

At his side, lugging the clanking army bag which the butcher had brought, was Hat, wearing a duffle coat and a green woolly hat pulled down over his ears. His scarf was neatly tied. He looked as if his mother had dressed him for school on a cold day.

Tahira, along with two other students, Tariq and Nina, stood behind them in the hall, also warmly dressed. Tahira's dark eyes, practically all Shahid could see of her, smiled encouragingly at him. She noticed him looking at Hat and said, "His Dad thinks he's visiting his auntie in Birmingham."

Chad uncoupled himself from Shahid. "There's something else I haven't had time to tell you about. Are you available?"

"For what?"

"There's an emergency on. Defense required. Our people under attack tonight."

"What are you talking about?"

Riaz looked at Chad and then at Shahid. Chad composed himself. Riaz's presence calmed everyone. He said, "You should be with us, Shahid, tonight."

"Shahid's always with us," Chad said, patting his shoulder.

"But I—"

Hat said, "Many others from college have also agreed to join us."

"Come along," said Riaz. "Collect your warm clothes."

Shahid felt he had no choice but to slip on the black puffa coat his mother had given him. He had, anyhow, been waiting to try it out.

"What are we doing, then?" he asked.

"Protection racket," Hat said. "Honest people abused."

"We're not blasted Christians," Riaz replied with considerable aggression for him, though the effect was rather undermined by the fact that he was, as usual, carrying his briefcase. "We don't turn the other cheek. We will fight for our people who are being tortured in Palestine, Afghanistan, Kashmir! War has been declared against us. But we are armed."

"No degradation of our people," said Chad, as they charged

downstairs. "Anybody who fails to fight will answer to God and hellfire!"

"We should call ourselves the Foreign Legion," Shahid told Hat on the stairs, getting into the spirit of the thing. His blood was warming; he felt a physical pride in their cause, whatever it was. He was one with the regiment of brothers and sisters. "What d'you say, Chad?"

Chad put his arm around Shahid. "I knew you were with us. Sorry I shouted and all. I get into a state."

"Foreign Legion!" Hat chanted.

Riaz's army were squeezing past the bicycles in the downstairs hall when the phone on the wall rang. Hat snatched it up. "Foreign Legion!" Then he called, "Hey, Shahid, it for you."

"Is it Chili? Say I'm—"

Hat shook his head. "A lady."

Shahid took the receiver. He'd been alarmed at the idea of letting Deedee down; she would be waiting for him. Now he could explain he was on an urgent errand. He would catch up with her later, lean his head on her shoulder and explain.

"Shahid?"

He recognized the voice but couldn't place the person. All the same, he shivered.

"It's Zulma."

At home he would hide in the toilet to avoid Chili's wife, dreaming up ways of harming her. She loved to complain that he was lazy, and moaned that "strange human smells" oozed from under his door and polluted the house. To Chili she would say, if Shahid's so intellectual, why doesn't he ever pass his exams; or, why are his girlfriends so badly dressed and mousy? Can't he find a beautiful Pakistani girl? Our women are the most delightful in the world!

"Oh, Zulma, great to hear from you. What's up?"

He imagined her lying on a couch in her silk salwar, looking like a film star, her black hair, which reached the floor, shining like patent leather.

"How are your studies coming?"

So friendly today: what could she want?

"Fine, fine, Zulma."

"Working hard?"

"Never harder."

"Making friends?"

Through the open door he could see the others waiting for him in the street.

"The best ever."

"Have you seen Chili?"

Why was she asking him? She was Chili's wife. She would be seeing him, if anyone was.

"Yes."

"Shahid, tell me when."

"When? He comes by to say hello."

"Chili never said hello to anyone. What's his number at the moment in London? My pen's hanging."

Outside Chad started gesturing to Shahid. Two minicabs had drawn up.

"I don't know, Zulma."

"Where's he's staying?"

"You know what he's like, he's probably staying with friends. They play poker all night and all."

She became fierce. "What the hell, Shahid, which damn friends? You better tell me, because you know."

"Do I?"

"Last time he said, you'll be seeing me. Where? I said. On the TV news, he said. What madness did he mean, eh?"

She was pressuring him. But why should he start doing her favors?

"Listen, Zulma, I gotta run to the library. You know Chili, or you ought to, and he doesn't tell no one what he's doing."

There was a pause. She was wondering whether to believe him. Whatever happened, she couldn't put her hands to his throat here. Outside, the first cab drew away.

She said, "I'm coming to London. I need to see you. We're all thinking of you, learning so much."

"Cheerio, Zulma."

"Wait! You haven't got in with a rotten crowd, have you? You know how easily influenced you are."

"Bye-bye."

"Shahid!"

He replaced the receiver and was about to ring Deedee when the second minicab started to move, beeping its horn. Shahid rushed outside, Chad threw open the door and he squeezed in beside Riaz. The car was driven by a man in salwar kamiz over which he wore a sleeveless pullover. Strings of beads flailed against the windshield.

To Shahid's relief, there was silence, affording him time to think about Zulma. She had lost Chili; or Chili was avoiding her; or something worse had occurred. To admit so much—she must have been concerned.

She came from a prominent, land-owning Karachi family and, like other such types, lived part of the year in Pakistan and the rest in England. In Karachi she zipped around the camel carts and potholes in an imported red Fiat Uno, a Hermès scarf knotted around her head. In London she went to her friends' houses and pursued the shopping, gossiping, and general troublemaking-in-other-families she enjoyed so much. She was light-skinned, beautiful, Zulma, but never beautiful enough: it took her two days to prepare for a party. She brushed her hair, of which she had sufficient for three people, with a hundred strokes and washed it only in rainwater. At the first hint of a shower Zulma would shake Tipoo awake and have him dash into the garden with bowls and saucepans.

Intelligence wasn't requisite for such women so it was significant that after marrying Chili she didn't stay in bed or practice aerobics, but accompanied him to work, where she learned everything she could about the business.

Also she made it her business to have Papa adore her. She would do everything he required; Bibi, Shahid's mother, had never been easy in this role, knowing it would be never-ending—from cooking tandoori chicken to buying records by the Ink Spots and listening to his accounts of the war. And when, each night, as Papa's cronies—the Indian and English owners of local businesses, restaurants, and garages, as well as any relatives who were staying—came to drink whiskey, watch movies, and "shoot the breeze" around Papa's bed, Zulma would sit with them, the only woman.

At first she merely greeted the cronies, fetched ice, offered crisps, and drove to the video shop. But it soon became clear that catering was not to be her finest accomplishment. The men started encouraging her to say what she thought. There in the bar-thick cigar smoke, her dissections of mutual or absent acquaintances, along with her nicknames for them and accounts of their misfortunes, were so disparaging and precisely cruel that the fearful cronies were left blanching and choking with laughter, as well as being terrified that they too would become her victims—which they did. Papa cherished this malicious talent. He exhibited her to the cronies as if she were a sleek tiger about to slip its diamond-studded leash.

Chili was proud of her, too. He loved walking into a party with Zulma and waiting for people to gather around. At home her phone never stopped ringing. The two of them went to dinner with politicians, bankers, businessmen, film producers like Ishmail Merchant, and fashionable actors like Karim Amir, with whom she was photographed by *Hello!* magazine. Her brother was an international pilot, and Zulma could fly aircraft. She took out hired planes as often as the local wives went horseback-riding, buzzing the cronies as they drove up the lanes. She contributed to Chili's glory; she was the best woman he'd ever had. However, there was a part of him that became not only jealous of the attention of other men, but, more importantly, envious of her attributes. He felt put down by her. He was supposed to know more than she did, and he didn't.

Chili returned to his old life, staying out late, disappearing to London, going to clubs with girlfriends; but he was careful with Zulma—rarely disrespectful, and he never hit her.

Zulma had few objections to his absences; she had her distractions. She socialized keenly with the Pakistani cricket team when Papa invited them to the house. Shahid caught her kissing a fast bowler—a very fast bowler—in the kitchen. Her family had a flat in Knightsbridge where she went to stay during the major matches, and where, so Shahid heard, she dealt with certain overdue virgins.

Shahid's mistake was to try to have political discussions with her, for, like Chili, she was an arch-Thatcherite. She would patronize and incense him, personalizing everything, saying, "It's typical, you're living off a business family, this isn't a commune, is it? Your father's a businessman, you're a hypocrite, aren't you?" Zulma could reduce him to near-tears of frustration if he talked about fairness or equality or opportunity, or the need to reduce unemployment. She'd laugh; the world couldn't be like that. What was needed was the opposite—enterprising people (like her and Chili, presumably)—who weren't afraid to crush others to get what they wanted.

He argued she was a dupe, explaining what racists the Thatcherites were. She might imagine she was an intelligent, upper-class woman, but to them she'd always be a Paki and liable to be patronized. She appreciated the truth of this, but it was a colonial residue—the new money knew no color.

Then she and Chili moved back into the house. Papa was dead. Shahid knew he had to get away and do something that had meaning while Zulma insisted, for the sake of the family, that he "go into travel."

He had traveled—to London. And now he was literally moving further and further away from her and all of them. He had escaped, but into what?

"Where are we going?" Shahid repeated to Riaz.

He and his new friends had driven through the City and were, it seemed, making for the East End. He needed to know what they were doing; he was anxious about missing Deedee later.

Riaz said, "I've written a poem on this subject. 'The Wrath.' Have you reached it yet?"

"Which one?"

" 'The Wrath.' 'The Wrath.' "

"No, not yet."

Chad interrupted: "How rapidly is the conversion onto computer coming along, then?"

"It couldn't be coming along faster. Riaz, brother, when do you want it finished? I have done a little but—"

"Please don't get into a rush."

"Thank you," Shahid sighed. "Also—"

He wanted to inform Riaz that some of the language wasn't as telling as it could be and that the thought was occasionally muddled; he'd reorganized it a little. He was about to tell Riaz this when they pulled up at a windswept project.

"Let's go," said Chad. He picked up the bag of weapons, extracted a machete, and put it under his coat. "This is it, brothers and sisters."

T hey parked, got out of the car, and started off behind
the shuffling driver, who had tied a scarf under his chin
and knotted it on top of his head as if he had toothache.

A somber sky, misty pathways, and dead grass bound
the blocks together. Small trees, in wire wrapping, had
been snapped in two, as if they gave offense. There was
graffiti, but only tags, nothing more to say, apart from
the strange legend in foot-high gold-and-silver letters,
"Eat the Pig."

The streetlamps shed little light. The shadows of the
posse rode beside them, like figures on horseback. The
silence was broken by car alarms. There was the sound
of a man running, followed by another, and shouts. The
group stood and waited as one, anticipating attack. They
were ready; indeed, they wanted, required, confrontation. But the moment passed. Menacing silence resumed.

The muffled boys and hooded girls were led into a
creaking lift. Then they moved through passageways
made ghostly by the reflections of jutting concrete
cliffs. They were plodding through one gully when
Shahid recognized the weeping brass of "Try a Little
Tenderness" coming from an open window. Chad heard

it, too, and stopped dead. Tariq crashed into him, and Tahira trod on Hat, marking his white trainers. The driver trotted on and disappeared around the corner.

Chad bent down and tied his shoelaces, twice, for as long as the music played. Getting up, he saw Shahid regarding him. Chad's eyes were wet. Shahid wanted to put his arms around him, but he marched on.

They arrived outside a flat which belonged to a Bengali family who had attended Riaz's "surgeries." The father of the family had been the man talking to Riaz when Shahid had gone into his room.

The family had been harried—stared at, spat on, called "Paki scum"—for months, and finally attacked. The husband had been smashed over the head with a bottle and taken to hospital. The wife had been punched. Lighted matches had been pushed through the letter box. At all hours the bell had been rung and the culprits said they would return to slaughter the children. Chad reckoned the aggressors weren't neofascist skinheads. It was beneath the strutting lads to get involved in lowly harassment. These hooligans were twelve and thirteen years old.

Through his contact on the council, George Rugman Rudder, Riaz had arranged for the family to move to a Bengali estate, but it wouldn't happen immediately. So Riaz had taken action. Until the family moved, he would guard the flat and seek out the culprits, along with Hat, Chad, Shahid, and other boys and girls from the college.

Their driver whispered through the letter-box and the woman, after the rattling of many locks, opened the door. The flat, with its busted furniture, boarded windows, and mauve view of the city below, was lit by only the TV and one shaded lamp. The woman wanted her enemies to think the family had fled.

The four young children were not frightened but playful, and they took to Chad. On entering, he emptied his pockets of sweets and pressed all his change on them, though their tiny hands couldn't catch it.

"What's wrong, Chad?" Shahid said.

"I'm moved by my people's suffering," he managed to say. "I can't keep it together."

"If you keep blubbering, the woman's not going to have much confidence in us."

"You're right." He blew his nose. "You stubborn but sometimes sensible."

Hat tipped up the green bag and out clattered cricket bats, clubs, knuckle-dusters, carving knives, and meat cleavers donated by the butcher.

"Used a weapon before?" Chad said.

"No," replied Shahid. "Can't say I have. You?"

"Yeah. I'll show you."

While Chad enthusiastically demonstrated the best way to handle a meat cleaver, Hat checked the layout of the flat for entrances, exits, and vulnerable junctures, just like a television cop. Then, to Chad's amazement and Tahira's giggles, he unpacked the overnight bag his mother had packed for him, putting his toothbrush and dental floss in the bathroom and hanging his red baseball cap in the hall.

Meanwhile Tahira prepared a little study area for him in the corner of the room.

"Hat always studying," Chad said, watching him. "He clever and his father putting too much pressure on him to be an accountant."

"Doesn't his dad run that restaurant Riaz likes?"

"Yeah," Chad said darkly. "But he don't like us. He think we stopping Hat being an accountant. But we ain't. We only say accountants have to meet many women. And shake hands with them. They expected, too, to take alcohol every day and get involved in interest payments. We not sure Hat won't feel left out, you know?"

Shahid was about to pick up the phone in the hall and ring Deedee when Riaz announced it was prayer time.

In Karachi, at the urging of his cousins, Shahid had been to the mosque several times. While their parents would drink bootleg whiskey and watch videos sent from England, Shahid's young relatives and their friends gathered in the house on Fridays before going to pray. The religious enthusiasm of the younger generation, and its links to strong political feeling, had surprised him. One time

Shahid was demonstrating some yoga positions to one of his female cousins when her brother intervened violently, pulling his sister's ankles away from her ears. Yoga reminded him of "those bloody Hindus." This brother also refused to speak English, though it was, in that household, the first and common language; he asserted that Papa's generation, with their English accents, foreign degrees, and British snobbery, assumed their own people were inferior. They should be forced to go into the villages and live among the peasants, as Gandhi had done.

At home Papa liked to say, when asked about his faith, "Yes, I have a belief. It's called working until my arse aches!" Shahid and Chili had been taught little about religion. And on the occasions that Tipoo prayed in the house, Papa grumbled and complained, saying, why did he have to make such noises during repeats of his favorite program, *The World at War?*

Now, though, Shahid was afraid his ignorance would place him in no man's land. These days everyone was insisting on their identity, coming out as a man, woman, gay, black, Jew—brandishing whichever features they could claim, as if without a tag they wouldn't be human. Shahid, too, wanted to belong to his people. But first he had to know them, their past, and what they hoped for. Fortunately, Hat had been of great help. Several times he had interrupted his studies to visit Shahid's room with books; sitting beside him, he had, for hours, explained parts of Islamic history, along with the essential beliefs. Then, clearing a space on the floor, he had demonstrated what to do.

While praying, Shahid had little notion of what to think, of what the cerebral concomitant to the actions should be. So, on his knees, he celebrated to himself the substantiality of the world, the fact of existence, the inexplicable phenomenon of life, art, humor, and love itself—in murmured language, itself another sacred miracle. He accompanied this awe and wonder with suitable music, the "Ode to Joy" from Beethoven's Ninth, for instance, which he hummed inaudibly.

Later that evening, the posse ate on the floor like guerrillas.

They'd brought college work with them; but they'd come a long way, they were stirred up, there was much to be avenged: no books were opened.

Around eleven there was a bang on the door.

Armed, everyone rose, including Tahira and Nina. Pigeon-toed Riaz hefted a sort of scimitar, not looking as if he could hoist it over his shoulder, let alone crack apart a skinhead's skull. Chad was already in the hall and at the front door. He was bearlike, but he was a swift mover. Meaning business, he turned back his sleeves, revealing his thick arms. Before unbarring the entrance he bent forward to listen for a voice through the door.

To everyone's surprise Brownlow leapt into the living room, not only wearing sandals with white socks but speaking words. His bony forehead shone. Shahid was surprised by how white he looked, as if someone had neglected to turn the color knob on the TV.

"Comrades!"

Apart from Riaz, they sat down again, relieved, disappointed.

"Good evening, comrades!" Brownlow declared. "Any sign of the lunatics?"

"Not until you arrived," Shahid murmured; the others smirked.

Riaz went to him. "Not as yet," he said. "But we know that immoral people surround us. Dr. Brownlow, we are so happy you received the message and were able to provide support."

Brownlow opened his arms expansively, as if he wanted to embrace everyone. They were fighting in the same trench.

"Ghastly—this estate! What has been done to these people! Crimes against humanity. Important to visit wastelands regularly. Lest we forget. Seeing them, one understands a lot. It's obvious, not surprising—"

Finally disclosed, Brownlow's voice was a fruity sound that could hail a taxi across Knightsbridge, send waiters scurrying like kicked dogs, and instantaneously put down mutinous colonies without being strained. Whether he barked, slurred, honked, or ordered, England had honeyed every rotund syllable. Poor Andrew spoke from the very thing he hated. On the day of the revolution his first job would be to tear out his own tongue.

"I beg your pardon?" Riaz said amusedly, looking at him with some intensity.

Riaz was invariably courteous to Andrew, calling him Dr. Brownlow and hanging on to his hand and cherishing it with little kiss-like pats, rather like the manager of an Indian restaurant greeting the mayor. At the same time Shahid knew by now that Riaz liked to have the advantage. His question, then, had a challenge in it. The group paid attention.

He continued: "What is not surprising to you, Dr. Brownlow, friend?"

But Brownlow was looking at Tahira with unmistakable lewdness; he was practically panting. He must have been on licensed premises a good few hours. Chad recognized it, too, and stepped back as from a blowtorch. Tahira pinched the end of her nose and made a face.

Shahid felt queasy. Brownlow seemed gay tonight, and capable of mentioning seeing him at Deedee's house.

"Not surprising they're violent," Brownlow said. "This place. Living in ugliness. I've been wading around, you know, an hour or two in Hades, lost in the foul damp. I have seen giant dogs, sheer mournful walls, silos of misery. Sties. Breeding grounds of stink, these projects, for children. Ha! And race antipathy infecting everyone, passed on like AIDS."

Riaz continued to look at Brownlow and, as Chad said, when Riaz looked at someone they knew they were looked at. Riaz took a few paces; a speech was coming on. He began, "But I could become fond of this project."

"Right. They've just decorated it up," Chad growled.

Brownlow sensed a trap and became puzzled. "Go on," he said.

"I'll tell you, I would change places with the lucky buggers here tomorrow! Tomorrow!" Riaz's voice rose and rose. "See how well fed they must be—they are so gross they can barely rouse their fat bottoms from the TV!" Everyone laughed, apart from Brownlow. "They have housing, electricity, heating, TV, fridges, hospitals nearby! They can vote, participate politically or not. They are privileged indeed, are they not?"

"The people here can't oppose the corporations," Brownlow said. "Powerless, they are. Badly fed. Uneducated and unemployed. Can't make jobs from hope."

Riaz went on: "And do you think our brothers in the Third World, as you like to call most people other than you, have a fraction of this? Do our villages have electricity? Have you ever even seen a village?"

"An' he's not talking about Gloucestershire," Chad muttered.

Brownlow said, "In Soweto. Three months living with the people."

"You will know, then," Riaz said, "that what I have said would be James Bond luxuries to the people there. They dream of having fridges, televisions, cookers! And are the people racist skinheads, car thieves, rapists? Have they desired to dominate the rest of the world? No, they are humble, good, hardworking people who love Allah!"

Shahid and the brothers murmured their assent. Brownlow must have regretted the moment he began to talk again. He was sensitive, and, with his belief in liberation, it must have cost him to take this from the man whose cause he supported.

He grimaced.

Shahid wondered if the others were as puzzled as he was. Here was someone who'd been granted breeding, privilege, education; his ancestors had circumnavigated the globe and ruled it. Shahid expected something more from all that had made him. At the same time he and the others couldn't help being pleased. The people who'd ruled them, and who still patronized and despised them, were not gods. Brought up to rule, to lead, now they were just another minority. Deedee had explained it to him. "They send them away to school at seven where they do something awful to them. From this they never recover."

Riaz politely indicated that he and Brownlow should sit together, at one side. Sadiq would unroll a clean Persian mat and bring a jug of water and tumblers. They could dispute in comfort.

Everyone was relaxing.

Shahid saw this as an opportunity to take out a novel. He hadn't read anything that day and missed the absorbed solitude. But even as he pulled a book from his bag he felt that somehow the others would disapprove of him reading on their night watch.

Instead, as Brownlow and Riaz began to talk, Shahid drew closer. When Riaz spoke at college or the mosque there was no debate, only soft questions. At the end Riaz's group would slap his back, compliment him and push back enthusiasts.

Shahid felt he had passed the point when he could question Riaz about the fundamentals. Shahid frequently fell into anxiety about his lack of faith. Observing the mosque, in which all he saw were solid, material things, and looking along the line of brothers' faces upon which spirituality was taking place, he felt a failure. But he was afraid that inquiry would expose him to some sort of suspicion. He could at least discuss his doubts with Hat, who said not to worry, let it happen. And when Shahid did relax he grasped that faith, like love or creativity, could not be willed. This was an adventure in knowing. He had to follow the prescriptions and be patient. Understanding would surely follow; he would be blessed.

But now Brownlow, sitting cross-legged opposite Riaz, was re-opening the wound of uncertainty.

"Often wished," he was saying, addressing Shahid as well as Riaz, "in my adult life, sometimes becoming desperate, that I could be religious. But read Bertrand Russell at fourteen. Expect you know him, don't you?"

"A bit," Shahid said.

Brownlow wiggled his damp toes in his sandals. "Deedee talk about him? Or does she only make you watch Prince videos?"

"She's a good teacher."

Brownlow grunted and went on: "Put the deity in his place, didn't he, Russell? Said that if He existed He would be a fool. Ha, ha, ha! Also said, quote, 'The whole conception of God is a conception derived from the ancient Oriental despotisms.' Good, eh? Since then often the people—me—felt abandoned in the universe. Atheism can be a terrible trouble, you should know. Having to invest the world with meaning. Would be marvelous to believe that soon after death by cancer one will slip—I mean, sip—grapes, melon, and virgins in paradise. Paradise being like Venice. Without the smells or early closing. Heaven, surely, as someone said, was man's easiest invention."

Shahid tried to smile. He wanted an alcoholic drink. He didn't know what had brought on such a sudden thirst—the fear or the company. Probably it was the talk of paradise.

Brownlow was becoming spirited.

"Wonderful on one's knees. Existing in an imaginary realm ruled by imaginary beings. Wonderful to have all rules of life delivered from on high. What to eat. How to wipe your bottom." His bunched fingers were now inches from Riaz's nose, as if he were about to pluck it off and wipe his arse with it. "How abhorrent too! The slave of superstition."

Shahid balked. Brownlow was calling Riaz a slave of superstition! No one spoke to him like this! How would he react?

Brownlow went further: "Magic realist tales from distant centuries! Bondage—surely you recognize bondage? And don't some of us weaklings prefer that to free will? Trading on infantile dependence—aren't you? D'you see?"

It must have been Brownlow's alcohol fumes which made Shahid yearn for the darkness of a pub. A pint of Speckled Hen, Southern Comfort, Heineken, Tennent's, Guinness, Becks, Pils, Bud—what lovely names, like those of the poets! His mouth was parched.

But Shahid struggled. He didn't want to be swung here and there by desire. Chili's excess and selfishness, for instance, disgusted him. Yet images of Brownlow's wife kept tempting him. At this moment, he could have been gripping her well-exercised calf, pressing her knee, cosseting his hand into her thigh, and sliding inward.

"Surely," Brownlow said, "surely the act of believing—"

"Believing as opposed to what?"

Riaz was not disconcerted by Brownlow's counterattack, but looked on with the confidence of a chess player who has anticipated the next moves.

"As opposed to thinking. Of thinking without preconceptions and prejudices. Yes, surely the strain of believing something that can never be proven, or shown to make logical sense must seem, for an intelligent man like you. To be. To be—" Brownlow searched for the least tendentious word. "Dishonest! Yes. Dishonest!"

Brownlow wasn't restraining himself tonight.

Shahid examined the smile which was so frequently on Riaz's face. He was balding, he had a wart on his chin and one on his cheek; he could smell of sweat. But Shahid had taken it for granted that his smile indicated humor, a love of humanity, patience. Yet if you looked closely, it was disdain. Riaz not only thought Brownlow was a fool, but thought him contemptible too.

"People must decide good and evil for themselves," Brownlow said.

Riaz laughed. "Man is the last person I would trust to such a task!"

Shahid stood up.

He would ask Chad if he could go for a walk. He could phone Deedee from the street. He wanted only to hear her voice now. But what if Chad refused him, which was quite likely? He'd be stuck then. Deedee would think he'd let her down.

Why did Shahid have to be scared of Chad? Chad had experienced unforgettable highs, and now he forced interminable restraint on himself. No wonder he was frantic and vexatious; everyday reality would always let him down. All the same, Chad was just another brother, albeit one who required forgiveness. Shahid would have to stand up for himself.

"Please excuse me," Riaz was saying to Brownlow. "But you are a little arrogant." Brownlow chuckled. He was enjoying the argument. "Your liberal beliefs belong to a minority who live in northern Europe. Yet you think moral superiority over the rest of mankind is a fact. You want to dominate others with your particular morality, which has—as you also well know—gone hand-in-hand with fascist imperialism." Here Riaz leaned toward Brownlow. "This is why we have to guard against the hypocritical and smug intellectual atmosphere of Western civilization."

Brownlow dabbed sweat from his forehead and smiled. His eyes scattered about. He didn't know where to begin. He took a breath.

"That atmosphere you deprecate. With reason. But this civilization has also brought us this—"

"Dr. Brownlow, tell us what it has brought us," Shahid said.

"Good, Tariq. A student with curiosity. Let's think." On his fingers he counted them off. "Literature, painting, architecture, psychoanalysis, science, journalism, music, a stable political culture, organized sport—at a pretty high level. And all this has gone hand-in-hand with something significant. That is: critical inquiry into the nature of truth. It talks of proof and demonstration."

Riaz said slyly, "Like Marx's famous dialectic, you mean?"

For a moment Brownlow halted. He continued: "And steely questions. Without flinching. Questions and ideas. Ideas being the enemy of religion."

"So much the worse for the ideas," Riaz said, with a snort.

They both looked at him. It was an argument Shahid felt barely able to participate in. He cursed himself for being inarticulate and ignorant, just as he had been when Chad had asked him why he loved literature. But it was a spur, too: he would have to study, read more and think, combining facts and arguments in ways that fitted the world as he saw it.

Shahid glanced across at Chad. He got up and moved to the door.

"Just popping out," he whispered to Riaz, leaving the room as quickly as he could.

In the hall he picked up the phone and dialed quickly.

"I'm scared," Tahira said. "Aren't you?"

He nodded. She wasn't going to move away. When he heard Deedee's voice he replaced the receiver.

"I'll just be back," he said to Tahira, pulling the bolts, turning the keys and releasing the chain on the door.

"Where are you going?"

"One of us should case the neighborhood. Check the layout and all."

"Good. But not alone. Let me come."

"No, no."

"I'm really not afraid."

"But I'd be afraid for you."

Shahid slipped out of the door.

It took him a while to get off the estate. He doubted that he'd find a phone even then. Fine drizzle fell, it was like walking through a cloud. He smelled the rain; it had been some time, in this city, since he had smelled anything so fresh. It was humid, too, and the pavements steamed, like in a music video. He wouldn't find his way back now. Nor would he be able to find his way home.

This area was notorious for racists. He began to jog, and then to run. Under a somber railway bridge he spotted the taxi driver who'd brought them, dropping off a customer. Shahid went up to him. He remembered Shahid and led him into the taxi office. Unearthly noises were coming from the back room. The man extended his hand, barring Shahid's way. He glanced around the door and saw the drivers playing cards while watching a porn video.

They let him call her from the front office. At last he got through.

"Where have you been? I've been waiting here for two hours! Couldn't you have called before? D'you think a woman would do such a thing to a man?"

Before the humiliation and annoyance in Deedee's voice could affect him, he explained that he'd been called out on urgent brother business. A year ago Sadiq's fifteen-year-old brother had had his skull crushed by a dozen youths. This particular duty had to be taken seriously.

She wouldn't accept it. It was as if she blamed him for the disappointments other men had given her, and for the hope which he, evidently, had stirred in her.

"Sorry, sorry, sorry," he repeated. "What could I do?"

While they talked he saw, from the window, a boy standing outside, the red spot of his cigarette glowing through the sticky drizzle. Probably he was waiting for a cab. Then the boy turned, looked right at Shahid and nodded.

"Even now," Shahid said, "there are racists outside, waiting for me."

She told him to get a cab—which she would pay for—and come over now, at least for a drink. She despised herself for asking this, he could tell.

"But I can't," he said. "Not tonight."

"When, then?"

"Soon, soon. I'll ring you."

"Promise?"

"Yes."

He got off the phone as quickly as he could, and asked the driver to take him back to the flat. When they left the office the kid had gone.

The gang sat up all night, sleeping on the floor in shifts. The next morning those who had lectures and college work left, and were replaced by others. Shahid, who had a clear day, didn't get away until that afternoon, and by then a bomb had exploded on the main concourse of Victoria Station.

pparently they were bringing the bodies out, no one knew how many. The injured were being ferried to hospitals in the area. It was said that the station was burning, but it was too dark to see, since a dismal cloud had fallen over the city.

In the rain the police erected barriers, directing people up one street and then down the same street, shouting through megaphones. Helicopters circled above.

One thing was clear: no one knew anything. Naturally there was plenty of talk. On the street someone told Shahid that this emergency wasn't an orthodox random attack but that shops, cars and even the airports were being bombed in a concerted effort by several organizations to take London. Not that this could be confirmed: the TV screens merely showed blood-soiled faces and accounts by passersby of the blast.

Shahid had arranged to meet Deedee, not at her house but at her friend Hyacinth's flat in Islington, off Upper Street. He was crossing town to see her. The journey took hours. He had walked some of the way, through the City, up Fleet Street, and along the Strand.

It was hard to see how there could be more chaos. At the moment the railway stations were closed, as were the airports and the bus station. The roads were at a standstill. In the Marylebone Road, on the Talgarth Road, even in the City, police cars, fire engines, and ambulances careered around stationary traffic; the public craned to glimpse the faces of those heroes at the wheel, as if some special mark of bravery and comprehension would distinguish them from the worried mass who were not, despite everything, especially surprised by the outrage.

Thousands of commuters milled around in the rain, standing on bridges beneath the low sky, staring into the foul water below, wondering what time they would get home that night, if at all. Some drivers lay down on the back seats of their cars; others abandoned their vehicles altogether and gathered around each other's radios. People went without prompting to the nearest hospitals, queuing silently to give blood, as television crews moved among them like disinterested scientists. Churches were opened and the perplexed waited in buildings they hadn't entered for years. The cafés and pubs were full; apparently they were being drunk dry. Illicit lovers, adulterers, and opportunists took advantage. The hotels were booking up.

Once he'd started, Shahid was reluctant to give up his journey through this strange forest. He wanted to be in the midst of chaos, not watching the event on television, where it would already have a form and explanation, robbing viewers of involvement.

After two hours walking he discovered that some trains had started running, on certain lines. This was the only possibility of movement in the city tonight. He went into the underground and after an hour boarded a hushed northbound train. To the passengers' wonder and relief the train passed through several stations. The proximity of others comforted him: they all sat guarded, scared, wet. Such a tragedy was the closest a city like London could come to communal emotion.

What did they feel? Confusion and anger, because somewhere outside lurked armies of resentment. But which faction was it? Which underground group? Which war, cause, or grievance was being demonstrated? The world was full of seething causes which required vengeance—that at least was known. While inside the city, gorging on plenty without looking up, were the complacent. And today "the lucky ones," those with mortgages and jobs, wandering the streets in search of a working phone, were meant to know they could be stalked, picked off, besieged. For they were guilty. They would have to pay and pay.

The driver made an announcement over the Tannoy, though what he said, apart from the word "urgent," was lost. Passengers were so alarmed they spoke to one another. Many of the stations were still being inspected by the security forces. The train would stop when it was able to. A woman sitting opposite Shahid gasped. The passenger next to her hushed her abruptly. When it did stop, the train would terminate. Terminate!

The train slid through darkened stations. Men with dogs and flashlights patrolled the platforms. Bright cones of light criss-crossed the normally busy areas. Shahid watched his companions in the carriage as the possible safety of each station was forfeited.

It was a relief to escape when the doors finally slid open a couple of stations away from the one he'd been heading for.

He ran to the house but stopped outside. He knew he shouldn't have come. All the same, not wanting to go back, he started down, guessing she would be listening for his feet on the stone steps. Now she would know he'd stopped; she would recognize his reluctance.

Only bad people lived in basements—but these people couldn't be bad enough, not like the boys from the housing projects. It was soft and easy here, cut off from reality. Already he felt guilty about leaving his companions in danger. He would talk to Deedee for a couple of hours before ensuring he returned to the gang later that night. He feared, too, what this woman might want or expect from him, the demands she might make, the emotion she might feel, and induce him to feel. But in ways he didn't understand, he needed her, though he could not allow himself to acknowledge this.

She had left the iron gate and front door open. He went in, throat tight, sniffing marijuana. The small, low-ceilinged room was lit by two candles. He just about discerned a couch, a television, a sound system playing "Desire." In the shadows he could barely make her out.

"Sorry I'm late. There's been a—"

"Don't think about it."

She was sitting on the floor, back to the wall, wearing a loose red skirt, black sweater, black tights. A paperback lay face down on the carpet. She smoked a thin joint and sipped from a tumbler of wine. She didn't get up; obviously she didn't feel like it.

He couldn't go to her, couldn't talk, he was shaking, he would only say the wrong thing and she would think him an idiot. He threw off his coat, under which he wore a short leather jacket and T-shirt. He walked up and down with the joint she'd prepared for him, glancing at her. She let him pace and look at her as much as he had to.

Then he started laughing. Maybe she found him eccentric, but she only tilted her head in amused inquiry.

He remembered that the previous night, not for the last time, Hat and Chad had been planning their response if the skins attacked. Chad was sitting on the floor with his knees up. His armory, a hammer and knife, lay between his legs. For a while Tahira had been giving Chad sharp looks. When she couldn't contain herself anymore, she said, as he crowed about the damage he would do to the racists, "Chad, could you close your legs, please?"

Chad frowned but brought his knees together, shrugging at Hat.

She went on, "Chad, I've noticed that you like wearing tight trousers."

"I do, yes."

"But we women go to a lot of trouble to conceal our allures. Surely you've heard how hard it is to wear the hijab? We are constantly mocked and reviled, as if we were the dirty ones. Yesterday a man on the street said, this is England, not Dubai, and tried to rip my scarf off."

"Sister—" Chad said in horror.

"You brothers urge us to cover ourselves but become strangely evasive when it comes to your own clothes. Can't you wear something looser?"

Chad looked at Hat and said, a little archly, that he had been looking out for some Oxford bags for a while.

Tahira said, "That will be progress. But aren't you thinking of growing a beard? Look at Hat, his is really coming on now. Even Shahid has got something bushy on the way."

Hat was smiling smugly.

Chad replied, annoyedly, "My skin needs a breathing space, otherwise I develop an itchy rash."

"Vanity should be the least of your concerns," Tahira said.

This finished Chad off. He sat there rubbing his chin and sucking his teeth, sounding like a wet log flung on the fire. He refused to talk to anyone, even Hat.

Later, when Shahid, Hat and Chad were in the kitchen, Hat turned to Shahid and said, "Is it true you've got something bushy on the way?"

"Too right," Shahid replied. "And Chad hasn't got anything bushy on the way!"

"I'll put something bushy on your face in a minute!" retorted Chad.

He didn't feel like telling Deedee the story. He had imagined she would be impressed by the anti-fascist work they were doing, but when, on the phone, he described Chad trying on his knuckle-dusters and Hat teaching Riaz how to make the machete swing through the air, he felt disapproval.

"Are you thinking about your mates?"

"Yes."

She said, "You should know, that boy you call Chad—"

"Why are you putting it like that?"

"He used to be called Trevor Buss."

"Chad? I don't believe you."

Deedee shrugged.

He repeated, "Chad?"

"He was adopted by a white couple. The mother was racist, talked about Pakis all the time and how they had to fit in." Deedee handed him the bottle of wine. "Feeling more like a drink?"

"These days I'm trying to keep a clear head. To respect limits."

"Chad would hear church bells. He'd see English country cottages and ordinary English people who were secure, who effortlessly belonged. You know, the whole Orwellian idea of England. You read his essays?"

"Not properly."

"Anyway, the sense of exclusion practically drove him mad. He wanted to bomb them."

"But why? Why?"

"When he got to be a teenager he saw he had no roots, no connections with Pakistan, couldn't even speak the language. So he went to Urdu classes. But when he tried asking for the salt in Southall everyone fell about at his accent. In England white people looked at him as if he were going to steal their car or their handbag, particularly as he dressed like a ragamuffin. But in Pakistan they looked at him even more strangely. Why should he be able to fit into a Third World theocracy?"

Even Papa had felt like that, Shahid wanted to say, and he had considered it his home. Surrounded by his brothers and sons, Papa had sat cursing in his club in Karachi, though the tables were covered with starched white cloths, the cutlery was silver, and the waiters wore white uniforms and turbans. On the walls hung autographed photographs of Cowdrey and May, and a print of George V broadcasting to the empire; *The Times* was open on an oak stand. Beyond were the veranda and the "top-notch" flower beds tended by an army of gardeners. The place enraged him: the religion shoved down everyone's throat; the bandits, corruption, censorship, laziness, fatuity of the press; the holes in the roads, the absence of roads, the roads on fire. Nothing was ever right for Papa there. He liked to say, when he was at his most depressed, that the British shouldn't have left. "Nineteen forty-five—a new country, a fresh start!" he'd cry. "How many people have such an opportunity! Why can't we run things without torturing and murdering one another, without the corruption and exploitation? What's wrong with us?"

He'd boast about England so much that his brother Asif said, "What, are you personally related to the royal family, yaar?" Yet Papa's eyes filled with tears when he left, like a boy going back to prep school.

Deedee continued: "Trevor Buss's soul got lost in translation, as it were. Someone said he even tried the Labour Party, to try to find a place. But it was too racist and his anger was too much. Too much for him, you know. It was fermenting and he couldn't keep it under."

Shahid sighed. "I didn't know all that stuff about him. I haven't even asked him."

"He said to me once, 'I am homeless.' I said, 'You've got nowhere to live?' 'No,' he replied. 'I have no country.' I told him, 'You're not missing much.' 'But I don't know what it is to feel like a normal citizen.' Trevor Buss dressed better than anyone and he made me tapes of music I'd never have heard. Does he still love music?"

"Yes and no."

"He was drinking and he got stoned. One day I caught him doing coke in a classroom and banned him. He'd stand outside with one shoe balanced on his head, staring through the window. He was dealing, and he was spring-loaded, a gun about to go off."

"But he didn't go off, did he?"

"No."

"Why not? Because he met Riaz?"

"Maybe."

"I knew it." Shahid snapped his fingers. "He could take the shoe off his head! What happened, then?"

"He changed his name to Muhammad Shahabuddin Ali-Shah."

"No!"

"He'd insist on the whole name. He played football and his mates got fed up saying, 'Pass the ball, Muhammad Shahabuddin Ali-Shah,' or, 'On me noodle over here, Muhammad Shahabuddin Ali-Shah.' No one passed to him. So he became Chad." Deedee took another swig of her wine. She shivered. "But it's not him that scares me. Not Trevor."

"Who, then?"

She said, "Riaz is the worst."

"Is he?"

"Oh yes."

On the way over Shahid had been thinking about Riaz. Hadn't they all grown up at a time of admiration for rebels, weirdos, outsiders of all sorts, from Bowie to Idol, Boy George to Madonna? Shahid's childhood friends had sported mohawks and pierced their noses—one even had his tongue punctured—turning their bodies into an offense. But it cost little to rebel. Only the old could remember what "respectability" had been. His friends, bent over the pub pool table every night, were phantoms, not the undead, as they called the elderly, but more like the unborn.

Riaz, however, in an era of self-serving ambition and careers, had taken on a cause and maintained his unpopular individuality. In the end he was more of a nonconformist—and one without affectation—than anyone Shahid had met. Where everyone else had zigged, Riaz had zagged.

Deedee held up the bottle once more.

Shahid shook his head. "You're slurring your words. Why are you always trying to make me take things?"

"Alcohol is one of the great pleasures."

"Is life just for pleasure, then?"

"What else is there?"

"I'm not sure. I know you're just trying to provoke me. But pleasure isn't enough, is it?"

"It's a start."

"What about making the world better?"

She made a face. "Is that what you think Riaz does?"

"At this moment he is risking his life guarding the flat of a persecuted couple."

"Riaz was kicked out of his parents' house for denouncing his own father for drinking alcohol. He also reprimanded him for praying in his armchair and not on his knees. He told his friends that if one's parents did wrong they should be thrown into the raging fire of hell."

"Don't expect me to believe that, Deedee."

"Sorry?"

"Riaz is one of the kindest people." Before she could protest

Shahid went on: "And he's an individual who's gone against the whole society. You know it takes bravery to do that. Don't start on him. I'm only asking you what happened when he met Chad."

"He took Trevor in hand and his mixture of kindness and discipline sorted him out better than any rehabilitation center could have."

"I thought so. Without him—"

"Yes, Trevor, or Chad, would probably be dead."

"Now Chad himself is looking after people in all sorts of ways you don't even know about."

She was looking at him. "But don't they scare you?"

"Who?"

"Your friends?"

"Why should they?"

"They're devoid of doubt."

He shook his head. "Some people have anger and passionate beliefs. Without that nothing could get done."

"Do you have anger and passionate beliefs?"

He flushed. "The thing is, Deedee, clever white people like you are too cynical. You see through everything and rip everything to shreds but you never take any action. Why would you want to change anything when you already have everything your way?"

"I don't know you well, Shahid, but I'm just saying I wouldn't want you to get hurt."

"Who by?"

"Your new companions."

"But we're the victims here! And when we fight you say we're getting worked up about nothing! You sit smoking dope all day and abuse people who actually take action!"

She sat with her eyes lowered, as if she didn't want to make it worse. But she wasn't going to withdraw.

He said, "I don't know why I bothered to come all this way."

"Didn't you want to see me?" She said this so forcibly that he started. "Have I imposed myself on you?" She got up. "I thought that was what it was." She grasped her bag and started stuffing things into it. "I've made a bloody fool of myself. You're a student.

I must have gone out of my fucking head. What have I been thinking about? I'm desperate, that's all. I wish I weren't. I suppose that's
what you think of me." She smacked the palm of her hand into her
forehead. "I want to forget this whole thing."

"Deedee . . ."

"Let's do that and get back to our lives!"

She turned off the music and the heating, jammed the cork in
the wine, and washed the glasses furiously, sobbing all the while,
her back to him. He wondered what Chili, who knew about such
things, would say to improve the situation. The bastard would
probably butter her up; flattery was a technique you could use on
men and women alike, Chili said. But he always added that you'd
better be able to locate the ticklish spot, or you'd be a creep.

He went to her before she got her coat on, and said, "You look
ravishing today, you do."

She put her head to one side and smiled. "Do I? Thank you."

"There have been so many distractions. We had a stupid argument. I'd forgotten how attractive you are. Don't leave."

"All right."

"What do you want to do?"

"Lie down."

"Why not?"

She said, "The bedroom's this way. And please—can you not
look at my body?"

"Sorry?"

"Look at the curtains or something. You're too young to be
ashamed of the way you look. But I have started going to the gym
again. Oh, and one other thing."

"Yeah?"

"Can you keep the leather jacket on?"

        Later the sky had cleared: it was
tranquil and diaphanous. Mouth to mouth, he and Deedee had
dozed but not fallen asleep. Then, satisfied and feeling adventurous, they'd dressed and got out of the basement. Now they were

laced together, and whenever he turned to kiss her—if, for instance, they were waiting to cross the road—she moved toward him, her arms were around him, they were all over one another. They had made love; she was his lover. He had liked lying there sweating in the leather jacket; she had really screwed him, getting on top, not sitting up, but lying on him, legs straddling his, shoving down on his cock. He had thrown his arms out, saying, "I want you to fuck me."

"Don't worry," she had panted. "Leave it to me."

Shops were selling T-shirts, cheap jewelry, belts, bags, wispy Indian-print scarves. Ex-students with pink mohawks and filthy dogs stood at small street-stalls selling bundles of incense and bootlegs of the Dead, Charlie Hero, the Sex Pistols.

The rinsed streets were busy. Some of the chaos had cleared; once more crowds gathered around the tube station, waiting for friends. People were magnetized by the pubs or the French-style brasseries which were becoming popular; or they queued for the late-nighter, Truffaut's *Fahrenheit 451*. It was rare to see anyone over forty, as if there were a curfew for older people.

Shahid watched his lover across the bookshop, a spacious place on two floors with the stock displayed on huge tables; in the past bookshops had always been so dingy. Seeing the piles of new volumes Shahid wanted to snatch them up, not knowing how he'd survived without them. Deedee bought *Lipstick Traces* and he followed her to the till, awaiting the bookmark and bag, with some stories by Flannery O'Connor and a couple of anthologies, bought with the money Chili had given him.

They went to a pub. The girls wore short skirts or white Levi's; the guys were in black or blue jeans, with holes in the knee; some wore black leather jackets over black polos or crewnecks. There were a couple of Goths in posthumous makeup, looking out of place. There were some smarter kids in business suits who had finished work and would get cabs down to Soho later, going to L'Escargot, Alastair Little, or the Neal Street Restaurant.

A lot of the kids, Deedee explained, were wasters, pretending to write scripts. But some worked in pop and low-budget film, they were runners, assistant editors, music video extras, young directors who'd be going on, later that night, to the latest clubs—Moist, the Future, or Religion.

In one corner was a pack of rougher kids, in hooded sweats and baggy jeans, handing out smudged flyers for raves. They were waiting for minicabs, with which they had accounts, they made so much money from selling Ecstasy. Raves were held in fields beyond the suburbs or in warehouses beneath the railway arches. She said they'd go tonight except there was an Asian punk band she wanted to catch, the Masters of Enlightenment.

He pressed her about herself. She became restless, turning on her stool, as she had the first time they'd talked properly, in the canteen. She wanted to speak of herself, but didn't know where to begin. She hadn't had time to digest and examine the past, her life had always been a rush, the years had flown, she hadn't rested.

Being an argumentative troublemaker, her school made her leave at sixteen. Early one morning, instead of going to her Saturday job, she put on "She's Leaving Home," threw some clothes into a rucksack, and got out of the house forever.

"I thought I should do everything at once, while I was at it, you know." Deedee's mother was a secretary on the *Daily Express* and her father owned a dusty shop where he was supposed to repair radios, music equipment, televisions. "They hated me going out in a black plastic bag, with lace gloves and scarlet lips. They had no idea of what I might be, they just disliked what I was."

She liked music, clothes, men, going out. She was speeding—toward what she had no idea. Nothing would hold her; velocity was all. She went to punk clubs; Louise's in Soho, where Vivienne Westwood and Malcolm McLaren held court, and to the Roxy, where Elvis Costello and the Police played. She worked in bars, ending up in a smart topless place in the West End.

"I did some escort work." She wasn't looking at him. "I'm only telling you because you might as well know everything. And I don't care anymore."

"Good."

"Those days London was full of Arabs, who thought they liked girls. They didn't treat you badly but they wouldn't talk. We were always saying things like, 'What's your wife like?' They didn't think much of us. We sat in their apartments all night, taking coke and waiting to be pointed at."

"Because of the money?"

"There'd be piles of it, hundreds of pounds, on my bedside table. Like cocaine, you could feel it drifting through your fingers, blown away on clothes, eating out, drugs. Until . . . until one of the other women gave me an article by Gloria Steinem. It was an account of becoming a Playboy bunny. I'd always thought of myself as a rebel, you know. Bad girls were individual, they stood out. The book made my brain bounce. I searched out other books and went through them, underlining. Not being stupid was—sort of—an everyday rebellion. I tried to join a women's group and got the bus up to Kentish Town hoping for discussions about why men were so hopeless. But the women had gone beyond that. They were lesbians only interested in each other. Two of them worked in a donkey sanctuary. That was the last straw. I put an ad in *Spare Rib* and started my own group." Her happiest day was being accepted for university. "My mother said, does that mean we have to support you? My old man said someone common like me didn't deserve an education."

University was grueling. She wished she weren't older than the others and yet academically less accomplished. She'd hardly written an essay before; libraries made her narcoleptic. She lived alone and worked harder than anyone, shunning the middle-class contagions: self-doubt, scorn for learning, ennui. After graduating she took her teacher's certificate. "Then I got my present job. I've been there a long time." She took his hand. "This pub's getting crowded."

They walked up the street to the Underworld.

"Is it all right, what I've said?"

He said, "It's OK, I think. I'm enjoying it. But it's confusing. Go on."

"At university I turned dour. Rather like you now, I had hard political purpose. From the middle of the 1970s there was always the Party. If I wasn't studying, I was at meetings, or selling papers or standing on the picket line. I met Brownlow."

"What did you see in him?"

"We liked the Beatles. We had activism and talk in common. We imagined we were on the Left Bank, running into our lovers in cafés, living without bourgeois jealousy, committed to personal and political change. Sartre and De Beauvoir have much to be responsible for. A lot of disillusioned people are looking to talk to them."

Everything they did was Party work. They were on picket lines, demonstrations, and at Greenham. Even now she didn't know how she felt about her commitment, except she feared that her politics had merely been an extension of nurturing, taking care of the oppressed instead of a husband.

Shahid bought drinks at the bar. The Underworld was a low-ceilinged black box behind the pub, packed with students. Lager seemed to be running down the walls. The lead singer, an Indian wearing glasses, was so nervous that, attempting to ram his guitar into an amp, he dropped it. The drummer was going off like a threshing machine. The band couldn't play much, and sounded like a heavy version of the Velvet Underground, without the tunes. Not that Shahid paid much attention. He was struggling to take in the facts of Deedee's life.

After a couple of songs Deedee slipped a pill onto her tongue and gave Shahid one. They decided to leave when the drummer, while taking a turn—clearly, as Deedee pointed out, no one had explained to him that the drums should never be a solo instrument—saw his turban fly off into the crowd, opening out like a kite.

They pushed through the crowd and onto the street, happy to be outside. The cool air and silence felt good. They walked slowly back to the flat. There she lay on the floor in a dusky light, pulling her clothes open, watching him stroke her. She asked him to massage her shoulders, neck, and upper arms.

"When I think about how far I've come—I'm proud of what I've done. Who's helped me? Some friends, but really no one. And I'm glad for that."

"Why are you sad, then?"

"Am I?"

"A little."

"Yes. It's painful to admit to. I s'pose I want to say that the price might have been too high."

She said that women in the 1980s, even the lefties, had aimed to get into powerful positions, be independent, achieve. But it had cost them. They'd worked themselves into the ground, drawing too deeply on their resources, having to support themselves as well as friends. Too many had forfeited the possibility of children. For what? In the end a career was merely a job, not a whole life.

How little enjoyment had there been! In those days of commitment while the world remained unchanged—and until the celebrations of "freedom day"—pleasure could only be provisional and guilty. Also, she'd rarely moved outside the political circle; it was felt, implicitly, that only those striving for change could be good. The others were callous, deliberately ignorant, or suffering from false consciousness.

"There was a period, in the mid-seventies, when we imagined history was moving our way. Gays, blacks, women, were asserting and organizing themselves. Less than ten years later, after the Falklands, CND, and the miners' strike, even I could see the movement was in a contrary direction. Thatcher had concentrated the struggle. But she'd worn everyone down. Where did we go from here?"

"Where, then?"

"Who knows? Ask Brownlow. It's been hard enough admitting to defeat and then to uncertainty. Now I don't even want to be certain anymore."

She would wait for experience and knowledge, aware of these particular certainties: there existed only the present, tonight belonged to them, and she liked him.

"You make me happier than anyone has for ages."

He undressed only a little coyly. She had said she liked him naked while she was dressed. But when he glanced at her, he saw she had drifted away. He folded his clothes and stood there. Suddenly she sat up and licked her lips. He shrank back.

"You're looking at me as if I were a piece of cake. What are you thinking?"

"I deserve you. I'm going to like eating you. Here. Here, I said."

On his knees he went to her. She put her lips to his ear and inquired if there were anything she could do. Hand in hand they went, once again, into the bedroom and lay on the mattress on the floor. There was a lot she could do, he thought. There was such a backlog he barely knew where to begin; the forbidden wasn't forbidden for nothing. He said, "I'm fine, actually."

She knew to persist. She'd been wanting him to wear makeup since she first saw him; she was certain he'd look good.

"Now?" he said.

"There's only now."

Surely it wasn't, as yet, his destiny to look like Barbara Cartland? Then he recalled their first night, when "yes" was a better word than "no." Why be afraid? Live, if you can, here, tonight. Tonight was forever. Didn't he know how to trust her? He had to. Oh yes.

She crossed the room and put on Madonna's "Vogue." Madonna said, "What are you looking at?" He loved that track. Deedee fetched her bag and lay everything out on a white towel. He sat beside her. She hummed and fussed over him, reddening his lips, darkening his eyelashes, applying blusher, pushing a pencil under his eye. She back-combed his hair. It troubled him; he felt as if he were losing himself. What was she seeing?

She knew what she wanted; he let her take over; it was a relief. For now she refused him a mirror, but he liked the feel of his new female face. He could be demure, flirtatious, teasing, a star; a burden went, a certain responsibility had been removed. He didn't have to take the lead. He even wondered what it might be like to go out as a woman, and be looked at differently.

To examine him she moved about, telling him to turn his head this way and that, to place his arms here and there, to do more of this or the other. It was easier not to resist, even when she had him walking up and down on his toes like a model. Beyond embarrassment, in a walking dance, he swung his hips and arms, throwing his head back, pouting, kicking his legs out, showing her his arse and cock. As he went she nodded, smiled, and sighed.

He bowed, took an orange from the bowl beside the bed, and started to peel it.

She said, "My turn?"

He nodded.

She went to the wardrobe. She'd brought over some things that he might like. Standing like a conjuror's assistant, she extracted a straw hat with a wide silk band in scarlet, and stockings. She sat on the bed to put them on. Then she tore open a condom, rolled the rubber onto a finger, and anointed it with K-Y.

He said, "I'll always think of you this way, particularly when you're teaching."

"Feel free. Sometimes, when I get home from work and want an orgy of relaxation, this is how I do it, before I eat. I look at pictures, too. Or read."

"What kind of thing?"

"*Crash*. Know that one? *The Story of O* is a good one-hand read as well. They spend hours preparing her, rouging her nipples. She wears black suede shoes with platform shades, and gloves, and fur and silk. When she becomes their slave and they whip her, she has to say, 'I'll be whatever you want me to be.' Her greatest shame is when they force her to masturbate in front of them. I'm thinking of compiling a literary wank list for my students."

"How do you turn the pages?"

"You daft boy."

She invited him to watch while she lifted one leg and pressed the finger into the muscle of her arse until it disappeared.

"Look," she said.

With splayed fingers she showed him her cunt. He picked up the candle and, holding it close, peered in. He was so pleased, and the drug, making her smiling face waxy, rendered her in magazine soft-focus; without losing her soul she was turning herself into pornography.

Rapt, he held his breath while Deedee picked up a deodorant bottle and inserted the top into her cunt. Had Riaz ever seen such a thing? Would he want to, secretly? Maybe Deedee would give him a demonstration so he might see its humanity.

The flesh around Deedee's stomach folded together like fingers. She fell forward onto her knees and frigged herself busily, with concentration, curling her hand into her crotch. Her breath came rapidly and her fingers moved between her cunt and her nipples, which had rose-petal aureoles. He got onto his knees and spat in his hand; face to face, they jerked off together, and fell over laughing when, simultaneously, they came.

She lay down and dozed off, almost as if she'd fainted.

He stretched out and dreamed. He couldn't help thinking of something Riaz had said a couple of days ago. In passing, Hat had stated that homosexuals should be beheaded, though first they should be offered the option of marriage. Riaz had become interested and said that God would burn homosexuals forever in hell, scorching their flesh in a furnace before replacing their skin as new, and repeating this throughout eternity. He said, "If you've ever burnt yourself on the stove you'll know what I mean. Think of that a million times over."

Riaz's hatred had been so cool, so certain. Shahid had wanted to mention it to Deedee but was nervous it might distract her. Was Riaz not, though, his friend? If only Shahid could understand where such ideas came from.

Later, half asleep and far away, he and Deedee talked a little, murmuring how much they liked watching one another in the classroom. She had written him the note inviting him to her house, but it had been hard placing it on his desk in the library. She had retrieved it, replaced it once more, and fled the college, imagining everyone could sense her excitement and turmoil. At home she'd felt like a fifteen-year-old, looking out of the window, thinking, will he come, what have I done, will he think me a fool? She'd never made such an advance before, not with a student. When they went out, she'd been so nervous, she didn't know why, she had to get stoned. At the end, after they'd parted she turned the cab around and come back. She'd driven up and down but couldn't remember where he lived.

She slept once more, lying still on her side with her legs pulled up, sucking her thumb.

Now, watching her sleep, and closing his eyes, he felt, in this particular intimacy—stowed beneath her duvet—he was intruding. At the same time, he knew, settling down, you couldn't dislike anyone you'd seen asleep.

He kissed her and left her to sleep. Later in the morning she knocked on the bathroom door where he was lying in the bath, coffee balanced between the taps, a flannel over his face. From the flat upstairs he could hear a Bach violin piece.

Deedee hitched up her sleeves. She soaped and washed him, his face, behind the ears, between the legs, everywhere, tipping water from a jug over his hair, pausing only to kiss his neck, the inside of his wrists, his armpits.

She helped him out, fetched towels from the radiators, rubbed him, and wrapped him up. She had him sit on the side of the bath and got him into a T-shirt. Then kneeling down, she dried his legs and sucked his cock. He'd never experienced lips that could make you feel they could inhale your soul through the end of your dick.

He felt a little bad about taking. She said it was OK, she liked pleasing him in that way, she'd had plenty of practice. Right now she was satisfied, she wasn't asking for anything. When she wanted something she would put in a request.

She stood naked in front of the mirror, wet a flannel, and washed herself. He handed her the clothes she'd laid out and helped her into them.

She said, "I've checked the fridge. There's nothing to eat. Shouldn't we go out for breakfast?"

For him this was a luxury: mornings had always been for hurry and work.

It was a cold day, but clear and bright, confirming their mood. Deedee put on her sunglasses and he took her arm. The place she chose was close by. The waitresses knew her because she liked to read there on her way to college, and hear about the clubs and bars they went to. It was warm enough and the baguettes and croissants were made in steel ovens on the premises. The aroma made them hungrier.

They put their gloves in their pockets and hung up their coats and scarves beside the counter. The few students, actors, and lovers didn't crowd the café. Deedee chose a red-checkered table by the window with a view of the street. There were theater posters, the music was Verdi, and the staff were actresses and not in a rush; they even brought the papers over.

Deedee ordered coffee and when the waitress came back they studied the menu. Asking her to wait, they ordered right away. The toast was warm, wrapped in a napkin: the bread was good and not sliced too thinly. The jam and marmalade came in jars, and were excellent. They ate quickly, hardly stopping to talk, though he did notice her glancing at him both fondly and as if she wanted to work something out. After, Deedee suggested they eat something else, scrambled eggs, maybe, and hot chocolate, with whipped cream. They discussed it and wondered if they were too fat, both denying the other was and patting their stomachs.

They were shyer of each other than before. One side of her face had gone blotchy; she kept turning her head, it was exasperating her.

"I wanted to look good for you," she said. "It's really bloody annoying. I have to avoid all mirrors I don't know."

There was plenty in the papers to discuss and when they'd decided to order *pain au chocolat* and cappuccino and both had undone their trousers, they smoked. People came and went, but he was the only person there with dark skin. That would be the fact in most places he went with Deedee.

She looked out on the street and said she still enjoyed London. Given the choice—not that she had one now—she liked to think she couldn't live anywhere else: the streets weren't as narrow or enclosed as in Paris or Rome, or as dangerous as in New York; you could usually see the sky.

She'd hitched around Europe with a rucksack, and yearned for more. He said he wanted to go to Barcelona and see Jean Genet's Barrio Chino; Shahid could get them cheap tickets through his mother. They would take T-shirts, jeans, and a bundle of books; they'd strike out for heat and indolence, and nothing would matter except what happened that day. Despite London, things could get small in England. You wanted to put your arms out and push everything open; you had to get away from the dismal tiredness of the place, the decay, political bickering and drift, the absence of optimism everywhere.

The thought of getting away made them feel better. They sat there drinking cognac until the waitresses were laying the table for lunch.

When they got out on the street he took her arm; but that wasn't sufficient: he kissed her until someone whistled at them and they almost tipped over. She had the day off, she didn't want to work ever again, the college was stifling her. In the best of spirits now they'd eaten, they walked around aimlessly, thinking of what else might distract them, as if London existed only to provide them with satisfaction.

They tried on clothes and jewelry and she wanted to buy him some boots. But although he wanted them, he forbade it and she gave way. She pointed out houses in the neighborhood that she liked; they inspected an old shop sign above a butcher's. For old times' sake she bought some Dylan bootlegs from a kid hawking a box of them outside the tube station. Finally she took him to a pub for lemon vodka. They stood at the bar and whacked back three shots each, taking a breath between each, then gasping at each other.

The only thing to do was to return to the flat, pull the curtains, and undress one another. He wanted to fuck her again, even more this time. After the second time it got better and better, once the fear was gone.

While she dozed he sat in bed drinking sour wine from last

night, and reading a Márquez story. He thought about Chili and wrote about him in his notebook. After a while, not sure if it was day or night, he kissed her and pulled on his T-shirt. He tried to get into his trousers without waking her up.

She opened her eyes and asked him why he wanted to leave.

He didn't want to leave her. He didn't need to, he was free, he knew that. But when she asked him if he wanted to see the new Woody Allen at the Gate, he said he should go home and study. She said he could study with her. No, he said, not today, he had things to do.

She gave him a searching look. But he didn't like being slotted into her plans, as if he were being hired for a job, the specifications of which she had prepared already. She didn't argue. Now that things were good between them she was happy to be alone; the rest of the day would be wonderful now.

She got dressed and walked with him to the station. She stood on the platform to wave, watching him until the train disappeared into the tunnel.

This journey, as he headed home, involved a different disturbance. It had been the best night. Now he wanted to dream it again, luxuriating in what he remembered.

But sitting on the faded seats of the Northern Line and strolling the tunnels between stations with her cunt, arse, and sweat on his tongue and fingers and smeared around his mouth, he became aware of a carnal atmosphere. A matchless orgasm, like a fine night out, can last you the day, she was right.

Also, maybe, the mood had been conjured up by a fantasy Deedee masturbated to. She would be walking around the city in high heels, lipstick, and a long transparent dress, her nipples and cunt visible, not being touched, but looked at. And as she walked she would watch men watching her; and as they masturbated she would stroke herself.

But it was mainly because he could see that today, although the secrets of desire were veiled, sexual tension was everywhere. He couldn't doubt its circulating tangibility. Beneath the banality and repetition of this ordinary day there ran, like the warm inhabited tube tunnels under the city, flirtation, passion, and the deepest curiosities. People dressed, gestured, moved, to display themselves and attract. They were sizing each other up, fantasizing, wanting to desire and be adored.

Skirts, shoes, haircuts, looks, gestures: enticement and fascination were everywhere, while the world went to work. And such allure wasn't a preliminary to real sex, it was sex itself. Out there it was not innocent. People yearned for romance, desire, feeling. They wanted to be kissed, stroked, sucked, held, and penetrated more than they could say. The platform of Baker Street Station was Arcadia itself. He had had no idea that the extraordinary would be alive and well on the Jubilee Line. Today he could see and feel the lure. She had turned the key on his feelings.

As he walked, Shahid was reminded of something his brother once said. A girlfriend was attacking Chili, saying she'd never met such a boy-tart. That kid, especially if he was wearing his Comme des Garçons suit, would run into some beauty on the street and practically go down on her then and there. He'd hardly bother to look at her face. Chili agreed. His lovemaking could be unselective because he reckoned he could find something unique and inestimable in any woman. "Under the sheets you're always diving for pearls."

Chili was confident, too, that they would find something alive in him. The girl argued that he was merely justifying vampiric behavior, but Chili said that was the least of it. He wanted to stick by the idea that somehow, sometimes, something sacred could exist in impersonality. "And isn't that what the Christians believe?" he said.

"God Almighty, Chili," replied the girl. "This time you've gone too far!"

"Nah," he said, "I can be very Jesus in bed."

Now Shahid got out of the tube and stood in the street near his digs. He must have paced around there for ten minutes, heading off decisively in one direction, stopping, and tramping off in another. He wished he were swallowing buttered croissants and coffee in the café with Deedee. Why did he have to leave her? What was it he so badly wanted to do?

Yes—there was something important. He couldn't leave his friends; they had something to fight for; they were his people; he had pledged himself to them.

He hurried back into the station. He got into another train, traveled back into the East End and walked briskly through the project, past the rusting and burned-out cars.

"Where you been?" Chad's eyes were dim with fatigue. "You're well late."

Shahid was aware that in the dismal flat his own eyes were shining like diamonds. The last thing he wanted was for Chad to see light streaming from him. He adopted his unhappiest expression.

"You can get some sleep now. I had some errands to run."

"Errands, eh? What's this?"

"A baguette. French bread."

"Indian food not good enough for you?"

Chad was wearing his familiar casual clothes with a white cap. But today he had hung around his neck a silver whistle on a luminous green length of string. It charmed Shahid, reminding him of the Trevor Deedee had talked about, the Trevor that Chad now denied. It was that part of Chad which Shahid wanted to reach out to. He had decided to tell Chad he knew who Trevor was.

"Listen, Chad—"

"Yes?"

"Brother, I want to say—"

But Chad turned away and tried a few strokes with his weapon. Shahid sat down and crooned "Sexual Healing" to himself, Chili's anthem. All day you'd hear Marvin whispering, "Get up, wake up, let's make love tonight," from the back room of the travel agency or addressing the country lanes from Chili's car.

Shahid said, "What's wrong? Nothing's happened, has it?"

"Nah. They cowards, when it comes to it. What's up with you?"

"Will you listen to me?"

Chad squatted back down on his haunches with his armory around him, as far from Nina and Sadiq as possible. The pair volunteered for the maximum duty. Forbidden to kiss or touch, they liked to fight: Sadiq had pinched her and now Nina was poised for the chance to pinch him back, regarding Chad and Shahid suspiciously, as if they were teachers. Chad didn't like the sisters accompanying them, though it was they, being devoted to the cause, who insisted; it was they, encouraged by Riaz, who had to make excuses to their parents.

"D'you remember, Chad brother, the first time we met, in Hat's restaurant, an' I told you that as a Paki, I went through a lot of shit?"

"So?"

"I was going to say, I reckon you went through some bad things, too."

"Yeah," Chad drawled. Clearly, his mind was bothered, but not by what Shahid was saying.

"And I wanted to say to you, Trev—"

Chad interrupted. "You been with your brother?"

"Chili?"

"Say, that's him. You seen him?"

Shahid was about to deny it. But the edge in Chad's voice halted him. Yet why shouldn't he have been with Chili? He didn't know why. But whatever happened, he didn't want to ruin his mood—the traces of his lover's kisses lay on his face, her body scent on his hands—by disagreeing with Chad.

"Why, brother?"

Chad picked up a sweater and flung it at Shahid. "Chili sent this over. He say warm your arse."

"How does he know where I am? How did he get this?"

"How he get it? How d'you think? He been staying in your room. Brother Riaz had the delectation of meeting him in the hallway. An' you know what happened? There was an incident."

Shahid's throat went dry. Nina and Sadiq stopped playing.

"What incident?"

"Chili threatened brother Riaz."

"Sorry?"

"He claimed the brother wearing one of his shirts."

"Oh no."

"Riaz didn't know what he was talking about."

"What happened?"

"Riaz ignored him. Now, answer this: didn't you let Chili into your room?"

"No! Doors don't stop my crazy brother. He come and go like a cool breeze."

"That OK, it ain't him nuisancing me right now. It you."

"Me?"

Chad leaned forward. "You were somewhere else that night. Where did you sleep?"

Chad assumed that Shahid was their possession; they wanted to own him entirely; not a part of him could elude them. But Chad had been wrong to anger him.

"What are these questions for? Don't you trust me? Is that what you saying?" Shahid looked at Chad steadily. "And can you tell me where Chili is now?"

Chad grunted. "You holding something back, Shahid?"

"Like what?"

"Who knows?"

"Please, Chad, don't be such a bad-tempered brother. I've been trying to deal with a few family things. Didn't I tell you they have an apartment in Knightsbridge?" At this Chad scowled. "But I'm right here now! Can't you see me?"

"I see you all too clear."

Shahid needed to know why Chili had stayed in his room; normally his loafers wouldn't grace such decayed linoleum. However, Chad wasn't the person to discuss this with.

Chad was still running his eyes over him. Shahid prayed that Deedee had scrubbed all the Molton Brown eyeshadow and Auburn Moon lipstick from his face.

Chad's voice rose: "Earlier, did you say Paki to me?"

"Yeah, I was trying to say—"

"No more Paki. Me a Muslim. We don't apologize for ourselves neither. We are people who say one important thing—that pleasure and self-absorption isn't everything!"

Shahid murmured, "Riaz says it is a bottomless basket."

"Ain't that a wicked phrase?" Chad had become inspired. Shahid knew his anger had passed, for a time. "One pleasure—unless there are strong limits—can only lead to another. And the greater the physical pleasure, the less respect for the other person and for oneself. Until we become beasts. The people paint their faces."

"What?"

"They wear aftershave. Inside they are filthy and bankrupt. But we people have made ourselves different."

"How can we be different?" Shahid noticed Nina and Sadiq move away from one another. "Living in all this ... decay."

Chad was gratified by the inquiry. "Excellent question."

Shahid listened attentively: a terrible torment was working itself up in his mind.

Chad said, "We have journeyed beyond sensation, to a spiritual and controlled conception of life. We regard others on the basis of respect, not thinking what we can use them for. We work for others, which is what we doing right here now."

"Yes."

"If we stick to this," Chad said, "however they try to corrupt us, we can resist."

"I understand."

"I glad, brother, I so glad, because I see weakness in you."

"Really?"

"It a serious business but Allah is beside us. What could be wrong with such an idea of pure living?"

"Nothing."

"That's right. Nothing. A man is more advanced, surely, if he conquers himself, rather than submits to every desire?"

"I think that is probably right."

"Right! One day there will be total change. I dream of it!"

Chad paced up and down as Riaz might have done, pleased with what he'd said and mouthing phrases to himself as if he were addressing the crowd in the mosque.

Riaz's absence was annoying. Without their leader the atmosphere was desultory, dispersed; the group could become childish, forgetting the reasons for their actions. And Chad did seem to enjoy imagining he had some authority over them. Shahid wondered if he didn't fancy himself in Riaz's place. All the same, Shahid understood what Chad meant. He'd been wrong to mock or dismiss his ideas. Chad could be overbearing but he spoke from harrowing experience.

Shahid sat quietly, but the flat felt airtight. The woman who lived there had initially enjoyed their company. But now she'd taken to frowning and retreating to her bedroom with the children. This may have been connected with Chad's insistence on talking Urdu to her, which he had taken up again. She would look at him as if he were speaking Welsh, and the frantic mimed motions that accompanied his attempts obviously agitated her.

And so in this overlit, grubby room, with everyone looking tired, sunk once more in the ordinary—and afraid, too, of racist attack—Shahid's mind returned to Deedee. Thinking of her was like listening to his favorite music; she was a tune he liked to play. He wanted to consider the way she nudged his head to one side so she could kiss his ear, as if, for then, only that part of him appealed to her. He thought, too, of the way she kissed his hand and pressed it against his eyes, cheeks, mouth, stamping him with love.

But instead of bathing in the warm memory of the love they'd made and the pleasures she'd introduced him to, which they could delectably repeat and extend into the future, he became aware of a bitter, disillusioned feeling. How he'd been drowning his senses in the past hours! What illusions he'd been subject to! What torrents of drug-inspired debris he had allowed to stream through his head! What banal fantasies he believed were visions! And on Baker Street Station, too!

Fortunately, his thoughts were interrupted by the arrival of Tariq. During the distraction Shahid informed Chad he was going to visit the mosque. After, he would patrol the walkways, keeping an eye on things outside.

Chad couldn't refuse him. "Just watch out," he warned. "They might want to pick us off individually."

Something about Shahid must have affected Chad, for then he said he had something to give him. While Shahid collected his notebook and favorite pens, Chad fetched a plastic bag and handed it over.

"For you."

"What is it?"

"Look."

Shahid extracted a white cotton salwar kamiz, shook it out, and held it up. "It's beautiful."

"Yeah!"

Shahid put it to his cheek. "Is it for me?"

"Course. I got my own. Will you put it on?"

"Now?"

"Go right ahead."

He watched as Shahid changed, for the first time, into "national dress." Chad looked him over before taking, from behind his back, a white cap. He fitted it on Shahid's head, stood off a moment, and embraced him.

"Brother, you look magnificent!"

"Thanks, Chad."

"I been thinking it would suit you. Wait till Riaz sees you. And Tahira. They'll be so proud. How d'you feel?"

"A little strange."

"Strange?"

"But good, good."

"Great."

Shahid pulled his sweater on, slipped into his jacket and went out. Chad watched him from the door, waving as he turned the corner. Feeling even more conspicuous in the salwar's full and comfortable folds, Shahid took the tube three stops.

He prayed as best he could, hearing in his head Hat's exhortations and instructions; he asked God to grant him realization, understanding of himself and others, and tolerance. Feeling empty of passion and somewhat delivered and cleansed, he settled down with his notebook.

Arranged on three floors, the rooms of the mosque were as big as tennis courts. Men of so many types and nationalities—Tunisians, Indians, Algerians, Scots, French—gathered there, chatting in the entrance, where they removed their shoes and then retired to wash, that it would have been difficult, without prior knowledge, to tell which country the mosque was in.

Here race and class barriers had been suspended. There were businessmen in expensive suits, others in London Underground and Post Office uniforms; bowed old men in salwar kamiz fiddled with beads. Chic lads with ponytails, working in computers, exchanged business cards with young men in suits. Forty Ethiopians sat to the side of one room, addressed by one of their number in robes.

Among the praying men on the vast carpet ran little boys in their best suits and girls in white dresses, with bows in their hair. Some visitors sprawled on mattresses against the wall and slept; they had kettles, water bottles, and their possessions in plastic bags around them. Others sat against pillars for hours with their legs crossed, talking. Some people lay flat on their backs, asleep in the center of the room, an arm across their eyes. There were dozens of languages. Strangers spoke to one another. The atmosphere was uncompetitive, peaceful, meditative.

Yes, Shahid reflected, he had plunged into a river of desire and excitement. And surely, soon, he would be bloated but not sated; such sensations wouldn't be sufficient. Requiring more, he would be flung into "the bottomless basket"! Riaz understood that. Shahid had to learn from him and Chad.

He had been tempted. He had dived headlong. But coming here was a good idea. He had returned to his senses before it was too late. If he hated himself, he had to commend himself, too, for regaining his purity. Hadn't he swum away from the whirlpool and redeemed himself by returning to this place? Yes and no. He still felt uncomfortable; he couldn't relax. Even in these cool rooms where he felt more tranquil than anywhere, his mind was working, justifying, and excoriating. He knew only one thing. He would leave Deedee before more feeling was released. He would tell her this tomorrow. He could concentrate on his work with Riaz.

Once this was decided, he got up, pulled his shoes from the rack, and went back out, blinking, into the street. He walked through a market where the noisy stalls sold suitcases, watches, tapes; shouting men tried to peddle machines for threading needles, gadgets for crushing oranges, and plastic geegaws for ruched curtains. It was a sharp transition; he found it difficult to reconcile what went on in the mosque with the bustling diversity of the city.

His friends told stories, in religious form, about the origin of everything, about how God wanted them to live, about what would happen when they died, and why, while alive, they were persecuted. They were old and useful stories, except today they could be easily mocked and undermined by more demonstrable tales, which perhaps made those who held to ancient ones even more determined.

The problem was, when he was with his friends their story compelled him. But when he walked out, like someone leaving a cinema, he found the world to be more subtle and inexplicable. He knew, too, that stories were made up by men and women; they could not be true or false, for they were exercises in that most magnificent but unreliable capacity, the imagination, which William Blake called "the divine body in every man." Yet his friends would admit no splinter of imagination into their body of belief, for that would poison all, rendering their conviction human, aesthetic, fallible.

He could see, though, where Brownlow had been wrong. All this believing wasn't so much a matter of truth or falsity, of what could be shown and what not, but of joining. He had noticed, during the days that he'd walked around the area, that the races were divided. The black kids stuck with each other, the Pakistanis went to one another's houses, the Bengalis knew each other from way back, and the whites, too. Even if there were no hostility between groups—and there was plenty, if only implicit; his mother, for instance, liked to make derogatory remarks about blacks, saying they were lazy, while middle-class whites she revered—there was little mixing. And would things change? Why should they? A few individuals would make the effort, but wasn't the world breaking up into political and religious tribes? The divisions were taken for granted, each to his own. But where did such divides lead to, if not to different kinds of civil war?

More pressingly, if everyone was so hastily adhering to their own group, where did he belong?

Back at the estate his heart sank even as his instincts were alert. Taking out the knife he was carrying now—Chad let none of them go out without a weapon—he watched for possible attackers. There were few people about. He kept lookout, sitting on a wall, "Sign o' the Times" on his headphones, alone with the black note-books he was rapidly filling. In the back of the latest book he began composing an erotic story for Deedee, "The Prayer-mat of the Flesh," which he would send to her as a good-bye present.

But it wasn't sensation alone that he and Deedee provided for each other. Last night, when he told her about giving Chili *One Hundred Years of Solitude*, she said she'd recently got through *The Sentimental Education*. It contained brilliant scenes, she said; she could imagine them being filmed. But a lot of it she'd had to force herself through, as she drove herself in the gym. *Little Dorrit*, too, she'd tried over Christmas. Serious reading required dedication. Who, now, believed it did them good? And how many people knew a book as they knew *Blonde on Blonde, Annie Hall*, or Prince, even? Could literature connect a generation in the same way? Some exceptional students would read hard books; most wouldn't, and they weren't fools.

The music her students liked, how they danced, their clothes and language, it was theirs, a living way. She tried to enter it, extend it, ask questions. It wasn't a pleasure telling people that culture would benefit them, particularly if they couldn't see what it was for. As it was, they were constantly being informed of their inferiority. Many of them regarded the white élite culture as self-deceiving and hypocritical. For some this was an excuse for laziness. With others it was genuine: they didn't want to find the culture that put them down profound.

But there was something in the book area that she did love at the moment. Deedee confessed to reading "shopping and fucking" novels secretly, as others ate chocolate in bed, for the clothes, sex, restaurants, hotels. She was, though, more ashamed of the dozens of self-help books she got through. Many women read them, she said, trying to figure out why they weren't happier, and why their expectations hadn't been fulfilled. She was interested in thinking what needs such books supplied rather than attempting to disturb people with literature, which only academics imagined central to anything, and real people only read on holiday.

Shahid, in a stubborn mood, stalked up and down, saying he couldn't go for that stuff. He'd tried it, but literature was better in every way, the difference hit you instantly, look at the first few pages of *Tom Sawyer*. That was why it was called literature. He intended to embark on the migraine reads. Turgenev, Proust, Barthes, Kundera: what did they have to say? Why were they respected?

And another thing. He didn't always appreciate being played Madonna or George Clinton in class, or offered a lecture on the history of funk as if it were somehow more "him" than *Fathers and Sons*. Any art could become "his," if its value was demonstrated. He wouldn't be denied the best.

They argued passionately but without acrimony, both modifying their views. Deedee always stimulated him to think. And now he was going to leave her.

He jogged along the walkway outside the flat to warm up. An old man passed him, a black kid walked in the other direction, and, once, a stroppy young kid walked straight at him, forcing Shahid to step aside. Otherwise there was no one around.

Then, not far away, he heard voices. Three or four men were singing. But what? He racked his brains before recognizing "Rule Britannia." To his relief it broke off. It began again, minutes later, somewhere above him, then below. He was convinced the words were aimed at him. He kept walking, turning here and there. He was going to get his head kicked in.

These people in the project, those surrounding him now, for instance, when they didn't terrify him, they perplexed him. He wanted to bring Deedee here to talk about it. He wanted to say he didn't like striding around the estate like a Britisher in India.

In the front of the notebook he was making word sketches of the block's inhabitants, who, despite being neighbors for years, regularly robbed each other. A young woman who'd been chatting Shahid up while he was on patrol—calling him her darlin' darkie and thrusting her hands into his hair, because she couldn't resist—said that one time, after she'd popped out to get her dole check, her flat was stripped: carpets, radiators, lightbulbs, beds, toys—gone. She said you'd be clever, if you went out, to stash everything in one room, behind a reinforced steel door. Or you got a Rottweiler, 'cept it would be half-starved, because there wasn't the money to feed it, and it might bite the face off a child.

The kids with initiative, who weren't going to be nothing, maybe the ones who would go after him tonight, they scavenged, robbed cars and houses, selling weed and coke. Some were adept at burglary. They carried knives, trained, knew they had to be ruthless. Weren't there stories of boys like them who had BMWs, Docklands flats, smart pussy, cute babies? Except the money wasn't there to be made. All they'd get were habits, facial scars, and five years in jail, minimum.

Sometimes Shahid found himself agreeing with Riaz. Surely these people had just enough to make their lives bearable? None of them was starving. They were not peasants. But in this place there was no God, political belief, or spiritual sustenance. What government or party believed that these people mattered? Any available work was of the meanest kind. The woman told Shahid that their condition might improve only if they drew attention to themselves.

"How could you do that?"

"By burning the fuckin' place down."

All around Shahid were people whose eyes burned with blame and resentment. Maybe they were the sort who operated the concentration camps. Didn't they have any pride or shame? How could they bear their own ignorance, living without culture, their lives reduced to watching soap operas three-quarters of the day?

They were powerless and lost. It occurred to Shahid that Riaz's group should do something amongst the people in the block, listening, handing out information, not dismissing them all. He made up his mind to talk to Riaz about it.

Riaz didn't arrive until the following evening. Shahid had patrolled all evening and stayed the night. The cold, fear, and strange singing had exhausted him. As Sadiq and Hat sat up, listening at the kitchen window for "Rule Britannia," he could only doze in his sleeping bag on the floor; finally he went into the kitchen to read. He ached for Deedee, as if he had already parted from her. He was convinced that she would forget him in a couple of days, and that it was better to end the relationship before they became too entangled.

But when Riaz did turn up, he didn't want to hear about the hexing "Rule Britannia"; he barely had a word for Shahid or the others as Chad led him away into the kitchen. Shahid pursued them and stood by the closed door. Riaz was explaining something in a low, forcible voice. Then Chad exclaimed, banging his fist on the table, "God has spoken to us. He has said, yes, he is there! He can see what is going on and will punish malefactors!"

Minutes later, Shahid stood on a balcony to watch Hat and Riaz hurrying away across the estate to the bus stop. Hat had been put in charge of organizing the patrols and would bring back fresh volunteers from college, as well as obtaining food from the restaurant. But even Hat had been looking worried lately, as his father was beginning to suspect that instead of working at his books, he was spending time with Riaz.

Someone must have been watching them. Not long after Riaz left, and about an hour before Shahid's shift was due to end, something happened.

Chad was in the kitchen. Sadiq had gone. The other boy hadn't appeared yet. Shahid and Tahira were sitting down with their college books. Tahira offered Shahid a bag of sticky gulab jamans, which she knew he could eat all day. "Let's spoil ourselves," she giggled. While they were together they had begun to take it for granted that the racists knew of their presence and didn't want a battle: either that or they were awaiting an opportunity. A bottle had been lobbed at Sadiq from a passing car but, living in the East End, he was accustomed to dancing around glass.

Now there was a rattling of the letter box followed by the sound of a brick being hurled at the reinforced window beside the door.

Chad jumped to his feet, seizing his weapon. Shahid picked up a carving knife. For a moment, to instill courage, they clasped one another's free hand.

Chad unbarred the door. Tahira threw on her coat.

"Stay there," Chad warned, looking around the door.

He saw nothing. Cautiously, he and Shahid moved outside. Tahira followed. Some of the walkway lights had been smashed; the air was so cold it hung like a gauze. In the wan light it was difficult to make anything out.

"Better ring for reinforcements," Shahid whispered to Tahira.

The two men looked both ways. Shahid discerned a young woman standing along the walkway with an object in her hand. She was accompanied by two kids, neither of whom could have been older than eight.

"Hey," Shahid called.

At this, the woman, who was wearing slippers, flung half a brick at them and tried to dash away. Chad and Shahid chased them. The smallest kid slipped at the top of the stairs and Chad seized her by the collar. The mother, with a dingy raincoat thrown over her heavy shoulders, stopped and stared defiantly at them, clutching the other kid.

"Chad!" Shahid said. "No!"

Chad clenched his weapon over the child's head, and waved it about. He might have wanted restraining.

The posse had required a cleansing jihad, but this wasn't at all the sort of thing they'd considered. Around them lights went on. A door opened and a tattooed face peered round. Dogs barked. No doubt the police were on their way.

In the hope that this might satisfy Chad, Shahid yelled at the woman: "Can't you leave these people alone? What have they ever done to hurt you? Have they come to your house and abused you or thrown stones? Did they make you live in these mildewed flats?"

The child escaped Chad's grasp, ran to her mother, and turned screeching at them. The woman, who was unafraid, jerked her head forward and spat at Chad and Shahid. But her saliva blew back and spun through her daughter's hair.

"Paki! Paki! Paki!" she screamed. Her body had become an arched limb of hatred with a livid opening at the tip, spewing curses. "You stolen our jobs! Taken our housing! Paki got everything! Give it back and go back home!"

She and the kids fled.

"You stay out here," Chad told Shahid. Both of them were trembling. "There might be more trouble. But don' worry, Hat, Sadiq, and Tariq rushin' this way, reinforced up!"

Alone, Shahid paced the walkway, knowing the woman would return with rat-faced brutes carrying bats. He wanted badly to go away, but his father had not been a coward, it wasn't in his family. Not that Chili, he reflected, could ever be described as an orthodox defender of his community. One of his black girlfriends did once persuade him to go on an anti-racist demonstration; and when the National Front yelled, "Get back, Pakis!" Chili, wearing a mink-colored suit, had annoyed everyone by taking out his fat wallet, waving it at the racists, and shouting, "Get back to your project flats, paupers!"

For distraction and out of frustration, Shahid wrenched his mind around to Deedee. He thought of her picking hard seeds out of her weed as she prepared a joint, before flicking them with her nail at the window. As she shredded the grass, distributing it in the paper, she'd glance up at him and smile. After, she'd tuck the spliff between her lips and park it there, removing it only for the demonstration of a point, lifting it to her face as if it were heavy. She loved listening to music then, turning it up and leaning her head back to blow smoke rings, lost in a luxurious indolence.

Shahid recalled slamming vodka with her; he thought of how her hands played on him, with a knowing life of their own, and how sex for her was like dancing, all of her alive and responding. He felt inept, only wanting to stick his dick in her; he couldn't feel or touch like her. She'd said he hadn't quite located his sensuality. He was keen to know if, by practicing, it might be winkled out. Oh, if only he could be lapping her cunt, not standing on this precipice, terrified that some white boy was going to plant a knife in him!

He spotted the kid's shadow behind a pillar and heard him laughing.

He shouted, "Hey!" and moved toward him, just to see.

The kid was alone. He wasn't big. But he was already gone. Without thinking Shahid pelted up a corridor and turned the corner. He went through a door and kept going. From the glimpse, he knew he'd seen the kid before. Where?

He was standing in the lift, boot jamming the door. Shahid wasn't entering that steel box. They stood watching one another. Good-looking, with soft, blond hair, the boy was soiled. But he'd come out in reasonable loafers, Chinos, and black zip-up blouson.

"Want anything?"

Shahid feared a trap. He looked behind him. "What?"

The kid put out his hand. "Know what I mean?"

Shahid breathed out. "Maybe." He touched the boy's hand. The kid smiled.

Shahid asked, "What you got?"

"It's always a party with me, man. Skunk, trips, E. You had my confection before. You know it scenic."

"Had it before?"

The kid took off, walking with a mixture of swagger and limp. Shahid had been on holiday in Jamaica and he recognized some Jamaican attitude in him. He wondered if he'd picked it up at school.

"Coming for a walk?"

Shahid hesitated.

The kid said, "Don't worry, there's no real Paki-busters out tonight. They're all indoors watching the match on TV."

Shahid called out, "Show us where those fuckers live, then." He caught up with him. "You know who they are. Show us."

"Sure you want to meet them? What are you gonna do, burn them out? For that you'll want specialized assistance. I can fire places up, if you like."

His name was Stratford, known as Strapper. An Asian family had fled their flat months ago, which Strapper was now squatting.

Shahid tried hard to think where he might have met him. He claimed to be a businessman. After some pressure—Strapper clearly reveled in mystery—it emerged that Strapper had been at the swimming-pool party Deedee had taken him to. "You don't re-member me? I'm the euphoric dealer on the stairs. I also followed you one time, round here."

"What for?"

"To check you. You phoned from the taxi office. I reckoned you were arguing with some girl." He had a filthy laugh. He added, as if the two remarks were connected, "The white capitalistic civiliza-tion has come to an end."

"Yeah?"

"You know that, don't ya? That's why you're dressed against it."

"Right."

Strapper led a watchful Shahid out of the block and across a patch of frozen earth. A car stood on blocks and two kids were busily pulling pieces off it; seeing Strapper and Shahid they hesi-tated, before continuing.

"You sure it's finished?"

"I'm telling you, man. I've had experience of it." Strapper went on: "Police, courts, kids' homes, rehabilitation centers, social work-ers. I truly been inside the law, man. I can tell you, it's the white people who've treated me like shit. None of them believe in love outside the family. Blacks and Pakis, the Muslims, the people put down, and outside, they generous and lovin'. They know what mistreatment is." Strapper stood there with his hands in his pocket. "If you aren't going to buy nothing, I gotta swing over to west London. Business is steep over there. So—later."

"I'm just off that way myself. That's where I got my digs."

Strapper said, "Wanna go back together? We can talk."

"Great."

Strapper asked Shahid to wait. He went behind a garage and reemerged quickly, slipping something into his pocket.

"Can't carry the stuff on me."

Strapper didn't mistrust him. This made Shahid feel that he could ask the boy something personal, that Strapper would like to talk about himself.

He said, "What would you really like to do with your life, if you could choose? D'you know?"

"If I tell you, you'll think I'm winding you up."

"I won't."

"Well, I'm not taking the piss," Strapper said. "I always wanted to do something with archaeology."

"Why don't you, then?"

"You think I could?"

"Why not you demand what you want?"

"Yeah, yeah, why not?" Strapper kicked out at a passing dog and hawked at its curled tail.

"Didn't you learn a trade?"

"I could marble your bathroom for you. Got a bathroom?"

"Not of my own."

"Well, when you get one remember I did painting and decorating in prison."

"Prison?"

"Yeah."

"OK."

Strapper accompanied Shahid back to the flat so that Shahid could check that the others had arrived. If they had, he would be able to get away.

As they rode up in the lift, Shahid repeated, "Where are these racists, Strapper? Just point at their door and we'll do the rest."

Strapper kept laughing. He was confident; he seemed to know more about life than anyone Shahid knew of that age. He enjoyed saying he'd survived stuff that people only see on television. His intuition, if not his schooling, went deep.

Shahid said, also laughing, "What's the problem? I'm not asking you to write down their names."

"You wanna find someone who hates another race?" Strapper stopped scratching himself long enough to motion at southern England. "Just knock on any door." They had pushed into the tiny hall of the flat. He added, "Course, I used to be a skinhead, meself."

"What?"

"I liked football, see. Millwall. Me black mates were always chasing me."

"For God's sake, keep your voice down."

"One time they tied a noose round me neck and tried to throw me over a bridge."

Following the scare earlier, a few of the group had already gathered: Sadiq, Tariq, and two of the sisters were sitting on the floor in their coats, cradling weapons, while Chad was reporting the earlier events. They looked up in dismay when Shahid strode in with Strapper. The two women turned their faces away. Strapper stood back, chewing his cheek as if it offended him, but grinning, too, still thinking about being tossed over the bridge, probably. Fortunately, he knew how to be friendly.

"That's Strapper," Shahid said. "He's on our side. Lives here."

But the frost didn't thaw. Mind you, Shahid was yet to see his new mate in the light. Now he noticed that despite his good-boned face, Strapper's skin was pockmarked and raw in patches, his eyes were bloodshot, and there were five gold studs in his ear. A marijuana leaf was tattooed onto the back of his hand.

Shahid recalled a phrase that Chili had used frequently in the 1980s: "useful contact." Surely Chad would appreciate Strapper, a street kid who lived in the block and knew the area?

"He'll be a useful contact. Maybe he can help us."

Strapper said, "How you doing, Chad, mate?"

Chad had turned furiously pale, or paler, and was watching Strapper. He said nothing.

Shahid hurriedly began gathering his Maupassant story collection, a half-finished essay, his gloves, and a woolly hat.

Strapper sucked his teeth. "Respect, eh?"

Chad folded his arms. Shahid didn't dare look at him again. He shook hands with everyone but Chad, changed out of the salwar in the bathroom and got out, feeling as if he were betraying them by leaving.

He and Strapper walked toward the station. After fifteen minutes, when Shahid saw the blue-and-red tube sign he felt relieved, as if he were, at last, out of danger. At the station Strapper told Shahid to wait until the guard looked away. Shahid inserted his ticket and Strapper shoved through the barrier close behind him.

In the train Strapper said, "I know your man, Trevor, Chad, or whatever he calls hisself. I see him up here the other day, sharpenin' his machete. He wouldn't give me respect—an' he used to love me so much."

"You?"

"Yeah, me, man. What do you know?" Strapper sneered. "Everyone loves me—at certain times. I can get as popular as punch. I used to sort rocks, crack, you know, for Trevor. An' anything else he wanted. He had money, see."

"How come?"

"He was running a couple of girls. Through it all now, is he?" Shahid nodded. "He's the lucky one. How many can do that? Chances are low, man. Low, low, low. His people saved his life. They're pure." Strapper sank back in the seat, looking abstracted. "I feel as if I've known you for a while," he said. "D'you know why that is?"

"Why is it?"

"You a Paki, me a delinquent." He had a dirty, sarcastic laugh which thought it cut through all pretension to the basic things. "How does it feel to be a problem for this world?"

When they got off the tube Strapper said that if Shahid wanted to get hold of him, or knew anyone who wanted to lighten their life, he could be found in the Morlock. It was nearby. Though Shahid didn't imagine he would need them, he listened to Strapper's instructions.

"Later, man."

"Later."

B ack at his place Shahid picked up two notes marked "urgent" that Riaz had left on the hall shelf. Both informed him that Zulma had rung. Shahid put them in his pocket and went upstairs apprehensively.

He pushed at the broken lock and stood in the doorway, looking everything over, scared his brother might step out from a corner. His room seemed no different, yet everything seemed to have been moved. Why had Chili hidden here? He'd never needed Shahid before. Who was chasing him? What had he done?

Shahid couldn't help being glad that Chili was in trouble. He'd got away with lying, deceit, and contempt for others for as long as Shahid could remember. If there was such a thing as natural justice, Chili deserved punishment. When younger, Shahid had, himself, continually attempted revenge. He'd sneak into Chili's room and scrape a metal comb over his favorite records; he'd drop one of his Armani ties behind a cupboard and feign innocence when Chili erupted. Nevertheless, Shahid didn't want Chili to be destroyed. He wanted him to recognize something about himself and change as a result. There was a part of Chili which Shahid admired even as he hated him, the part of him that stated, "I don't give a fuck."

It took defiant courage, much arrogance and some nobility to be so reckless with oneself, to risk others' anger and retribution. Even Chili's greed, and the idea that the accumulation of everything he wanted would make him feel better, now seemed more touching than bad. Hope and fearlessness were not qualities which Shahid naturally possessed himself. Compared to his brother, he knew he rarely took risks.

Shahid wanted to sit and think. But on the desk sat Riaz's poems like a reproach. Shahid had no inclination to open them or any other book. The silence of his room felt unnatural and oppressive. It seemed like days since he'd been alone. Who would be solitary if they could avoid it? He had been resisting his own company, running from himself. It wasn't mere boredom he feared; the questions he dreaded were those that interrogated him about what he had got into with Riaz on one side, and Deedee on the other.

He believed everything; he believed nothing.

His own self increasingly confounded him. One day he could passionately feel one thing, the next day the opposite. Other times provisional states would alternate from hour to hour; sometimes all crashed into chaos. He would wake up with this feeling: who would he turn out to be on this day? How many warring selves were there within him? Which was his real, natural self? Was there such a thing? How would he know it when he saw it? Would it have a guarantee attached to it?

Lost in such a room of broken mirrors, with jagged reflections backing into eternity, he felt numb. His instinct was to escape, to seek out someone to talk to. Even Chili would have been better than nothing.

But he forbade himself to move from the chair. When he had returned to Sevenoaks after first meeting Deedee Osgood, he had thought about his future. He knew he wasn't naturally brilliant like some at school. But his father, who was capable of quite indecent dissipation, had worked all hours, as did his mother still. They had been good examples. Shahid, during this time, had made up his mind to be a disciplined person and not waste his life.

Now he laid his watch on the desk. He would continue working on Riaz's stuff, as well as his own material, not moving for three hours. Even if a bomb exploded outside, which wasn't entirely unlikely, he would burst with his arse adhered to the chair.

After a few minutes he didn't have to force himself to sit still, for he liked this, attempting to do something well, to the limit of his ability, on his own terms. What would turn up? Inconceivable ideas entered his head, exciting him. He went over the same piece again and again, until the original idea had been extended, even transformed, into something he'd never thought before.

There was, too, something he was sure of, even as his life shifted daily: everyone had their story; and what went on in his mind occurred in others', too, the current of life flowing through all. Writing could be as easy as dreaming, except the dreams spread in concentric circles, one coloring another. When it dried up, he found it best to wait, and it would begin again.

He'd done enough. He was hungry, but there was only a rancid lump of cheese and some bad milk in the fridge.

He lay down on the bed. He would take a nap; he didn't feel so good now. His earlier excitement and enthusiasm had been misplaced. Why wasn't his work better? How come, when he read the words over, they were only a muffled echo of what he wanted to make sharp and clear? Would it ever improve? Was he fooling himself; should he give up? Surely Prince, from whom music gushed without respite, never felt like this?

He closed his eyes and considered visiting the mosque, which always calmed him. But, moving the pillow, a paper handkerchief fell out. Maybe Chili had wanked—although that was unlikely, since Chili liked to state, "Why do yourself what you can have others do for you?" There were two spots of blood on the handkerchief. Lying back to consider what Chili was up to, Shahid's hand trailed on the floor, resting on a crumpled copy of *New Directions*, a magazine he'd consulted until the people in it were like old friends. He didn't need to stop himself extracting it and brushing away the fluff, as the day had already been justified by the work he'd just done.

He turned to his favorite section, "Get It Together," which featured Polaroids readers had sent in, to meet similar others. He perused one picture.

An arse and cunt filled the frame, photographed from behind. At the top of the thighs, prying apart her cunt—the grip not unlike that of a fast bowler bisecting of the seam of a cricket ball—were the woman's fingers, the nails red. Beneath this he read, "Young Lady, twenty, seeks elderly gents, preference given to gray hair and big males. Likes being licked, sucked and shagged. Can accommodate. Adventurous spirit. Essex."

Licked, sucked, shagged! Young lady! Not only could she accommodate, but the adventurous Essex woman had troubled to have the photograph taken. She'd penned a letter, addressed it, posted it!

It was stirring; he fondled his cock. Maybe it had stirred her to think of being looked at? But what made her go for gray hair? Was she really twenty? The angle didn't assist. He turned the pages. He liked the positions the women were in. There was a page of women straddling their husbands' cars in stockings and high heels. What were they doing at this moment? Listening to the radio, or dancing? Washing up? He wouldn't recognize them if they walked into the room.

He read through some "readers' letters." Many of them concerned a couple going to a pub or disco where the woman got picked up by a couple of strangers or a pair of his friends. The husband would watch her being fucked by the anonymous pair, often in his own front room, eventually joining in. The prose was standardized, unexpressive, and never humorous, for that would undermine it, though the writers favored exclamation marks.

Shahid wondered why for him, whose eyes dashed from the words to the pictures, from the pictures to the words, with ever-increasing excitement, but whose cherished reading was the ironically bawdy *Thousand and One Nights*, full of farts, impotence, and trickiness, such banal tales were riveting. Maybe pornography presented a complete and uplifting adventure, like the world in children's books. The other pleasure was the way pornography differed from real sex: there was no need to think of anyone else.

Now he was taking down his mirror and setting it against the desk at a complimentary angle, so he could slink backward and forward, viewing the top of his legs as he played with himself. Clumsily, not entirely sure where to put his fingers, he tugged on one of the stockings Deedee had given him, and a pair of her French knickers, which were a little tight. He was applying lipstick—inaccurately, like Chili's daughter Safire—when there was a sound. He crept to the door.

Riaz was going into his room.

Shahid was giggling. He would get changed, invite Riaz in, leave the magazine open, and pretend to go for a pee. Through the crack of the door he might see Riaz lift the page to peruse Greta from Acton. He could witness any possible fly movement. Surely Riaz had some weaknesses?

Maybe he did, Shahid reckoned. But Riaz lacked a taste for the vulgar; he wouldn't yet be tainted by corruption and probably not much by curiosity. He wouldn't wonder why the women were lying in the childbirth position, in those clothes; or wonder which expression was his favorite. He wouldn't consider what the women, whose eyes said nothing, were thinking of and why they exposed themselves for money; or what the men who masturbated over them wanted; or why it was that everyone seemed to be voyeurs these days, armchair sex being the coming thing. People's eyes were popping. But who was actually doing it, unless they were getting paid?

No; Riaz had one thing on his mind: the future and how to forge it.

Shahid put everything away. He stood outside Riaz's closed door. He was about to knock but stopped himself. Shahid didn't like to criticize Riaz, but there was one thing you could say about him: his laughter was always astringent and sardonic. Folly didn't entertain him; he wanted to correct it. Like pornography, religion couldn't admit the comic.

Shahid was ashamed, too. The prank would have delighted Papa and Chili, but they enjoyed taking the lowest view of human nature.

Why couldn't Riaz help him? He had, after all, opened him up and pulled him into this. Yet now he asked nothing but obedience, and gave little. Shahid had imagined Riaz possessed some understanding or wisdom about living; there would be late-night arguments and illumination. But only Chad really had access to Riaz, and Chad kept everyone else away. Shahid found some change in his pocket and went downstairs. He needed to talk to someone.

"Hi, it's me," he said into the receiver.

Music was playing in the background. She sounded excited. "Shahid. My God. Where are you? You do sound sad."

"Do I? I'm not. Well."

"I've just been to my therapist."

"Are you in need of help?"

"Yes. Now I'm writing my dissertation and waiting for you to call. And you did. Thanks for being reliable."

"Do men fuck you around?" he said impatiently. "Don't categorize me, Deedee."

"I have a healthy suspicion, all right? Even more now, I'd say." Her voice softened. "Maybe you're not old enough for that. What have you been doing?"

He hesitated; they were arguing already, he couldn't start up about Chad and Riaz. He told her about running into Strapper.

She said, "I hate not having any drugs in the house. Sounds like a good dealer."

He asked her what she was doing later.

"Do you really want to see me?"

"I can't wait," he said.

There was a tube station nearby where she would meet him. He went straight there. He knew she wanted to see him, but she made him wait forty minutes. Maybe she imagined the anticipation would do him good.

It did. He'd never been more impatient to gaze on someone's face, and give them a long look of marveling curiosity. It puzzled him how, but he made her happy. She didn't want anyone else; she would do anything for him. How had it happened? And what was she really like? Was he yearning for someone he didn't know at all? Would she be as he'd remembered? Or less attractive? Had he invented or written her in some way? He knew one thing: he wanted to listen to her.

She knew to dress unobtrusively, in black Levi's; but she liked her breasts and wore a low-cut top. Her hair was still wet. He handed her some music tapes, containing dance stuff he'd listened to at home, mixed with some INXS and Zeppelin tracks, because she liked boys with guitars.

"Thanks, thanks." She gave him a full kiss, her face adhesive with makeup. "But you're in a funny mood.

When you've been with your friends your mouth curls down."

"And when I'm with you does it curl up?"

"When you're with me, man, all of you curls up."

They walked toward the Morlock, having located it without trouble. It could be heard at the far end of the residential street.

"All right," he said. "My friends."

Outside a few kids were leaning against cars, eating fish and chips. At least they appeared to be kids, but in fact they were men, in their mid- to late twenties.

"It's difficult for me."

She took his arm and held him tight. "You've admitted it, at least. Maybe now we'll get somewhere."

He pushed the door. They looked in.

Just inside was a trestle table with two turntables on it. A jumping white boy rubbed and dipped his fingers in the records, as if he were putting a pattern on a pot. Behind him an old man sat on a bench with a slobbering mongrel on his lap. Further along were a couple of withered women in their seventies, looking as if they'd been sitting there since the war, oblivious to their surroundings.

"We going in?" he said doubtfully.

"Oh yes."

The Morlock didn't favor decoration. The flock wallpaper was faded, the two photographs of Irish boxers were yellow, and against the walls stood a few shaky tables and chairs. A kid sat with his head cradled in his arms. Joint roaches and silver paper littered the threadbare carpet.

"Where's the boy?"

"Dunno."

Shahid and Deedee hustled their way through, peering into the dark corners and alcoves which a few intermittently flashing colored lights were failing to illuminate. A lot of men wearing Joe Bloggs jeans, trainers, baggy sweatshirts, and leaning against the pool table, observed her.

"What?" Shahid asked.

"We can score here," she repeated.

"Expect so."

The dealers, of whom there appeared to be many, were the ones looking around furtively, passing money and drugs from hand to hand and moving back and forth to the toilet, although the bar staff were oblivious or indifferent, standing back with their arms crossed, as no one was buying drinks.

Shahid and Deedee sat on stools near a group who, shouting above the music, were discussing how one of them had passed drugs over the table to a mate in prison. Deedee ordered vodka and ginger beer in long glasses, with ice, and watched the crowd, nodding her head. The barman set out the drinks.

"Am I going to see you dance?" she said.

Shahid was wondering if they shouldn't leave. These weren't their people. And wasn't Deedee looking at them with a too objective eye, as if they were specimens of theories she might have about music, fashion, or street life?

"Doubt it."

"Oh, why not?"

"Wait."

Shahid pushed his way through the Morlock. As he moved toward the back, which got darker as he went, kids were toking and tripping. Pockets of girls and boys clutched the walls to stand up. Others stood alone, sweat forced through their skulls, mad-eyed, suddenly dancing with their arms above their heads as if trying to communicate with someone far away, abruptly stopping as if told bad news, all the time possessed by some inner boiling, impossible to reach.

Shahid stepped on the wet toilet floor and saw across the gloom people smoking crack pipes; a boy was leaning against a wall in conversation with another kid, while vomit dribbled from his mouth. A piece of graffiti declared, "People can be cunts." Shahid considered Chad's strictures against self-poisoning. Maintaining your humanity these days was an accomplishment. You had to be resolute not to fall into the maelstrom when most people were diving in head-first.

He told Deedee, "I feel like being fit and well, my mind working."

"You are fit and well. Your mind works, don't it?"

He was watching a girl. They were young, this group, only thirteen or fourteen, long-haired, dressed up—one wore spangled shorts. They danced for one another, watching themselves in the mirrors, being watched by the men at the bar, passing joints.

Amongst them was a woman in her fifties, maybe someone's mother, in a spotted party dress, dancing grotesquely, and occasionally scattering the crowd with a deranged jig. She had black eyes and a smashed mouth. She heeded Shahid: when his eyes returned to her, she scrutinized him, as if to say, "You might come in here and think I'm rubbish. But I'm not, and I can punch."

The girl passed them.

Deedee said, "What is it you like about her? Legs, shoes, hair, tits?"

He gestured with his glass. "Yes."

"What would you like to do with her?"

"What I'm going to be doing with you later."

"Goes without saying that I can do more for you than these adolescents—and with knobs on. You know that you can do whatever you want to me, don't you?"

He kissed Deedee on either side of her mouth; she held his arse and kissed his eyes. Her sexual pride, and the way she held him proprietorially yet carelessly, made him shiver. This casually intimate way said she knew him; they were together.

She said, "You missed my James Baldwin lecture. I played Miles Davis. I've been wanting to see you. Sometimes . . . I just can't wait. But there's been a silence."

The DJ turned up the music.

"I know, I know. Here I am, though."

People were dancing wildly, like they were having nightmares.

"It's not easy for me. I'm so attracted to you. But I can't make a mistake. It would be too much."

"What d'you really mean, Deedee?"

"I mean . . . Tell me what your friends say about women."

"What do you think they say?"

The DJ shouted, "Let's have a good time tonight!"

"I've got some idea. I do have to teach some of them."

He took her wrist. "People make assumptions. I've never known one of them to leer at any woman or even look at one. They've got respect, not like Englishmen—" he indicated the pub—"who consider women bags of slop to come into." He leaned back. "OK?"

She laughed at him. "Come off it."

"What d'you mean?"

She got up. "Just don't give me that shit."

"Listen," he said.

"I need another drink."

She went round to the other side of the bar. The volume of the music rose.

Looking over, Shahid saw his father. Or at least it resembled Papa. Then Deedee, who was standing beside him trying to get served, leaned forward and concealed the person. A moment later she moved back and Shahid was able to watch the man talking to her. It was Chili, chatting her up.

Chili loved going out; he liked clubs and enjoyed pubs. In the old days, when there was the opportunity, a final match, for instance, Mum and the assistants ran the business while Chili and Papa went to the pub to watch the match on TV. Papa always said, as he careered through the bar door, that pubs were the only glory of England now and the single reason for existing in such a godforsaken country. After a few hours, if Imran had been swinging the ball or Zahir Abbas was building a double century, or if the Indian spinners or West Indian fast bowlers were cutting through the English batsmen, or even if the Australians—they were colonials, after all—were putting down England, Papa and Chili became quite ebullient.

After enjoying oysters with a shake of Tabasco and a pint of stout, he and Chili took great pleasure in scoffing pork pies, bantering that if only the mullah were here—which was, admittedly, not a regular occurrence in the Sussex Castle—they'd jam it in the self-righteous fucker's beard and then skewer a hot kebab up his hypocritical arse. Chili would get rowdy, but Papa would get worse, challenging people to arm wrestle. Chili had to pick him up and carry him out of there with Papa bellowing, "I fought for your lives, you bastards, kiss my MBE!" and kicking his legs like a bride crossing the threshold.

Chili would drive Papa up to London for the evening. Only God knew what turn their terrible pleasures took, from which Shahid was excluded. But he was aware, through Tipoo, of a wager they'd taken with each other, the subject of which was "love in uniform." The winner would be the first to fuck a nurse, traffic warden, and policewoman. Naturally there had to be proof—an item of the uniform, which was why the trophy of a traffic warden's cap took pride of place on Chili's desk.

But at least Chili had been under control as long as Papa was there, because he loved Papa, and was afraid of hurting him. Now Papa was gone, and what was Chili doing now, here, tonight?

Deedee walked back around the bar with the drinks. Chili followed her until his Guinness-dark eyes rested on Shahid. He tipped his glass to his brother as if they met in the Morlock every night. Chili was about to get up when Strapper struck his hand on Chili's shoulder. The two of them began talking, even arguing, their faces close.

Deedee put down the drinks. "Is that the lad?"

"Yeah. With Chili."

"Your brother?"

"My brother."

"Wow."

"Exactly."

She looked across at them. Several people, when passing Strapper, greeted him, touched him. Others nodded in his direction. Not that he was impressed.

"Do they know each other?"

"I didn't think so."

"What's wrong, didn't you expect to meet your brother tonight?"

"I didn't even know he came to this kinda place."

"He could say the same about you. Do you want me to meet him?"

"I'd rather get out. I don't really want to meet him myself."

"But why?"

"I only want to be with you."

"Good."

They were finishing their drinks when Strapper and Chili got up.

"Fuck, it's too late," Shahid said.

Deedee took his hand and kneaded his fingers one by one. "He's not as good-looking as you. And I can't imagine him blushing. But he has a refined face, doesn't he?"

"Yeah?"

"Like a priest."

Chili insisted on putting his arms around Deedee, hugging her, kissing both cheeks, and looking into her eyes.

She smiled back at him. "Hi, Chili, whoever you are."

"Right! How come you're bringing my baby brother into these dumps? I might have to put my foot down."

"I'm a bad influence."

"What are you called?"

"Deedee Osgood."

"I like bad influences, Deedee Osgood. The worse the better, in my book. Not that I read books. Strapper does, don't you, boy? Babe, I hear you're in the education business. Let's have a drink. What's everyone having? Deedee? Shahid?"

Deedee pushed their glasses forward.

"Nothing for me," Strapper said. "I don't touch alcohol."

"Strapper's on a health kick," Chili chuckled, waving at the barman. "I've never seen him so hearty. He's a walking advertisement for Lourdes. Give them one of your raps, Strap. This boy can really talk. And how many people can you say that about?"

"Fuck that, what you fuckers want?" Strapper said. His eyes were sunken; light appeared to enter them, but none was given out. Compared to earlier, he was wary and withdrawn. "I'm towering here."

Deedee said, "That's exactly what we want. To Eiffel Tower."

"Eiffel this wondrously sexy woman right up, Strap," Chili said. "She deserves the very best and right now, you bum."

Strapper scrambled to fetch the drugs from where he'd concealed them, behind the baseboard, so that if there was a raid he'd be as innocent as always.

"He's a good boy," Chili said, waving Deedee's money away. He informed Strapper, "I'll pay you later."

Shahid put his arms around Deedee and pulled her away from the bar.

"Now I want to dance."

They moved close and slowly, though the music was fast and the occupants of the pub were heaving as one, waving their fists and cheering.

"You do know how to swing," she said. "How are you feeling?"

"All the better for being with you."

She said, "You can be quite sweet, and it's not all put on either."

"It's true. Oh yes."

"What's that?" She wiggled against him. "You're getting hard."

"Certainly am."

"We can't spend the night together."

"Why not?"

"Oh, dear, a little pout!"

"Deedee."

"There'll be awful trouble if the students in the house find out I'm being shagged ragged by a student. Intercourse with the lecturers isn't on the curriculum. And Brownlow's wretched face still depresses me most nights, though he claims to be moving out." She took his hand and led him across the pub. "Come on."

"Where?"

"We really can't leave you this way."

They fell kissing against the toilet door. He had envied gays who could retire to a nearby stall, pull each other's cock, and then be "gone like a cool breeze," without having shaken hands first.

She opened his trousers and took his cock into her warm hand. Then she spit in her palm and began rubbing him, alternately weighing and squeezing his balls in her other fingers.

"Harder."

"Isn't it hurting yet?"

She worked. He abandoned himself. She interrupted herself to ask, "What would your friends say?"

He laughed, yanked down her fly, and thrust his hand into the front of her jeans.

"Don't put me off, Deedee."

"Don't turn me on, then. Would they say you're a hypocrite?"

He pulled his fingers out of her and tasted them. "What?"

In the next stall someone put the seat down.

"Isn't that what you are, technically?" she said.

"Technically, wank me."

"Hey, I'm good at this when I want to be. But tell me what you're going to do about them."

"I'm—"

The occupant of the adjacent stall began talking into a portable phone.

"What?"

"I'm going to leave them."

"Yes? I wish when you said something it was the truth."

"But I've been so miserable and frightened. It's all going wrong."

She stood back to listen. His trousers had fallen around his ankles, resting in the wet; his pants were around his knees, his arms across his chest. The stink of vomit rose around them.

She laughed. "I like looking at you like that."

"Thanks."

"But you're shivering."

"Please, Deedee. I never like being told what to do. I've got to make up my own mind about things! I can't stand this harassment."

"Leave them to God and they can leave you to me. Say this: I am an atheist, a blasphemer, and a pervert. Say it on your knees in a toilet. Don't you ever have such thoughts?"

He covered himself with his hand and shook his head.

"No, no! Are you mad? I don't always want to be on the outside of everything."

"Is that what it is, then?"

"I want to follow the rules."

"Even if they're foolish?"

"There must be a reason for them. Those rules have been followed by millions of people for hundreds of years."

"I expected more of you than some dismal orthodoxy."

"Oh, Deedee, don't do this."

"You like books, don't you? And most novels, like most lives, could be entitled *Lost Illusions*. Isn't that what's happening to you?"

"Can't you just make me come? You don't usually lecture in such venues, do you?"

"I might have to start," she said, "the way education is being run down these days."

He did himself up. "I need to get out."

"Fine."

She followed him. Two boys standing at the urinal smirked. Chili was blowing his nose at the sink. His eyes were bright. He put away his handkerchief but not before Shahid noticed the blood on it.

Chili kissed Shahid on the side of the head and said, "I thought I recognized that whining voice."

Deedee fixed her hair. The pub was closing. They went out into the street.

Shahid said to Chili, "Where's your car?"

"I'm coming to your place."

"Why?"

"Don't ask stupid questions."

Shahid said, "You feel pretty comfortable round there, eh?"

Chili raised a warning finger. "Watch your mouth as well."

Deedee saw a cab and waved it down.

"Deedee—"

He thought he saw tears in her eyes.

"You've got some serious thinking to do. Cheerio."

She didn't even kiss him. As she walked away she tossed her hair. Suddenly he was afraid he might not see her again. He wanted to run after her but she was gone and he was with his brother.

Strapper tore out into the street and went to Chili.

"Where's my money? Where is it?"

Chili started walking and tried to brush him away. "Don't worry, boy, it's waiting for you." But Strapper clutched his arm. Chili said, "Don't you know me, you little shit?"

"I know you. You're a quality guy," Strapper said. Chili drew back his fist. "Pay me," Strapper said, "so I can buy some chips."

"Get off my fucking back tonight."

"When, then?"

"Little boy, your useless troubles bore everyone."

The hurt look which broke across Strapper's face was weary rather than angry, as if he'd experienced this scene numerous times but still found it an unbelievably bitter pill that this was all his life had brought him, as if he'd won the booby prize and didn't know why.

"Chili," he implored.

Chili thrust his flat palm into Strapper's chest and sent him reeling across the road, where he toppled into the gutter. He picked himself up and ran away like a child, following some people coming out of the Morlock.

Shahid and his brother got back to his building but at the bottom of the stairs Chili lurched back against the wall. Looking into his ashen face and seeing the mauve shadows beneath his eyes, Shahid could see what Chili, having been, until now, a young man, would look like as he aged. There will be a day, he thought, when someone will look at me like that. Not that Chili gave a damn about anything at the moment.

"What have you been taking, Chili?"

"Not enough."

To get him up the stairs Shahid had to take his weight from behind and push. Fortunately, the speed-freak from upstairs was on his knees beside a bucket of water, washing the floor. He was happy to give Shahid a hand with his load. Shahid just wished he'd stop murmuring, "He Ain't Heavy, He's My Brother," as they heaved.

The three of them were making their unwieldy way when Shahid heard Riaz's voice at the top. What was worse, Riaz was talking to Chad. Why would they be standing in the hall unless they were intending to come downstairs? Shahid ordered Chili to stand still. "Try not to sway," he whispered. "Keep your mouth zipped."

"What?"

"Shut it, Chili!"

Chad and Riaz were standing at the top of the stairs. Shahid nodded and smiled at them as casually as he could, but was afraid to speak for fear they would detect alcohol. As usual Riaz looked anxious and was impatient for them to pass; Chad glowered at the entire group.

Shahid shoved Chili into the room and was pleased to see he could stand. Chili removed his jacket, brushed the shoulders with his fingertips, and hung it over the back of the chair. He sat down and rubbed his forehead as if trying to calm himself. He was used to ignoring Shahid and Shahid was accustomed to silence from his brother. Shahid changed into his pajamas and went up the hall to the bathroom.

Chili was on his hands and knees behind the cooker when Shahid returned.

"Chili."

He continued rooting around but said, after a while, "You and the woman still like each other? What's her name?"

Shahid addressed his brother's backside. "Deedee Osgood. But it's so difficult. And it has to be kept secret, for lots of reasons."

"Maybe, but she didn't want to part from you tonight. She'll do anything for you. Take full advantage."

"She hates my friends."

"Jackpot!"

"Eh?"

Chili plucked a plastic bag from behind Shahid's fridge, opened it, and extracted a small envelope. There was sufficient coke for two thin lines, which he cut out on one of Shahid's college books. He snorted them both, then licked the paper, the 10-pound note and the book.

Shahid muttered, "Your closest brush with literature, ever."

When Chili looked up again he'd forgotten what they were

talking about. He sat there with his arms crossed. A red bead had appeared in one nostril; then it rolled from his nose, like a tear, and dropped into his lap.

Shahid got into bed. Chili lay down on the hard floor, his eyes open, smoking, staring at the ceiling.

"Got a drink?"

"Fortunately not."

"You got an objection to drinking?"

"I didn't have, no," Shahid said.

"But you do now?"

"It would be better if people looked after themselves, wouldn't it?"

"How many times you prayed today, you moralistic little shit?"

"Chili, why don't you go to sleep?"

"Floor's very hard. Where's your landlord? I want to complain. He's a fucker."

Shahid got up and found his brother a blanket and a cushion.

"Please try to sleep. Close your eyes and try to take it from there."

Chili pulled the blanket over himself. "It would be easier to die."

Shahid went and sat on the floor beside him.

"Who are you running from? I know there's someone. What were you doing in the Morlock?"

"What are you, a detective?"

"You wouldn't be here otherwise. You don't even like me. Is it that you miss Papa?"

"D'you?"

"Of course."

"Thought so," Chili said. "He did his best by us. Still, I'm pretty glad I haven't got him on my back right now."

"Why?"

"If he were alive, we'd be giving him heart attacks. Which of us, d'you think, would he be more horrified by?" Chili started to laugh. "I'd love to take a picture of you praying on your knees and send it to him in heaven. He'd probably say, what's my boy doing down there, looking for some money he's dropped?"

"Have you done something? Is it really terrible? Why won't you tell me?"

"That poor fucker, worked his arse off, and for what?"

"To live a decent life."

Chili gripped Shahid by the front of his pajamas and pulled him toward him. "And what is that? Do you know? Are you saying you do?"

"No! Let go of me!"

Chili seized his brother's arm with one hand, and wrenched it. "No one knows!" With the other hand he slapped him. Shahid felt one side of his face burn and turn red. He was trembling with anger. He pulled his fist back. Immediately Chili struck him again.

"Now shut it!"

"Fuck, fuck!"

Shahid threw himself on his bed. All this reminded him of his childhood. He wanted to say: wait till Papa finds out. But Papa would never find out and there was, now—he was convinced of it—no one watching over them.

Shahid attended two lectures and went to the library. He was an organized student and could remember reams of matter which he'd wipe from his mind after an exam. He had figured out what was required, and with discipline and concentration would get through the course without panicking or studying at night. He found it increasingly tedious, but that was because things had been a little strange lately.

Going out into the street he saw the sun had come out. Londoners loved a temperate day, and at any glimpse of brightness they removed their overcoats, went to Boots, and bought sunglasses. At lunchtime they walked through the parks, where the daffodils and crocuses were coming up early this year, and angled their faces hopefully at the sky. Or, as the winter chill was still cutting, they went in groups to pubs and stayed out until two-thirty, eating steak and kidney pudding and drinking lager.

In an Irish pub nearby, Shahid had a cheese sandwich, toasted, with thick brown bread, on which he lashed mustard, Branston Pickle, and tomato sauce. He didn't want to drink; he knew the pub would be full of office workers not students. He'd see none of the brothers.

He rewarded himself for his morning's effort by propping up a novel. He read holding a pencil and tried to see how the author achieved an effect, which he would trace and then transform with his own characters, in his reporter's notebook. Then he embarked on a story which he wanted to call "The Flesh, the Flesh."

This was tremendous, more than satisfying; his imagination stirred and took grip. Strong and motivated, he felt what he might do. What could be better? Then a secretary danced across the pub, after putting "Kiss" on the jukebox.

Earlier he had sat in Deedee's class. That morning she must have had a meeting—she attended many, for the college was going to be privatized—and was wearing a black suit with polished oxblood loafers, worn down on the inside. Something must have put her in a brisk, stern mood. She incinerated a student who hadn't heard of Freud. She marched about the classroom and removed her jacket, under which she wore a red silk T-shirt. Occasionally she sat on the desk, swinging her legs as if kicking the students, while pressing her skirt down between her thighs. She did this, Shahid imagined, lingeringly. But then she did believe education should be exhilarating. At the end she thanked the students; by the time Shahid had gathered his things she had got out of the room.

"Deedee," he called after her. "Wait a minute."

On the narrow stairs, she was fenced in by the Three Degrees Zero, an Afro-Caribbean woman, an Indian, and an Irish girl with pink hair. Deedee had a handful of such groupies, who would swoon if Deedee unexpectedly turned a corner. But these three were her most devoted, dressing as she did and studying her as if she were Madonna.

Shahid pursued the groupies hurrying behind her and was about to push past them when Deedee stopped to talk to Tariq, one of the brothers. Knowing it wasn't sensible to be seen with her, Shahid circled the building a couple of times. When he returned, the groupies had been left standing outside the staff room. He waited half a hour but it was no use. He went to the pub.

Now he went home to see if she'd call.

He realized, walking upstairs, he'd forgotten about Chili. That morning when Shahid left for college, Chili had got up from the floor and collapsed into the bed without opening his eyes. But now he was gone, the cup of coffee Shahid had made him stood untouched by the bed.

Shahid was working on Riaz's manuscript when Hat knocked on the door, came in, and said, "We're needed up the East End." Shahid returned to his desk and carried on typing. Hat stood behind him settling his hands on his shoulders. "The family are moving out their flat and into the new place. The man's still in hospital. They need help getting their stuff out."

"Keep your eyes right off what I'm doing."

Hat automatically stepped back. "Don't you wanna come?"

"It's not my turn. I've gotta do this typing job for Riaz."

"Leave it for now."

"I'm just following orders."

Hat sighed. "Riaz want to see you. Something else has happened over there."

"What is it?"

"Chad keeping it under his hat."

"As usual."

"Oh, come on, Shahid, boy. I know Chad can get strange and all. But don't you fancy some bindi?"

On the way they stopped off at Hat's family restaurant.

Hat sat Shahid down and fetched him food and some of his father's spiced apple chutney. Then, picking from a bowl of radishes, Hat leaned over the table. "Try this chana, yaar." Hat even dug his fork into the chickpeas and held it to Shahid's mouth. "What's the problem, Shahid, boy? A few of us notice you get moody. Someone said you hiding somethin'."

"Do you think that, Hat?"

"I can't say I ever seen you do some bad actions."

"But someone did?"

"There's some deep emotion bothering you. Has something gone wrong? You still don't believe?"

Shahid said nothing. He liked Hat; he didn't want to get into a discussion with him that might turn into an argument. So although Hat looked at him soulfully, as if to say, "There's someone here to listen, if you feel like it," and Shahid was grateful, he merely said, "Don't worry about me, Hat, I'm just thinking 'bout some personal stuff."

"Don't forget I'm your friend," said Hat.

As they struggled to heave beds, wardrobe, fridge, television, and kids' toys down to the van, Shahid passed Chad on the stairs and heard him say, "Good, eh, what the Iranians saying?"

"The fatwah business?"

"Yeah."

Shahid said, "Someone mentioned it at college this morning. But I couldn't take it in. Surely they're not serious?"

Chad said, "That book been around too long without action. He insulted us all—the prophet, the prophet's wives, his whole family. It's sacrilege and blasphemy. Punishment is death. That man going down the chute."

"Are you sure that's necessary?"

"It written."

Shahid had liked *Midnight's Children*; he admired its author. He didn't see why Chad was so worked up.

He said, "If he's insulted us, can't we just forget about it? If some fool calls you a bastard in the pub, it's best to not think about it, you know. You shouldn't let these things get you down."

Chad looked at him suspiciously. "What are you talking about?"

"What?"

"What exactly are you saying?"

"Just what I said."

Chad shook his head disbelievingly.

It soon became clear how far things had already moved on. As they passed back and forth with the family's belongings, Shahid discussed it with Tahira, Sadiq, Tariq. The feeling was unanimous. Riaz had informed Chad they were rejoicing in the Ayatollah's action, and Chad had passed this on to the group.

Chad and Shahid stood in the empty flat.

"That's not all. There's been a further confirmation against him." Chad gave Shahid a severe look. "No one can doubt it now."

Shahid guessed that this was what Hat had been referring to earlier. "What confirmation?"

"I'm not telling you now—there's too much to do," Chad said, relishing the secrecy. By now the rest of the group, who had finished this leg of the move, had gathered around him.

"Oh, what is it?" Tahira said.

Chad was enjoying the moment but couldn't say more; yet he needed to give them something.

"All I can say, just to guide your curiosity, is that we have been given a miraculous sign."

Tahira clapped her hands. "A sign. We are so lucky! What sort?"

"An arrow."

"An arrow?" Shahid said.

"Yeah, it's an arrow pointing straight at the author."

"What type of arrow?" asked Hat.

"How many bloody type of arrows are there?" Chad said. "You idiot." He was about to abuse Hat but restrained himself when Tahira gave him a warning smile. "I'll just say this. It's an arrow in the form of a fruit."

They considered this.

"Must be a banana," Hat said.

"No, it's not a banana. I'll clip you upside your head!"

They shut up the van, drove it a couple of miles away and, supervised by the relieved woman, unpacked everything in a near-identical flat in a Bengali area. Then, when they were tired, Chad made them climb back in the empty van. Instead of taking them home he took them toward the north London suburbs.

After sitting in nervy silence for a few miles, Chad said, "This is fully confidential but I think I can let slip now that the arrow is an eggplant."

"What?"

"Just listen."

"What's an eggplant?" said Hat. "How can you plant an egg?"

"Farhat—zip up your mouth," said Tahira.

"How can an eggplant be an arrow?" Shahid said.

"You a bunch of fools!" Chad cried, lifting his hands from the wheel and banging his ears. As the car crossed the center of the road they yelled for him to glance, occasionally, through the front window. "Listen, then! Don't problem up a brother!"

He told them that a devout local couple had cut open an aubergine and discovered that God had inscribed holy words into the mossy flesh. Moulana Darapuria had given his confirmation that the aubergine was a holy symbol.

"And we're exhibiting it," Chad said.

"Where?"

Chad pointed ahead. "I'm at liberty to tell you that we are now approaching the site of the aubergine exhibition."

Chad said a squad of brothers, in collaboration with the enthusiastic locals who were already installed, had been volunteered by Riaz to watch the door of the house, ensuring the crowds were orderly and that the press didn't turn hot lights on God's rapidly withering message. As with the flat they'd guarded, there would be a shift system.

Shahid saw Riaz waiting for them with some of the other college brothers and sisters who lived in the area. Chad's group filed into the small suburban house. In the front room Shahid squinted into the mulch of the aubergine. Hat, Tariq, and Tahira stood beside him.

"I can just make it out," Tahira said. "God has granted me the sight."

"Can you see it, Hat?" Shahid asked.

Hat appeared to be nodding.

Shahid slipped outside to get some air, and settled down on a wall opposite. He decided not to go back in but to return to his room. He was heading for the bus stop when he bumped into Riaz, who was whirling anxiously, his eyelids pink with strain. He seemed relieved to see Shahid.

Shahid realized how rare it was to see Riaz alone; even as he worked at his desk someone was with him.

"Assalam alaikum," he said.

"Salam, brother."

In silence they watched the crowd. Shahid thought of what he wanted to say now he had the opportunity.

The excited but patient people were waiting four deep along the fences of several adjoining identical houses. It wasn't warm and most had wrapped up. They could have been queuing for an Indian movie, except that there wouldn't have been so many aged people who looked as if they would only go out to visit relatives, attend a funeral, or witness a miracle. They were in holiday mood, too, promenading, yelling hellos, gossiping.

An old man in the queue whom Shahid recognized from Riaz's surgery came over to them and complained that the local rich— restaurant proprietors, importers, the owners of sports shops and lucrative electrical stores—had their chauffeurs drop them outside the House of the Miracle. Or they double-parked, strolled over, and jumped the queue.

"Look, look," he said.

A couple were doing as he'd described. The chubby man wore a white viscose shirt and tight black toreador trousers. He had mirrored glasses, a gold chain around his neck, a gold earring and a thick gold bracelet. A bunch of keys swung from his crocodile-skin belt. His hair, piled in a dense mass on top of his head, was a hennaed, brickish color, looking as if a golden loaf had been placed on his skull like a crown of bread crumbs. The light-skinned woman accompanying her darker husband wore a tight pink T-shirt, white Levi's, and white high heels. She wore no jewelry; she couldn't compete with her husband.

Shahid said he and the others would do what they could to prevent such behavior.

Then he asked Riaz suddenly, "Would you kill a man for writing a book?"

Riaz had little physical presence. Shahid imagined him in a corner of the school playground, his hands across his face, shying from the bully blows.

"Stone dead. That is the least I would do to him. Are you suggesting this is something wrong?"

"It makes me feel a little sick."

"Why is that?"

"It's such a violent thing."

"Sometimes there is violence, yes, when evil has been done."

"But aren't we loving people, brother?"

Riaz put his hand on Shahid's back; they walked away from the house.

"Are you an anarchist?"

Shahid hesitated. "I don't think so."

"So, then? There must be order in society for the elements to cohere. We all of us are angry."

"I know, but—"

"Are you not with your people? Look at them, they are from villages, half-literate, and not wanted here. All day they suffer poverty and abuse. Don't we, in this land of so-called free expression, have to give them a voice? Aren't we the fortunate ones, after all?"

"Fortunate, brother?"

"We are educated, a little. We are not slaves day and night in some shop or factory. But that means we have other duties, doesn't it? We cannot just forsake our people and live for ourselves."

"No."

"If we did, wouldn't that mean we had totally absorbed the Western morals, which are totally individualistic?"

Riaz paused to greet someone.

Shahid noticed that in the adjoining garden an elderly white man and his wife had set up a trestle table from which they were selling fruit juice and sandwiches, passing the food and drink over the fence and tossing the money into a tin box. They'd hand-painted a sign with the word "hallal" on it, which they suspected guaranteed some kind of immunity.

Shahid watched the man he had wanted as his friend and who, like him but with less reason, seemed strangely out of place here. Riaz loved "his people," but, unless offering assistance, he appeared uncomfortable with them. Riaz had little: no wife or children, career, hobby, house, or possessions. The meaning of his life was his creed and the idea that he knew the truth about how people should live. It was this single-mindedness that made him powerful and, to Shahid now, rather pitiful.

Riaz rejoined him and, with the naïve enthusiasm he adopted when speaking about this subject, said, "Tell me, how is the typing coming?"

"I've been wanting to tell you, brother—"

"Yes?"

"That there are a few things in it I've corrected."

"Excellent." He clapped his hands. "Are you having to translate my work into English?"

"No. It's more like—"

"Smoothing out?"

"Yes."

"Good. Chad has informed me that you bang away into your computer night after night."

"It's true."

"I am obsessed like that when I begin to compose." Riaz thought for a moment, before saying, "Tell me, in your own work, what exactly do you write on?"

"On life, I suppose."

"In general or from which standpoint?"

"There is," said Shahid firmly, "no standpoint."

"No standpoint? I always have a standpoint. If only I had more hours to write. How do you make time?"

"Surely, brother, you have the discipline?"

Riaz grimaced. "So many people need me. I have one hundred answered letters in my room. One's own needs seem unimportant. Chad says you have had some work published."

"A story. In a magazine. It was written a while ago."

"But I am impressed."

"Thank you."

"What was it called?"

"What? Oh . . . it doesn't matter. But the thing I'm working on at the moment is called 'The Prayer-mat.' "

"Will it be published?"

"Maybe."

"I am interested, because I would have thought that outsiders like us would have had trouble gaining acceptance. The whites are very insular, surely they won't admit people like us into their world?"

"Oh no, there's nothing more fashionable than outsiders."

Riaz seemed puzzled. "Why is that?"

Shahid shrugged. "Novelty. Even someone like you, brother, could have a wide appeal if the media knew of you. Think how many people you could address."

"The media, yes. That is the right direction for us to go in. We must utilize all channels for the message of devotion. I hope you will soon be submitting an article on this matter of blasphemy to the national newspapers. Have you so far considered this?"

"No . . . I haven't."

"But isn't that the work you should be doing for your people? Remember, the masses are simpler and wiser than us. There's much to learn from them. Do you think someone should abandon the others to whom he belongs?"

"This matter of belonging, brother. I wish I understood it. Do you, for instance, like living in England?"

Riaz blinked and looked around; it was as if he'd never considered the question before.

"This will never be my home," he said. "I will never entirely understand it. And you?"

"It suits me. There's nowhere else I will feel more comfortable."

"We were very concerned about you. I hope brother Chad, who I have put in charge of your welfare, has been helping you."

"Chad? Oh yes."

"And are you happy now?"

"Happy? Riaz, there are so many questions I have."

"Dismiss them!" Riaz said with the energetic confidence that had made Shahid admire him.

"But, Riaz—"

"Just believe in the truth! These intellectuals tie themselves up in knots. Look at Dr. Brownlow. Who would want to be such a clever, tormented fool? In the end there is the leap of faith and trust in God. But there is something in what you say, too."

Shahid looked keenly at Riaz. "There is?"

"You know how some people love to say we are undemocratic. Why shouldn't we fully discuss this entire thing?"

Shahid said, "Surely we should talk it over without prejudice."

"Why not? Will you speak to the interested brothers and sisters about a time and place?" Shahid nodded. "We must do it soon. Why not tomorrow morning? And please, will you write a draft of an article about Western arrogance with regard to our right not to be insulted?"

"After the discussion," Shahid said.

"All right," said Riaz. "You have a very persuasive quality, I think."

"Thank you."

At that moment everyone turned.

A red Escort had screeched to a halt outside the holy house. For some reason, perhaps because the whole day had been so unlikely, Shahid thought the house or crowd was about to be attacked.

A boy in a black fishnet T-shirt and leather trousers sprang out of the car and glared at the crowd, daring it to challenge him. He opened the rear door and another boy, with pageboy platinum hair and a bandaged ear, tumbled out. The two of them stood to attention beside the car like children pretending to be tough, bickering the while.

Riaz gave a little satisfied nod. "But this could not be topped."

Shahid noticed Brownlow standing by the gate of the house, smiling at the car. With everyone else, he watched as a big man with a vivid smile slapped across his florid, polished face, who had appeared to be lying upside-down on the back seat of the car, hauled himself onto the pavement before the watching crowd. He said sharply to the boys, "Quieten down, kittens. This is a cultural celebration."

"God Almighty, it's the Rubber Messiah," guffawed a white on-looker.

"Hello there, people! Hello, all!"

The man waved at the crowd and didn't seem discouraged when no one, not even the children, waved back.

"He's not Muslim, is he?" said the onlooker's companion.

"Not yet."

"What's he doing, then?"

The onlooker shrugged. "Interferin'."

The Rubber Messiah appeared to tiptoe toward the house, for, relative to the rest of him, his feet were tiny. And with his elbows protruding like a pair of rails beside him, his hands floating freely at the end of them, he seemed to stroke people as he passed. He wore the correct clothes—a shirt, waistcoat, suit, and tie—but none of the items fitted, some being too tight and others too bil-lowy; the shirt, for instance, was both at the same time, in the wrong places, and the green tie appeared to be stiffly appended to the front of his shirt like a cucumber.

"George Rugman Rudder," Riaz told Shahid. He looked across at Brownlow, who winked. "The Labour leader of the entire elected council. Our friend Dr. Brownlow knows all those local politician types. He's succeeded brilliantly on our behalf."

A photographer had begun to take pictures. Riaz, Brownlow, and Rugman Rudder shook hands for the lens. Then Brownlow stood aside and allowed Riaz and Rudder to be photographed to-gether. Meanwhile a journalist scribbled.

"Thank you for coming, Mr. Rudder," Riaz said to him. "We knew you would pay your respects."

"Naturally, naturally. What a marvelous crowd, worshipping the fruit of the earth! What a popular aubergine, top of the vegetable table! What a sound method of communication the miracle is! Thank God a Tory borough wasn't chosen!"

Brownlow looked a little dismayed, but Riaz said, "Mr. Rudder, many thanks again for confronting on our behalf all police and traffic problems. And for letting us use a private house in this public way. We understand how illegal it normally is. Our whole community, so often put down, is eternally grateful. You are a true friend of Asia."

"He is our friend!" Chad shouted, bouncing on his toes.

"The friend of Asia!" echoed Hat.

"Asia's best friend!" Tahira trilled.

Riaz began to applaud; Chad and Hat clapped, and even Brownlow allowed his hands to meet in a kind of Hindu greeting. Others in the crowd began to show their appreciation. There was a chant of "Rudder, Rudder, Rudder—he's our brother!"

"Yes, and I will be rewarded, in heaven, no doubt," Rudder said, beaming at his scowling boys. He said more quietly to Brownlow and Riaz, "Naturally I have been generous enough to use my influence, as you surely appreciate, against very racialist opposition, to open a private house in this way." He lowered his voice further. "It is because our party supports ethnic minorities, you have my fullest assurance of that. The Seventh Day Adventists have expressed deep satisfaction, and, it is said, mention my ailments in their prayers. Rastafarians shake my hand as I walk my dog. This is widely appreciated all over east London. But you are also smart enough to know, Riaz—and you are a smarty—" for a moment it looked as if Rudder were about to tickle Riaz under the chin—"that it can't last forever."

"We are aware of that, Mr. Rudder," Brownlow said. "Which is why we have been thinking so much about the Town Hall."

"Yes, the Town Hall," Riaz said.

"Sorry?"

"For the preservation of the sacred miracle in public," Riaz went on.

"The Town Hall?" said Rudder, as if Riaz had suggested the aubergine be placed on his nose.

"There's no reason why not," Brownlow said confidently. "You have just affirmed your faith in different faiths."

"For which we thank you from our hearts," said Riaz.

"And thank you again," said Hat. "Friend of Asia!"

"Rudder brother!"

"Shh!" said Tahira.

The journalist's hand flew over the pages.

"Yes, yes, perhaps the Town Hall," said Rudder, rearranging something in his wide paunch. "There's plenty of room." He offered his mouth to one of the boys: "Most of it between the ears of the people who work there."

Riaz pressed on. "It will have to be the foyer."

"There it will be prominent," Brownlow said.

"Yes, it would be," Rudder said, pursing his lips. "In the foyer."

Riaz said, "Besides, there is already hanging there a picture of Nelson Mandela."

"And the African mask," added Chad.

"We will not be ghettoized," Riaz said.

"No, no. No ghettoization."

"That's going to be arranged, then." Riaz motioned to Chad and Hat. "It's all established."

"Great, great," said Chad.

"Go, go, go," Hat said. "A friend of Asia! A friend of Asia!"

Some of the others called out, "Friend of Asia!" and "Rudder Brother!"

The journalist was writing, the photographer was snapping.

"Let's shake hands on it," Brownlow said.

Rudder pushed his boys into the house ahead of him. "Nothing is settled. Now let me witness this wondrous example of God's signature. Come along, boys."

"Repulsive, reactionary fellow," Brownlow remarked when Rudder was out of earshot. "But bent over the barrel. Best place for him."

"Top marks," Riaz said.

"Full on!" said Chad.

"Yo!" went Hat.

Shahid followed Rudder into the house.

"This your first miracle, Georgie?" said one of the boys, as they went in.

"It is until the Labour Party gets reelected." In the hall he said in a stage whisper, "Of course, revelations are faith's aberration, an amusement at the most. Let's hope they curry this blue fruit. Brinjal, I believe it's called. I could murder an Indian, couldn't you, lads?"

That night it took Shahid hours to locate the group and inform them about Riaz's promised discussion. He was determined that everyone should be there. Some people, like Tariq, weren't at home, or they were eating with their family. One room, belonging to Sadiq's family, was covered with mattresses. Four or five children slept and played; their grandmother, who knew no English, sat cross-legged as if she were in her village; washing was strung across the room on lengths of string. Shahid had to sit with them for an hour, eating until he was stuffed, waiting for an opportunity to convey the message and escape. Or three or four of them were, he was told, upstairs at Hat's restaurant, playing video games; or, according to Hat's uncle, they'd just left Hat's for Riaz's place and would be, apparently, popping in to see Shahid on the way.

The other problem was getting people to commit to the meeting. It was only when Shahid took the initiative by saying that Riaz had issued instructions to miss college if need be that people promised to attend. The brothers and sisters couldn't see the point; they thought everyone had made up their minds.

At each place he visited, Shahid asked if he could use the phone. He wanted to ring Deedee; they could get together when he finished this errand. He dialed her number a couple of times but each time replaced the receiver before she answered. Deedee always liked to say, "And what have you been doing?" How could he say he'd been overseeing an aubergine?

So, he went back to his room, made himself sardines on toast, and continued typing Riaz's manuscript on to the disk, making adjustments here and there.

Then he lay in bed thinking about the next morning and what he might say—if he was able to speak.

C rammed in Riaz's room, they had to wait forty minutes for him. He was, Shahid had observed, late for most
things. He seemed to enjoy creating anticipation, and
then, when frustration had accumulated, making an entrance. It was odd, because Riaz was essentially unas-
suming and reticent. Perhaps he thought the others
required him to show more authority.

Apparently, today, Riaz was having a meeting with
Brownlow and Rudder. Fortunately, as they waited, Hat
turned up carrying a bag of his father's food, which he
distributed cheerfully. Three of the women were there,
including Tahira in a crisp, long white shirt, black
trousers, and gray-and-white checked scarf.

At last Chad hurried in, holding the door for Riaz,
who was wearing a new gray salwar. He stood there a
moment, put his briefcase down and sat on the floor
beside his desk.

"The progress, as you will want to know, with Coun-
cilman Mr. Rudder of Labour Party, is looking good,
looking good," Riaz told them immediately. "He understands the position and importance of the minority
in this country. He has stated to us personally that he
will put his big back right into our cause."

Hat slapped hands with Tariq. "Friend of Asia!"

"My sentiments, too. This sympathy for our people is as rare as an English virgin." Riaz giggled at the remark, which he made often. "But now there is this other filthy matter which we must quickly go through, as I am informed by Shahid here that you are all busy studying nonstop."

Laughter rippled through the room once again. Shahid realized that Riaz was looking at him, and waiting, as was everyone. This he hadn't expected.

Riaz said, "Kindly remind us of the topic, brother."

"Sorry?"

"Better remind yourself, too," Hat chuckled.

"You called us here," Tahira added. "And for what, please tell us, when the issue is so obvious?"

Shahid tried to speak carefully, as if translating from a foreign language, but still the words came in a rush and his own voice surprised him.

"The ... er ... book," he began.

Chad said, "That book."

"Right," Sadiq said.

"And storytelling. This is the issue! Why we need it. If we need it. What can be said. And—and what can't be. What mustn't be said. What is taboo and forbidden and why. What is censored. How censorship benefits us in exile here. How it might protect us, if it can do that. That—that kind of thing."

"All right," said Riaz. "This should keep us awake—for a short time."

He gave the group a sudden hard stare to abolish any frivolity he might have aroused. Having taken control, he began to talk in his preferred fashion, launching an idea onto the sea of upturned faces and letting it go where his wind blew it. Shahid was relieved; Riaz hadn't judged him, but—so far—used him only as an excuse.

"You see, all fiction is, by its very nature, a form of lying—a perversion of truth. Isn't the phrase 'telling stories' used when children tell lies? There are harmless, perverted tales, of course, which make us chuckle. They pass the time when we have nothing to do. But there are many fictions that expose a corrupt nature. These are created by authors, who cannot, we might say, hold their ink. These yarn-spinners have usually groveled for acceptance to the white élite so they can be considered 'great authors.' They like to pretend they are revealing the truth to the masses—these uncultured, half-illiterate fools. But they know nothing of the masses. The only poor people they meet are their servants. And so, really, they are appealing to what is filthy in us. It is easy to do. Dirt attracts us. Not Hat, of course."

Hat laughed nervously. People were already nodding in agreement.

"And as one would deprecate a disrespectful nature in another person, it is impossible to see how such a spectacle could be valued as literature. Does anyone want to comment?" Eyes swiveled toward Shahid. He pretended to be just another person sitting there, but was unable to avoid flushing self-consciously. "After all, for what higher purpose can such literature possibly exist?"

There was a silence. People sat with averted eyes; it wasn't that they were afraid to speak, they had nothing to say.

Shahid said, "Surely, to tell us about ourselves?"

"No!" Riaz shook his head. "But continue."

"Surely literature helps us reflect on our nature?" Shahid said.

"That is presumption and arrogance," Riaz said.

"Please," Shahid began. "Please—"

Sadiq decided to agree with Riaz: "Pure arrogance."

Shahid said to Riaz, "As a poet yourself—"

There was a knock on the door.

"Yes, I am a poet," Riaz said, paying no attention. "Thank you for reminding me. But I am telling you that it is not ourselves in general, not the people, but the mind of the author that we are being informed of. That is all. One man."

"A free imagination," Shahid said, "ranges over many natures. A free imagination, looking into itself, illuminates others."

"We are discussing here the free and unbridled imagination of men who live apart from the people," Riaz said. "And these corrupt, disrespectful natures, wallowing in their own juices, must be

caged as if they were dangerous carnivores. Do we want more wild
lions and rapists stalking our streets? After all," he went on, "if a
character comes into your house and spits out that your mother
and sister are whores, wouldn't you chuck him from your door and
do bad things to him? Very bad things?" There were many smiles.
"And isn't this what such books do?"

Shahid said, "They disturb us."

"Yes!"

"They make us think."

"What is there to think?"

"Sorry?"

"Must we prefer this indulgence to the profound and satisfying
comforts of religion? Surely, if we cannot take the beliefs of millions of people seriously, what then? We believe nothing! We are
animals living in a cesspool, not humans in a liberal society."

As usual Riaz pronounced the word "liberal" as if it were the
name of a murderer. He looked around the group.

The knock was repeated, only louder.

Chad fixed his eyes on Shahid, who opened his mouth and
shook his head, determined to say no more, afraid of what trouble
the discussion might lead him into.

Riaz said, "Even your great Tolstoy denounced art, didn't he?
You may like to think me a philistine, but somewhere I have the
book. Chad, will you look for it?" Chad nodded. "But see to the
door first."

"Must be for Shahid," Hat murmured.

Chad went out into the hall and closed the door.

Riaz said, "To me these truths about the importance of faith and
concern for others are deeper than the ravings of one individual
imagination."

"But the individual voice is important, too, isn't it?" Shahid persisted, aware that the fervent note in his voice was separating him
from his companions.

"Up to a point. And then no further. Is there one society in
which any individual can be allocated unlimited freedom? Anyhow, we must now move forward. People are getting restless. We

have to discuss what action we will be taking against this book."

"What sort of action?" Shahid asked.

"I said that that is what we will see."

Tahira, who was sitting beside Shahid, said in his ear, "You seem to have a problem. Please tell me if it is pure confusion, or something else."

"Both, I think."

The room was quiet but outside Chad's voice clashed with that of a woman.

Riaz said, "Are there any further questions?"

"Yes," said Tahira. "What are we going to do?"

The door was pushed open. Zulma stood there in canary Chanel and a black wrap. Chad was behind her, palms outstretched in frustration. Zulma took three firm but still languorous strides into the center of the room. People shifted urgently to avoid having their hands impaled by her heels.

A battle ensued between her scent and the odor of the room.

Zulma searched the faces with a mixture of politeness and irony until she located the purpose of her visit crouching in the corner with his hand over his face.

"Come." Was she intending to yank him out by his ear? "Attend, darling."

He got up onto his heels.

"At this moment?"

"Of course!"

"Zulma, this is a meeting."

"For what? Who is in charge here?" Her eyes settled on Riaz. "Professor, a crucial family matter is at stake!"

Riaz gave an impassive wave; he wouldn't waste words on someone like her, but Chad sniggered as Shahid got to his feet. Zulma ushered Shahid out of the room, throwing Chad a savage glance as she went.

He ran down the stairs behind her, unexpectedly gladdened by the sudden freedom.

"What are you doing in there, having a political meeting?"

"About the fatwah, as it happens."

"Oh, God. And these are all students?"

"Yes, Zulma."

"And they're going to demonstrate in his favor?"

"No. Not in his favor, I don't think."

"But you said they're students."

"So? Of course they're bloody students, Zulma. What d'you think they are, captains of industry?"

"Oh, Lord, you're attending the swearing classes, then?" She gave him a inquisitive look. "I've never seen you in such a froth. You used to be so shy about everything, making silly jokes and all, hardly able to open your rude mouth. You had a funny twitch, too. That cleared up?"

The car was half on the pavement. Zulma practically pushed him into the seat to stop him running off. She closed her thighs, tugged up her skirt to free her legs, and, flinging a hand out of the window, they veered out into the traffic.

"Is that what college students are like these days?"

"Some of them."

"Students are supposed to have bloody brains, aren't they?"

"What are you talking about, Zulma?"

"Don't raise your voice at me!" Her gold jewelry jangled. "I'm explaining that religion is for the benefit of the masses, not for the brainbox types. The peasants and all—they need superstition, otherwise they would be living like animals. You don't understand it, being in a civilized country, but those simpletons require strict rules for living, otherwise they would still think the earth sits on three fishes." She punched the steering wheel. He noticed the diamond wedding ring that Chili had bought her. "But these mind-wallahs must know it's a lot of balls."

"Zulma, they believe in it."

"And kill him and all?"

"Yes," he said despondently.

"These madmen are becoming far too mad. It makes the derangement seem general. Practically the whole world is ringing me about this hullabaloo, as if I wrote the novel personally. Darling, things are getting so extreme I may have to read it."

Zulma bought magazines like *Elle, Hello!, Harpers,* and *Queen,* preferring instructive literature on shiny paper, with photographs, to the merely imaginative on matt.

She said, "As if my head weren't burning up in flames with the problems your entire family has given me, thank you very much."

Zulma's family apartment was behind Lowndes Square, in a grand old block. "But why are you in with these people?" She looked at him with concern as they got out of the car. "Oh, Shahid, it's not true you've fallen into a religious framework?"

"Please, Zulma, leave me alone for a few minutes. I need to think."

"You will certainly be needing to cogitate, it is true, after this conversation, so I would wait until later."

The uniformed doorman who had been polishing the door put away his rag, placed his cap on his head, and dragged back the iron lift gate. As they slid upward in the narrow latticework box, like an inverted coffin, she lowered her voice to whisper, "You don't go for prayers, do you?"

"What d'you mean?"

"Tell me the truth now or I'll slap your face."

"You can't do that kind of thing to me, Zulma."

"No, I s'pose not, but I'm in the mood for some slapping."

He was curious to see whether she would carry out her threat.

"I have been to the mosque," he said. "I'm not ashamed. Should I be?"

She pretended her legs were giving way. "But you had a decent upbringing!"

He followed her out of the lift and wondered, as they padded down the hushed, curved hallway, if this was where she'd strike him.

"I can't tell you the problems Benazir has had with these cunning fools. She's such a dear girl, too, and endured so much."

"Whatever I might do, Zulma, at least I'm not like your husband."

She laughed, though her hearty ebullience was absorbed immediately into the walls of the silent, formal building.

"My husband. Next time I'm going to be demanding an

arranged marriage. Not a bad idea, eh? These free marriages, what are they but bad manners in the day and bad smells at night? They've gone too far!"

Shahid didn't feel like talking to Zulma about this, or anything else for that matter. He recalled that Deedee had told him, don't do anything you don't want to do—not ever. If you feel like walking away from someone, crossing the street, and fleeing, just do it—now.

Zulma's cavernous flat resembled a hotel suite. There were few personal adornments: a Persian rug had been laid over the ivory nap; a bucket full of lilies sat on the floor; there were onyx lamps and a marble table; three exotic pieces in the room had been lifted from Pakistan's unprotected monuments. Seeing her mistress, his niece's ayah collected some toys and took them out of the room.

Shahid played with little Safire, who had Chili's coffee-dark eyes. Shahid always liked to be carrying sweets in various pockets so she would climb over him, searching. But today he had none and she foraged for nothing. While they played, Shahid heard Zulma talking in the kitchen to a man with an upper-class accent.

"Safire, who's that?" Shahid whispered. She said it was Charles. Catching a glimpse of him, Shahid saw Charles was pudgy, in an expensive suit. He asked, "Does he smell of over-boiled Brussels sprouts?"

Safire was giggling when Zulma emerged with a glass and bottle of wine.

"You know I wouldn't normally be knocking it back before lunch. But seeing those fanatic types always makes me crave a cool glass of Sauternes. Maybe your papa's influence." She poured, and lifted her glass. "Well, chin-chin," she said, using the vernacular still current in Karachi.

Shahid got up and made for the door. "Heroin is illegal in Britain. Why don't we have some of that as well?"

"Oh, Shahid, we're not always the best of friends, but it makes me feel rotten to know you're running in that direction."

"Zulma, listen to me, I—"

"Sit down and shut up! Let me inform you what happened to me at a party in Karachi recently. I was saying to some empty-head who's been a close friend for years, 'That inane God stuff jolly well irritates me when we don't even have housing, hospitals, and education.' Guess what?"

"I can't guess."

"Can you believe it, Mr. Sulky Face, the bitch woman slapped my face—tuck!" She clapped her hands. "And threw me out of her house. My insides turned to ice. They will slaughter us soon, for thinking. Have you stopped thinking, Shahid?"

"Nope."

"Are you sure of that?" Zulma sipped her wine and put the glass down. "Safire, go to Charles for a minute. Good girl." To Shahid she said, "He's a decent chap, Charles Jump. Like most of them, he's not very bright, of course, and odd toward women. But he's a Lord. Or is he a Count? Count, I said, with an 'o.' He's got a stately home in Wiltshire. The buses stop outside and the tourists look in when one's having breakfast." She leaned toward Shahid and slapped her knee. "I've brought you here to help me. Tell me honestly—do you know where Chili is?" He shook his head. "Cross your heart and hope to die?"

"Yes."

"Well. He has gone AWOL, then. I don't care a damn, darling. Who wants to see that loafer again? We are going to be divorced. That's between him and me. He's a son of a— More badly, he is raining shame on your respected family and the reputation your papa created. You know how people chatter in Karachi."

"It's all those lazy bums have to do there—when they're not thinking of how to exploit their workers and run their money out of the country."

"Thank you for that thought. But don't you understand that Bibi can't run the business alone? How can you expect that from an old woman?"

"No. I know that."

"This is what you must do. Go back home and dedicate yourself to helping her and the travel business. If that scatter-head has gone crazy, then you become in charge of the family." She laughed at the idea. "From now you head the business your father and mother created, if you want it to survive. Who else is there, after all, but you?"

It hadn't occurred to Shahid that this would come up. He didn't know what to say. The freedom he had come to London for was being snatched from him. He was being dragged back into an earlier self and life, one he had gratefully sloughed off.

"Yes," she said, "you'd better take it in."

What would happen to him and Deedee if he became the manager of a travel agency in Kent? How often would they meet? More darkly, what would she think of him? What would he think of himself?

He said feebly, "But I have to finish my course."

Safire was playing with her dolls across the room. Charles Jump settled on the arm of the sofa beside Zulma, regarding Shahid with a mixture of commiseration and disapproval.

Zulma said, "Don't forget who is paying for these studies. Your mother and family. I'm reminding you that you have other responsibilities now."

"Oh, Lord, what serious responsibilities," Jump put in.

Shahid refused to acknowledge him. "Papa wanted me to be educated. Fools irritated him. He liked people with vigor, conviction, and intelligence."

Zulma said, "Why, then, are you spending all your time with those religious fools?"

"We have been making inquiries," Jump said.

"You have?"

Jump continued: "Isn't it a fact that you have joined the militant Muhammadans?" Shahid glanced at Zulma, who grimaced. "Because I'm telling you, we know they are entering France through Marseilles and Italy through the south. Soon they will be seeping through the weakened Communist regions, into the heart of civilized Europe, often posing as jewelry salesmen while accusing us of prejudice and bigotry."

"Pardon?" Shahid said.

"You can't walk ten steps without coming across a mosque. That is where the disorder is fomented."

"What disorder?"

"Don't be jejune."

"What?"

"You will slit the throats of us infidels as we sleep. Or convert us. Soon books and . . . and . . . bacon will be banned. Isn't that what you people want?"

Zulma raised her penciled eyebrows at Shahid. "If only it were so exciting."

"Surely this invasion of terrorists must be eradicated from society like a disease?" Jump lost confidence for a moment. "The other day in San Lorenzo you were saying that is the only way, weren't you, Zulma?"

Shahid appealed to Zulma. "Did you bring me here to listen to this pompous crap?"

"All right, all right." She hushed both of them. "Shahid, let's get back to the subject. Unless your brother returns to his senses, I'm afraid you're going to have to take charge. You can't both forsake the business your family has spent years building up. Surely that is clear to you?"

"But what about you? You made sure you understood the business."

She snorted. "It is not difficult to run, either. But I am going to think of myself for the first time. I will go away to Karachi. Naturally I am taking my Safire with me."

Shahid loved Safire; the thought of not seeing her for a long time upset him. It would upset Chili more.

She said, "When you see Chili, you should be kind enough to inform him that he is breaking your mother and that his place will be taken by you. You must know that she is in agony."

"Agony," Jump said.

"Go and make a phone call," Zulma said to him.

"Yes, my dear. Whom to?"

"Your accountant."

Jump went away.

"See how Jump jumps." She giggled.

Shahid got up. "What rubbish have you been telling him?"

"Don't be angry."

"Christ, Zulma!"

"Shahid, how am I responsible for what people believe? They see us on television behaving like fools and they think we're deranged. On the other hand, our people come here to this country and they get the Western habit. They forget they have families. And these families bust up. We become like everyone else then."

"I have to go."

"Where?"

"Thanks for being straight with me."

He walked to the door and opened it. It was easy.

She called, "Come here. We have some other things to sort out."

"And so have I, Zulma."

"Like what?"

"My life."

"Shahid, you can't just run out like this!"

He slammed the door as hard as he could.

F irst he needed to escape Zulma's part of town, with its embassies, hair salons, couturiers, and sleek traffic, where, off the main streets, he almost expected to see horses and carriages, men in top hats and women in hooped skirts. What was the hush?

He was becoming fond of the seedy variety of his manor, with its maniacs and miseries, where everyone wore bad shoes. *His manor*—that's how he thought of it now. In London, if you found the right place, you could consider yourself a citizen the moment you went to the same local shop twice.

He had to have money. Luckily he was carrying his cash-card, and he pulled out as much as he could from a bank machine. He walked quickly past the gloomy Knightsbridge Barracks and along the edge of the park. He was outside the Albert Hall when he jumped on a bus. He had to change twice to get back.

In the Morlock it was early. The only music was on the jukebox. The barman had a cut lip and a patch over one eye. As Shahid strode in the was passing a joint across the bar to the proprietor, a ruined woman in her late thirties who had, lined up in front of her, three vod-kas and orange. The barman recognized Shahid and even nodded, which gratified Shahid. He had become a regular. As usual, the kids stood around the bar.

"Half a lager."

Everyone looked up at him briefly, more alarmed by his energy than by anything else, and then continued whispering.

The barman shook his head. "No beer till tomorrow."

Shahid had never been in a pub without beer before. "Half a lager, then."

"Don't take the piss. Shorts only, unless you bring in your own beer from the pub over the road."

"Right. A Jack Daniel's."

Shahid sat down on a broken seat and watched the kids move back and forth between bar and toilet.

He didn't know what to do. He couldn't go home in case Riaz or one of the others required him; and he was too desperate to see Deedee. She wouldn't like him in this state; she was already angry with him. By now her patience would have run out.

When he fetched another drink one of the kids at the bar held up an unopened pack of cosmetics. "Want any anti-wrinkle cream for the old lady?"

"She could do with it," he said. "Where d'you lift it?"

"Boots."

"I've got to find fucking Strapper."

The kid shrugged. "The Strap might look in tomorrow lunch time. Or he might privilege us tonight. He's a cunnin' one."

"Is it worth waiting?"

"Ain't it always worth waiting for the Strap?"

Shahid sat down again and after an hour or so someone passed him a spliff. A lunatic tried to kiss him, thinking he was his wife, and Shahid had to be rescued by the barman, who was keen to practice his kick-boxing.

He lost track of the time. It was several hours later that his prize was helped through the door and propped up against the bar.

Strapper's jaw was shaking and his head was nodding. He was only able to ask why everything was "fuckin' disintegrating."

"Because it is disintegrating," one of his mates said.

"Oh yeah," Strapper said. "I forgot."

Shahid fetched him some beer from a pub across the road. When he returned Strapper was lying across some seats. Shahid bent over him like a doctor making an essential inquiry of a sick patient, and tried to make him hear, hoping a space would open in his rush. When the chaos did eventually clear for a few seconds, Shahid explained himself.

Strapper said, "Yeah, well, there's a lot of cunts looking for your bro's bollocks. And with good reason, man."

"Please, Strapper, you said the whites are selfish. I need your help. I thought you loved the Asian people."

"Not when they get too fucking Westernized. You all wanna be just like us now. It's the wrong turnin'."

"I'll buy some stuff off you—later. I've got money."

Strapper's eyes almost opened. "What was that?"

"I need to see if we can find him."

"Who?"

"Chili. I've got money."

"Where?"

Shahid showed it to him.

"Fuck, someone in your family's got real money."

Shahid helped Strapper onto his feet and they set off walking. Strapper, appearing to have recovered, swaggered along as new, almost, gobbing and cursing.

"In here."

They were a few streets away. Strapper swerved off toward the Fallen Angel, with Shahid sticking close behind him. Outside, Strapper held out his hand. "Gimme some money."

"What?"

"Gimme, man, gimme. Don't you want a good result tonight?"

After this transaction Shahid expected, somewhat optimistically, to see his brother at the bar of the Fallen Angel. Instead, Strapper followed a dealer into the toilet. Then he had a drink with the guy, making Shahid sit across the pub from them, before the landlord recognized Strapper and they were hustled out, with many threats made and almost a punch thrown.

With Strapper gaining buoyancy, for some reason, pub by pub, they were soon on their way. They legged it through poxy council estates and badly lit alleys, scrambled across gardens and down beside the tube line, where only suicides and graffiti merchants dared. Minutes later they even took the public highway, where they halted at a chemist's. Here Shahid was instructed to buy a bottle of cough medicine: Strapper quaffed it in one, wiped his mouth on his sleeve, and flung the bottle into a hedge.

As they progressed along the margin of the pavement in a part of "ancient Londinium"—as Strapper called it—that Shahid didn't recognize, he noticed that people regarded him differently. Women clutched their bags and zipped them. Younger kids stood aside. Others nodded their respect like soldiers at a senior officer. With certain people, across the street or through an open window or a pub door, Strapper would exchange an obscure semaphore, which started, via the eyebrows, with an inquiry, and was followed by an earnest look which featured the mouth, finally being topped by a question asked by hand. In reply the look would be inquisitive and then either affirmative or negative, confirmed either by a smile and good-bye wave from Strapper or by a finger message and another wave, which indicated, "See you later with the stuff."

Something must have made Strapper talkative. As they proceeded he gave a guided tour of his life and work in drugs, beginning with the dazzling Es he'd had recently and what color they were, whether they were burgers or caps, and how they were made, imported, and marketed, though he couldn't be too explicit about it, for security reasons. He expounded on the quality of the rush obtained from taking two, four, or six at once—Strapper had done ten (he was proud that, despite his efforts, he hadn't been able to overwhelm his constitution)—and the advantages to health of staggering or even limiting intake, and the effect when mixed with alcohol or grass or hash or coke, or various combinations of all, at different times in the trip; on evil and "snide" Es and how abominable they could be, especially if you overheated while dancing—people had combusted, he'd seen it with his own eyes in Liverpool, ravers reduced to slime, and others, "weekenders" usually, who'd overdone it and choked on their own vomit like in *Spinal Tap*.

The raves he'd been to in warehouses and fields last year, the "summer of love"—this was how he'd seen Britain, walking, hitching, sleeping rough, living with the travelers, staying in a tepee. The adventures involved in scrambling over the fence and crawling into a space containing three thousand virtually naked, high people, dancing as one without violence, the new acid dream, not over, not yet. The soulfulness and generosity of people he'd met on that scene who, mocked and outlawed by the straight world, would welcome him into their homes on this very day if he turned up, no questions asked, sharing whatever they had, for they understood one another, as if they'd been in combat together; it had been collective love and spiritual oneness. Adventures in several rehabilitation centers around the city and how many times he'd fled or been kicked out for drug-taking or fucking other inmates in the basement.

And an account of how, on Friday nights, the occupants of the Morlock liked to bundle into minicabs and shoot out to the country, where they'd find a secluded spot with a view, build a bonfire, and sit out until morning, tripping, talking, dancing around the fire.

"Next time," he said, "you should come with us."

"Can I?"

"You're welcome, man."

Drugs, the intensity and intimacy they created, were Strapper's element and area of expertise. As he talked up his adventures as a desperado, giving the impression he keenly scanned the hours of his carefree life for a moment of nefarious opportunity which he would seize and exploit, Shahid wanted Strapper's life of no responsibilities, no tomorrows, taking pleasure and money as they came and went, moving on. But all the while, despite a quantity of inward innocence, Strapper gave off such an unmistakable atmosphere of wrongdoing, deceit, and criminality that Shahid expected them to be seized by the police at every step, just for strolling insolently. At the very least it would have been impossible to get served in any restaurant. Clearly, if you were Strapper, there were many places you couldn't go. Tonight, though, Shahid could be like Strapper and bear it. But Strapper would have to be Strapper for always, probably, and when they stopped once more, this time in an Asian corner shop where Strapper stuffed his pockets with sweets, crisps, chocolate, and where under the neon Shahid could see Strapper's face once more, he knew he didn't want to be him.

London mingled with itself ceaselessly. Around him, Strapper saw lads his age in Armani, Boss, Woodhouse; he glanced into the road and saw broad BMWs, gold-colored Mercs, and turquoise turbo-charged Saab convertibles. He saw five-floor shuttered houses owned by men in their thirties, with nannies, cleaners, builders. None of it would be his—ever. It just wouldn't be. It didn't make sense.

Chili had promised Strapper a way up, telling him he knew big dealers, importers, money people. Cynical Strapper, who half-proudly lived this life, yet knew others saw it as worthless and sensed he had no future but disaster, fell for it. Chili must have really wound him up, injecting him with that misleading substance, hope, which, unlike the other drugs he took, had failed to wear off.

"When I first met Chili-Willy he took me to all kinds of hip apartments in his cool car, full of birds, impressing me up," Strapper told Shahid. "He was throwing money around. Said he'd taken a shine to me. I wanted to do a bit of big dealing, and the dude said I could help him out because I knew how the street worked."

"What did he want to do?"

"Kept saying England was too small for him—too small for his head, more like. Couldn't wait to get out to America. The bastard said we could make money and do a runner together."

"But where is he tonight?" Shahid was losing his temper. "Is it far?"

"I dunno. I've gone and talked myself out of seeing the fucker!"

Shahid took hold of Strapper's jacket and pulled him. "No! If we don't find him soon tonight I'm going to do you!"

To Shahid's surprise Strapper looked scared. Perhaps he thought the whole family was violent.

"All right, all right. But what if we don't reach him before the others do? Then they'll be waiting for us."

Shahid said, "What are you talking about? Who?"

"You don't know nothing, do you?" They walked some more. "In here, Paki boy."

Through a door and into a garden full of rusting car parts and old fridges; they climbed into the back of a semi-derelict house with bricked-up windows, where, inside, the doors had been replaced with dark curtains.

Strapper called, "Chili!"

They listened.

"Chili!"

From somewhere within the rank gloom Shahid recognized Chili's unmistakable grunt. "Come on."

They stumbled through to him. So this was where Papa's dream had been shipwrecked.

Shahid whispered, "If he could see you."

"Speak up," he said.

At home he had a wall of suits, linen for the summer, wool for the winter, arranged according to color, hanging in his wardrobe like a spectrum. There were cashmere coats, Paul Smith scarves, Cardin umbrellas. His luggage was the finest, the leather spongy. There was a drawer full of sunglasses, inscribed with their designer names; a cupboard was stacked with electronic toys—calculators, video players, a portable CD, personal organizers—all in the unyielding color of that time, matt black. On a shelf were his colognes, by Guerlain and purchased in Paris.

Chili had paraded for a quarter of his life before a mirror and caressed this booty for another quarter. Shahid had been forbidden to touch any object, though occasionally Chili would summon him to gaze on a new suit as he strutted it about, which Shahid would have to praise unreservedly. At parties Chili would open his jacket to virtual strangers, displaying the label, beautifully sewn pockets, or lovely buttons, and laughing. Another room in Papa's house had been converted into a gym where Chili had been "redesigning his body." In the drive Tipoo cleaned his cars.

Now, illuminated by an unshaded bulb which ran off a battery, he sat on a mattress leaning against a wall of crumbling plaster, wearing a smeared T-shirt and one blue and one brown sock. Half a cigarette was clenched in his face. His eyes squinted. He drank vodka from an unwashed mug.

Shahid and Strapper had passed through a room in which several junkies were lying around. One of them, a black woman, was naked, but no one paid any attention. Shahid had no idea what part of town Strapper had transported him to.

"We better talk," Shahid said.

Chili closed his eyes.

Shahid lay down beside his brother, who continually licked his dry and cracked lips.

"That's why I've come for you, Chili, to talk about some things."

"Yeah?"

But Shahid suddenly felt tired; he didn't feel like moving again that night. He would rest a few minutes until he felt stronger.

Across the room Strapper settled down with his knife, lighter, and dope bag, constructing a spliff. Wherever he was Strapper seemed as contented as he'd ever be, as if he couldn't afford to make the distinction between his and others' space.

Shahid drifted into sleep.

He awoke. It can't have been much later. Suddenly he sat up and said, "Please."

"Please?" Chili ruffled his brother's hair. "I would, I would tell you anything, but without a pick-me-up I'm dead."

"Don't gimme that." Strapper gave a devious little smile and held out an envelope. "Because I've sorted you."

Chili practically stood to attention. "Sorted! Toot sweet! This is excellent, Mister Strapper."

Chili's praise lifted him; Strapper loved pleasing his former friend. "Yeah, I reckon it is. But there's only a bit left. After this . . . you know."

"What?"

"It's gotta be rocks."

Chili glanced at Shahid, gave Strapper an imperceptible nod, and said, "Thing is, Strap, times are moody, I have to admit. You know that—temporarily—they've stopped my fucking money."

"You tol' me your missis is loaded."

"She doesn't like me so much, at the moment. Not sure why. Did I tell you she has a remarkable physical strength?"

"Why can't you just go back to work?" Shahid said.

"Work? What the fuck for?"

"It's only a suggestion."

"Well, stick it."

Strapper was sniggering now.

Shahid said with as much enthusiasm as he could, "Travel's a great business. Papa thought so."

Strapper agreed. "I fancy a bit of travel myself. People always need to escape."

Chili chopped out three lines and inhaled one. "Tellin' me. They lie in the sun, fuck each other, make a noise, learn nothing about what they see—and go home." Chili turned to Strapper: "He wants me to do that for the rest of my life."

"It's a job, it's work," Shahid persisted.

Chili inhaled the second line. "You see them, our people, the Pakis, in their dirty shops, surly, humorless, their fat sons and ugly daughters watching you, taking the money. The prices are extortionate, because they open all hours. The new Jews, everyone hates them. In a few years the kids will kick their parents in the teeth. Sitting in some crummy shop, it won't be enough for them." Chili anticipated Shahid's objection. "Not that sitting here is thrilling either. But—" Chili often became aggressive when he was most bored. "You go and work there if you like it so much! I give you my place! But you won't either. You're too fucking artistic. We ain't a generation to make sacrifices. Hey, Strap, look at the dreamer." Chili snorted the third line and indicated his brother. "He's a dreamer with big hopes."

"Like me," Strapper said.

"You?"

"Yeah, me, man."

Chili cackled. "They ain't dreams, they're drug hallucinations!"

Strapper's gob flew and spattered in the dust at Chili's feet.

"Watch your mouth! Fuck you!"

Chili tried soothing him. "But there's things Shahid really wants to do, that he believes in."

"I can draw a bit of a picture." Strapper searched his pockets for a pen. "Give us some paper!"

"Haven't you noticed that Shahid's got the artistic temperament?"

Strapper pointed his knife at Shahid. "He's got everything and the fucking money, too!"

Chili asked Shahid, "You've got money?"

"A little," Shahid said, trying to ignore Strapper.

"Give me a little, then," Chili said. "All this talk! Christ Almighty, Shahid, get it together! Aren't we family?"

Shahid had no power to refuse; he emptied his pockets to his brother.

Just then Chili looked up and Shahid saw that for the first time in years Chili was afraid and there was no strength of resistance in him. A small, middle-aged white man, dressed casually like a bank employee on a weekend, had come in, followed by a taller, ugly guy, whose head lolled and rolled as if his spine couldn't bear the weight. At the sight of this pair Strapper appeared to shrink into the shadows of the room.

"So?" said the first man, who was twitchy and quick.

Without a word, but with an obsequious smile, Chili leaned forward and handed over Shahid's money. The man counted it, snorted derisively and took a step toward Chili. Chili put up his hand defensively; he knew what he had to do. He extracted his car keys and dropped them into the man's palm.

"That's better," the man said.

"Full tank, too," said Chili.

"Pardon?"

"Full tank."

The men left. Shahid opened his mouth but Chili put a finger to his lips.

They sat there listening, afraid to move; after a couple of minutes

Chili shifted his position and tried to laugh, but it was a hollow, meaningless sound, more like a moan. Shahid could see that he had been humiliated.

To show he could still function, Chili got up and stretched, patting his stomach and squeezing his upper-arm muscles. Then he took a few steps across the room and knocked playfully on the side of Strapper's head with his knuckle.

"There's someone in there, oh, yes, I know there is."

"Christ," whimpered Strapper. "They . . ."

"What?"

"They gone?"

"For now."

"Right. Phew."

"Take it easy."

"That's what you say."

"Gimme that spliff."

"No man. I need it. I done shit meself." He pointed at Shahid. "An' so has he."

The kid resumed fretting and scraping at himself as if he would tear away the anxiety of the last few minutes from his skin. Shahid twisted his head to look through into the next room, where they were now playing "Electric Ladyland." Chili's voice had become normal again. He talked of Strapper as if he were introducing a landmark to a party of tourists.

"I'm glad you like him, because this little fucker can see things. Oh yes. He's in the shit but he knows what he's worth, what's been done to him, and the amount of hope he can take for granted, which is not a lot. That's why we've got to give him our help. Nothing terrible will happen to us, unless we will it." Shahid gave Chili an admonitory look here, but his brother was flowing: "But evil has been done to him, practically from day one. And he doesn't deserve to be wasted. Somebody must do something for him!"

As Chili's eyes filled with tears, Shahid realized Chili was talking about Strapper as if he were Papa talking to himself.

"Stop," said Shahid, sobbing. He was shaking. "Please don't go on about it."

"Anyhow." Chili turned away after giving the boy's head a final inquiring tap. "He reads the books. He's better than me in that respect. Strapper, what's the name of that one you were boring me about the other day?"

"What?"

Strapper was looking at Shahid with hostility.

"The book."

"*A Clockwork Orange.*"

"That's right," said Chili, chopping into a small bank of coke. The action itself brightened him up. "Know that one?"

"Just escapism," Strapper said.

He'd picked up a roll of wallpaper and unfurled three feet of it on the floor. Getting on to his knees he began to draw, rapidly, on the back of it, occasionally glancing at the brothers. Beneath the pictures he scrawled illegible words.

Shahid soon tired of watching this. "Zulma's had enough."

Chili looked up. "When did you see her."

"She's had enough of you."

"What else is new?"

"She's taking Safire to Pakistan."

There was a pause, after which Chili became a man who shrugged, who bore what happened to him with indifference, one thing not being any worse than any other. But, for a moment, a shadow crossed his face.

He lay down for a while and sat up only to drink.

"Where's your woman?" he said eventually. "Ring and tell her to come here. I could really talk to her. I can see into her, and she knows it. You still seeing her?"

"I don't know."

"By the way, what's her name?"

"Chili," said Shahid. "I think you're going to wind up dead, if you aren't careful. Please tell me what you've done that means you have to hide out."

"Mind your own business."

"At least tell me what you're going to do now."

"Ditto."

Shahid got up and shook his fists in frustration. "Chili, brother, if you can't give me a little more, I'm going to leave you now."

"I've got nothing to give you."

Shahid looked at Strapper. "You heard the man," he said.

"See you," Shahid said.

"Little brother—" Chili called.

"Yes?"

"Don't get lost."

Shahid stumbled through the house until he found the back door. On the street once more, he realized he had no idea where he was. He walked until he found a tube station.

Sorry, I'm a stupid fool. Sorry," he said,
    She stood shivering at the front door, pale and anxious, looking up and down the street. She wore an old T-shirt with an unraveling sweater tied over her shoulders, and torn black leggings. She'd removed her makeup; it was the first time he'd seen her in glasses.

He'd been running. Breathing hard, he backed away from the door to indicate she didn't have to let him in.

"Shahid," she called, as he reached the gate. "Why are you here?"

"I need to see you."

"Then come in."

"Are you sure?"

"No. But do it anyway."

She turned away, leaving the door open. He followed her upstairs saying, "Thanks, Deedee, sorry about this."

One of the live-in students was waiting on the landing. Shahid smiled embarrassedly at him. Deedee's room smelled sweetly of perfume and weed. This was her at home, unprepared, private. She had taken supper in bed with the TV on. Several books, a large journal with a fountain pen between the pages, and a hair dryer lay on the duvet. He felt safer now but was aware of her discomfort; she didn't like being seen like this, but didn't want to care.

"So?"

He began, "I had to drag halfway across London, but I found Chili. Strapper knew where he was. I'm in other trouble, too. Zulma wants me to run the business if Chili's gonna go all the way to hell."

"Really?"

"I couldn't believe she was saying it. But she's serious. What am I going to do?"

Deedee was not young—he noticed now how veined the skin of her hands was—and she'd moved beyond a certain stage of toleration. She'd been thinking things over and had hoarded them too long. She wasn't going to be diverted.

She shut the door and started: "I thought we'd stopped seeing one another, that's why I can't listen to this."

"Sorry?"

"It's been hard. But I've been relieved to think it couldn't go any further. I've been imagining that I'm . . . I'm too much for you, that I overwhelm you. I want to give up on us."

"But why?"

"Surely a wise woman would keep away from love and find some practical arrangement of sex, friendship, and art to replace it?"

He was half-listening; he couldn't take it in.

"I'm saying," he said, "what am I going to do? Chili was hiding—miles away. There's violent people looking for him. I think he did this horrible thing. He won't talk about it, but I've worked it out from something Strapper said. He smashed some dealer up and took their drugs and money, after doing some other bad things. Now there's people who want to knock him off."

"You could hardly blame them, could you?"

Clearly she didn't want to know this; it was a distraction. He sighed: "How are you, then?"

"Are you interested?"

"Yes, as long as I don't have to sit down."

"Most positions are agreeable to me, I'm a liberal. Or used to be." She sipped her coffee and then drank some wine. "The college finally admitted that they're going to make some of us redundant. Brownlow, too."

"That's good."

"You're telling me." At last she laughed. "So on the way home I was thinking about how scary that was, leaving college. And exciting, too, in another way. You know how I like to be ridiculously positive, because I can easily become self-pitying." He stroked her hair. "But it was difficult to bear. There aren't any jobs. I could be unemployed for years. I could never get another teaching job. Anyhow, I went to the supermarket, came back to watch *Brookside*, and stuffed some peppers. Usually I cook and eat with the TV news on, with a book propped up and drinking wine."

"I like doing that."

"I do a bottle or more most nights and, yes, it's better than some marriages I know. My friends with kids envy me the single life. I can go out to dinner. I fuck who I fancy. Or no one at all. What more could a girl want? But I can't carry on in the same way. I don't want to do everything alone anymore. I find this whole thing so hard because I've been having fantasies—"

He sat down and put his head in his hands. "What sort?"

"Those I'll tell you later."

"That's something to look forward to."

"Fantasies that you and I might be together more. Except you're not sure if you want that, are you?"

He couldn't say anything. There had been too much to think about, and now she had to start confining him.

She added, "I've been losing faith in you."

"Fuck off, Deedee. Who cares? I'm drained. I can't do a middle-class kind of relationship discussion tonight."

"You want me to be straight?"

"Why not?"

"I heard this worrying thing that made me wonder. And wonder."

"About what?"

"How can I put it?" She was looking intently at him. "You look very anxious, love. You can't sit still."

"Shit, Deedee, I can't stand this fucking sarcasm tonight! What have you heard?"

"That you're involved with this aubergine."

"I see." He shuddered. "Aubergine?"

"Yes."

She waited for him to break down.

"Deedee, I have heard about the aubergine. It's true. And I have been over there to have a peep. Definitely. I won't deny that."

"God has written on it, hasn't he?"

"That's what some people are saying. But they're simple types. Unlike you, they can't read the French philosophers. A few years ago they were in their villages, milking cows and keeping chickens. We have to respect the faiths of others—the Catholics say they drink Jesus's blood and no one jails the Pope for cannibalism."

"Is it true that you've persuaded the Rubber Messiah to place this . . . this manifestation in the Town Hall?"

"Mr. Rudder has stated publicly that he wants a closer association with our community. If aubergines are what we believe, it's gonna be respected. It's our culture, right?"

"Is it your culture? Is it culture at all?"

"You're being a snob."

"Really? And you're fooling yourself. What would your father have said?"

Shahid bowed his head and bit his lip.

"You know that Rubber's a totally cynical bastard?"

He shouted, "We're third-class citizens, even lower than the white working class. Racist violence is getting worse! Papa thought it would stop, that we'd be accepted here as English. We haven't been! We're not equal! It's gonna be like America. However far we go, we'll always be underneath!"

"The story is true. I gave you more credit than that."

"Deedee." He wanted to be held. He moved toward her. She took him in her arms but wouldn't kiss him.

"I don't like it when you're so critical all the time," he said.

"I don't give a damn. Because I've been around and this aubergine takes the biscuit. I'm not going to respect a communicating vegetable and I'm not going to compete with one either."

"I understand why you feel like this. But be reasonable—"

"What sort of people burn books and read aubergines? I'd heard books were on the way out. I never imagined they'd be replaced by vegetables. Presumably, libraries will be replaced by greengrocers. No, I'm giving you an ultimatum."

"What are you saying, Deedee? I'm on the verge of insanity here!"

"Who isn't? But it's me or the enchanted eggplant."

"Stop it."

They were sitting on the edge of the bed. "Which of us d'you want?"

He reflected. "It's not difficult."

"The turnip?"

"I think so."

"That's what I expected."

"Really?"

"It's OK, chéri. As long as I know."

"Kiss me good-bye."

"It's been a lovely time, at times."

"It has." He returned her kiss. "Give me your tongue."

"Undo your shirt." She bit into his lip. "I love that *café-au-lait* skin. Let me see it one last time."

"You undo it. I like that."

"I don't think I can," she said. "My hands are shaking."

"They are, too. But get this T-shirt off."

"Help me."

"Here. Now lie back. You're beautiful."

"Thank you," she said. "Touch me . . . please."

"That way?"

"Oh, God, exactly that way. Roll it, pull it . . . and tweak it. Christ. And that one, too. Oh."

"Too hard?"

"Not yet. Use your mouth. It'll calm me down. Put your other hand on my arse. Dig your nails in."

"OK?"

"Yes! You haven't forgotten you owe me a long suck?"

"Do I?" he said.

"Half an hour, at least, you promised."

"Half an hour?"

She closed her eyes. "Get to it."

He began to follow her urging, but soon sat up to look anxiously at her.

"Deedee. What is it?"

Her cheeks trembled; the corners of her lips lifted, her nose flared. Instinctively her hands went to cover her face.

"Deedee!"

Laughter exploded in her mouth, a cataract of glee. He started to giggle himself, which set her off again. Each time they looked at one another, and before either of them could begin to pronounce "aubergine," they were rolling around the bed, holding on to each other for fear they'd fall off. Tears ran down their faces. They slapped one another and kicked their legs in the air like babies. The only way he could stop howling was to bite her arms. She tried stuffing a pillow in her mouth.

Eventually she picked herself up and went to the bathroom to wash down in cold water.

He wasn't going anywhere else that night. The day was done. He undressed gratefully, threw down his clothes like a teenager, and slipped beneath her duvet as quickly as he could, smelling her on the bedclothes.

She came back, turned off the light, and slipped into bed next to him. Heads together, they still gave little occasional giggles, chortles, and cackles, but physical sensations were mercifully replacing their hilarity. This was what sex was for. She could lie there now, legs apart, hands behind her head, moving only to take his hand and urge him to a particular action on a certain site. He required no directions, though, but wanted to prospect for sensation and fondle and rub where he wanted, at his own pace. Her cunt was becoming familiar to him; he wanted to roam in it as if it were his; he'd had no idea you could feel so personal and proprietorial about a vagina.

"Give me your aubergine. Fill my cock-shaped hole," she said. "Stick it in my earth and let me bless it with my holy waters."

She began to laugh again, she couldn't hold herself back, and her cunt muscles alternately contracted and relaxed; he felt as if he'd placed his eggplant inside a concertina.

"Hey," he said, "this is the life."

"Right," she replied. "You couldn't be more right."

Next morning, attempting to avoid Deedee's tenants, Shahid was creeping up the hall. But the front door opened and Brownlow crashed in, spitting out croissant. "Hello there, Tariq! Are we fortunate enough to have you renting one of our rooms?"

"Pardon? Er . . . no."

"What are you doing here, then?" Brownlow gave Shahid a quizzical look before saying glumly, "Oh, I see. You're doing my wife."

"You could say that."

"Serious?"

"Quite."

"Fucking hell."

Shahid looked at Brownlow in surprise; a college professor and the word he used most was fuck.

"Course," Brownlow continued, "I have some interests like that myself, though younger. But I imagined your religion was severe about such things. I must have misread the Koran. Perhaps you would be good enough to put me right in that area someday. Or maybe I'll consult Riaz this afternoon."

"Good idea."

"On your way to college?"

"Yes."

"Wait a couple of minutes and we can accompany one another. We should talk. Snaffle a croissant."

Brownlow tripped over the bottom stair, regained his balance, and bounded upstairs.

Shahid was still waiting when Deedee came out in her pajamas. Her face bore the glaze of sleep; he kissed her eyes.

She snuggled into him. "So the cat's out of the bag."

"Yep. See you at college."

"Hope so. Shahid."

"Yes?"

"Give me another kiss."

He had to rush along to keep up with Brownlow, who was yelling, "My congratulations are in order."

"Thanks a lot," Shahid said, nervous of inquiring what he'd done to earn this accolade.

"I was at Cambridge in the late sixties, you know."

"The best years?"

"Not by a long way. But I took part in the rebellion. Sartre was my god." Brownlow glanced at Shahid, as if afraid he'd patronized him by mentioning someone he hadn't heard of. "And Fanon, of course, who Deedee sometimes takes a certain interest in. Students were a united force then—this was when humane education counted. I remember thinking, we've smashed through the barrier, the walls of fear and deference have come down, we no longer have to grovel to the gods of authority. We can write the terms of a more sensual history." Brownlow stopped then, waved his fist and began to sway from the waist down, while chanting to the rush-hour crowd, "LBJ, LBJ, how many kids you burned today? LBJ, LBJ how many kids you burned today?" He looked wildly at Shahid, then wanted to put his arm around him but stopped himself. "Know that?"

"Not till now."

"Sorry for saying this, but how incredible it is just that there are kids who never tasted that combustible freedom. But you guys, Riaz and Chad, and the women, too, in the most reactionary period since the war, you're doin' it, you're not isolated from the people and you're not intimidated! You are the modern—with grandeur and dignity on your side, oh yes!"

"But in the sixties, you know, man," Shahid said, "when society was on fire, you didn't like censorship, did you?"

"We were blowing all the doors open—blowing them off their hinges, blowing away their houses!"

"Really blowing times." Shahid continued, "But recently Deedee, Ms. Osgood, I mean, mentioned a phrase that was used then. She still stands by it, too: 'all power to the imagination.' "

Brownlow said impatiently, "She must have picked it up from one of our friends."

"You're in favor of censoring this writer, then?"

Brownlow withdrew his arm and blinked. "I see what you're getting at. If only—if only this were merely a book matter. But you don't believe the liberals—who are working themselves up into a pompous lather—are fighting for literary freedom, do you?"

"I think—"

"They're just standing by their miserable class. When have they ever given a damn about you—the Asian working class—and your struggle? Your class is arguing back. No one will colonize you, put you down, or insult you in your own country. And the liberals—always the weakest and most complacent people—are shitting their pants, because you threaten their power. Liberalism cannot survive these forces. And if you meet any of them, be sure to tell them that their pants are going to be on fire pretty soon."

"What d'you mean?"

"You know what I mean," Brownlow said with a fierce laugh. He swerved away past the security guards and gave the peace sign. "Ciao."

That morning Shahid worked in the library as calmly as he could. He didn't want to leave, he had a bad feeling about what was outside; yet it was ridiculous, he was a college student, he couldn't hide away.

At mid-morning he went to the canteen and saw no one he knew. He was returning to his desk, looking forward to some quiet reading, when he saw Hat and Sadiq talking heatedly as they walked. Spontaneously he tried to duck away into the crowd heading toward the classrooms. But Hat had spotted him and, even as Shahid kept his head lowered, he pushed through the throng, crying, "Listen, guess what she did, yaar! Just now. Sadiq can't believe it. Chad's gonna go through the roof."

"What are you on about?"

Hat took offense. "Come, come, don't be all stiff, it starting." He held Shahid's arm in friendship. "Where were you last night?"

"Busy—I—"

"What doin'? You missed the meeting. Not so funny without your funny comments, brother."

Sadiq was bursting. "Tell the people, Hat, yaar."

"OK, OK," Hat said, addressing Shahid even as he tried to move away. "That woman, this morning, Miss Osgood. She hold up the book. And you know what she say, waving it about like a sanitary napkin, she say, let's talk, it's literature, which is what this class is about today—Orwell and all. It being threatened, freedom going down."

"What happened then?"

"There's a Syrian girl and an Iraqi sister and that Pakistani—"

"Me, you fool," said Sadiq.

"Oh yeah. They upset having shit purveyed in their face. 'Any thoughts,' she say, stalking around like some dictator. 'Any thoughts?' 'I give you a thought, Miss,' I say. 'Put down that book before I . . . before I . . . You know what I'm saying, Miss Deedee Osgood?' "

"Why did you say that, Hat?"

"Hey, why not? What's your problem? I say straight out, our parents pay taxes, here should be British scholarship and brainwaves, the envy of the world, not curses."

"What did she say?"

"She keep going on, 'This is a classroom. There must be discussion, debate, argument!' "

"She's persistent, then."

"Until I start fisting the desk, brother. Then the others take it up, smashing down together. I don't expect it, I hardly know those people."

"Apart from me," said Sadiq.

"But big support they give me."

Shahid said, "How did she cope?"

"It shut her mouth right up. Democracy in action. Student protest full on. I tell Brownlow an' he say we have to be listened to. Our voices suppressed by Osgood types with the colonial mentality. To her we coolies, not cool. So Miss Deedee has to stick the book away before someone sticks it—"

"Was she upset?"

"Upset? That's not the end of it, man. We upset!"

"How come?"

"I just now pass the staff room and out she fly with a bunch of leaflets and bang this in me hand." Hat held out a photocopied sheet. "She putting up some course, starting tomorrow. The History of Censorship: Importance of Immorality. Plato, the Puritans, Milton." He studied the sheet. "How d'you say these? Baudelaire, Brecht. Anyway, just about the whole white doo-dah."

"Sounds good," said Shahid. "Where d'you sign up?"

"Hey, your humor make me laugh. But you better keep the joking to yourself, you know what I mean, for your own benefit in the long run."

Once more Shahid tried to move away. "See you later."

Hat nudged him along. "We going this way."

"I've got to get to my books."

"Too late for books! Foreign Legion full on!"

"Full on!" intoned Sadiq.

Shahid had never known the atmosphere in the group to be so excited, pent-up, ready.

Chad and the others had gathered in an empty classroom collating leaflets in several languages. But as Shahid watched Riaz confidently issuing well-prepared instructions, he was at first puzzled and then dismayed to see that Riaz was wearing the clothes Shahid had loaned him after they first met. Under his jacket Riaz was wearing the Paul Smith red shirt and dyed green Levi's along with Chili's dotted socks.

"Chad," Hat said. "Take a peep at this leaflet, yaar, it's dynamite from Deedee Osgood."

Chad looked it over. "I'll dynamite her later, brother, don't worry." He turned to Shahid, who was making his way toward the door. "Where you going?"

"Library."

Chad was jiggling on his toes, as if preparing for a run. "Don't be a prick, we gonna torch that moldy mother." He pulled Shahid aside. "Your job is to fetch a long stick—"

"A stick?"

Chad imitated him. "A stick! Yeah, a broom handle."

"You're a joker, man, if you think you gonna start beating people!"

"Fool! To suspend the burning filth so everyone can see our protest and cheer off their heads. You better get string, too! Go!"

"Chad, I—"

"Here's money—and bring me the change!" Chad slapped a five-pound note in Shahid's hand. "What are you waiting for—a bit of hurry-up?"

Shahid turned away, saying, "This man, whatever he's done, I know he hasn't spat on us or refused us a job. He never called you Paki scum, did he?"

Chad's face turned the color of clay. Stamping his foot, he pulled Shahid round. "How many times do we have to repeat, this bastard's smeared shit over our faces."

"I want more discussion with brother Riaz," Shahid insisted, taking a step in that direction.

"Don't start. We had a talk and you left with that air hostess! Brother Riaz more annoyed with you than ever. Where's the typing we entrusted you with?"

"Chad, I feel sorry for you. Without him you're nothing."

"I agree with you."

"Yes, a dog without a master."

"A dog, eh?"

Chad virtually embraced Shahid now, dragging down on his wrists so it was a struggle for Shahid, pulled forward, to remain upright.

"A dirty dog."

Chad said, "Least, least I recognize that a master is required. I not arrogant enough to think I can do everything myself. Did I make the world?" He started jabbing his finger into Shahid, just below Shahid's windpipe, as if he wanted to make a hole in him. "But I do know that, unlike you, I not a coward."

"Chad—"

"Because you are always talking, never taking action! And you know why? Because you had an easy life! That shit you tol' me the first day, you invent it to make yourself interesting! Oh yeah, I know how much you are a liar. Actions will be taken!"

Shahid recalled how Chili would throw his head back and laugh if anyone threatened him, as if the notion of being punched out was hilarious. However, Chili knew karate and wasn't unused to being hit. Nevertheless, Shahid gave Chad's smooth, broad face his nicest smile.

Chad grasped him by the front of his shirt, dragged him close, and flung him out of the door. Shahid left the college, not willingly, but at least he was away from them. He would have time to think.

He was walking along, in turmoil, hardly aware of the direction he was taking, when Tahira ran up behind him. Her scarf had slipped; wisps of hair broke the oval of her face, which she replaced carefully.

"Shahid, I saw what went on." She put a finger to his mouth. "Shhh . . . Don't be humiliated, but remember—this is only one step on the road. You're behaving as if it's the whole journey." She wanted to say something more but found it difficult. "From the beginning . . . I've liked you."

"Me?"

"Why so surprised? You are broader than the others. But why are you always thinking of something else?"

"My studies."

She gave him a sly look. "Or is it someone else?" There was a pause. She waited but he knew to say nothing. "I wonder who. Let me have a wild guess. I think it's—" He began walking. "Please, don't go. We have been trusted with something. Shahid!"

She led him briskly to a hardware store, where they bought a broom and some string. Outside he tried to dump them in her hands, saying, "Take these to brother Riaz."

She wouldn't concede; she knew what he intended to do. She hurried him back through the college.

"This isn't the time for giving up. We've got to believe in something and stand up for it, otherwise they'll have us."

It was before lunch on a fine and normal day; classes were full. Soon everyone would pile out into the playground. And there he'd be, guarding the flame with brother Riaz, Chad, and the others. Great!

He wanted to cooperate now, giving himself over to bitter nihilism, destruction, and hatred. He would love the madness coursing through him, as if he were at a teenage rave in Kent.

Suddenly Shahid spotted one of the security guards coming down the stairs. Surely the man would seize on his guilt? Assuming the broom handle was a weapon, he'd seize and question Shahid before marching him away. Shahid would be ejected from the college. By evening he would be accompanying his bags on the train. That night he would sit down with his mother while Tipoo fetched tea, having become "head of the family."

"What are you doing?" said Tahira. He stuck the string inside his jacket and started to sweep the floor. "Shahid!"

He couldn't begin to tell the sane from the mad, wrong from right, good from bad. Where would one start? None of this would lead to the good. But what did? Who knew? What would make them right? Everything was in motion; nothing could be stopped, the world was swirling, its compasses spinning. History was unwinding in his head into chaos, and he was tumbling through space. Where would he land? If the security guard had asked him to add two plus two, what would he have answered?

As calmly as he could, Shahid brushed a patch of floor, but he had no notion of what he was doing.

When the guard had walked on, Shahid, pursued by Tahira, went through the back of the building and headed toward the playground, where the demonstration was going to be. He wanted, on the way, to see Deedee's face again.

They passed the hut in which she was teaching "her girls," a class of black women fashion students. One of them was, somewhat embarrassedly, standing on a chair. The others were giggling and clapping. Deedee was also laughing and pointing at the woman's shoes. She was so brightly alive; how people enjoyed her classes!

He shut his eyes and walked on.

"What's the matter?" Deedee was behind him, dragging him behind the hut. "Are you ill?" It was an intimate roughness, her soft face and breath so close to him. Tahira stood back, watching.

Shahid's teeth were chattering. Deedee wanted to protect him and, at this moment, he couldn't have been more grateful. She stared at the broom and the string as if they were exhibits in a trial.

"Are you helping the caretaker now, or will you be riding on that broomstick?"

He dropped the string and picked it up. "There's been an accident."

"Where?"

"Something got broke. I should clear it up."

"Tell me what the string's really for!"

He pushed her hands away. "Get away from me!"

"I love you, you know. Have you got any of that sort of feeling for me?"

"Where did you get that idea from? I'm really on my way now."

"What were you doing?" Tahira said, when he'd pulled away from Deedee and they were continuing.

"She is marking one of my essays."

"That woman is very bad."

"In what way?"

"Riaz has evidence that her family are nudists."

"I had no idea they were so interesting."

"Shahid, do you like being so cynical?"

"On reflection—"

"Yes?"

"I think I probably do."

She was staring at him in fascination.

In the classroom, Shahid offered the broom and string to Chad.

"Good, good," Chad said, glancing at Tahira. "You're hard-core. Bring it along."

Sadiq had obtained a can of petrol. Hat had fetched some speakers from his bedroom and borrowed a college microphone. Meanwhile other brothers and sisters were distributing leaflets in the canteen, on the stairwells, in the common room, and had been posted outside classrooms as the students broke for lunch.

Shahid, Sadiq, Hat, and some others went out into the college yard, an enclosed and starkly asphalted children's playground, where the students played basketball. This had been chosen by Riaz as the site.

Soon the students were piling out of their classes and congregating there. Some climbed on abandoned school desks for a better view. Shahid took in the festive atmosphere, the laughter and idle curiosity, the kids spinning on roller skates. Around the yard windows banged open and scores of heads jutted out. There were cheers and shouts. Hat was ushering people into the playground and loudly ordering them to keep the noise down. To his surprise, Shahid noticed that Brownlow was assisting Hat.

The yard was nearly full when Chad strung the book on the pole and thrust it into the air. Nearby a couple kissed, mouth to mouth, looking up occasionally—the girl to rotate her finger at her temple—even as Hat poured petrol over the pages.

Two college security guards were moving toward Chad. They would have to stop this: permission couldn't have been given for such a demonstration on college property. It was almost over, surely? Yet Shahid didn't, now, want the event to be interrupted. He certainly wouldn't have turned away in disgust. He wanted to witness every page in flames.

As the guards approached Chad, Brownlow moved toward them, extending his arms in a calming gesture, and beginning an explanation. But his stutter had returned, and the guards exchanged amused glances, more interested by this senior lecturer's behavior than by the event, which was, after all, peaceful. However, Shahid knew that by participating in this display Brownlow was risking his career.

Shahid saw that Deedee had come out of the main building and was standing at the back with some of her students and groupies.

"My God," she cried, her hand on top of her head. "What is happening to us!"

Fiercely resolute she elbowed through the crowd to Brownlow. She was angry enough to clout him but people were gawking at her, it wouldn't have been a good idea. She berated her ex-husband, who stared at Riaz, shook his head, and stuttered even more, his lips making futile spastic gestures. She moved around him, trying to locate something she could appeal to, but the students began laughing at them for having "a domestic" at such a time.

Riaz took a breath. Then he stepped up onto the little box placed there by Hat and took the microphone from Sadiq. Until now, waiting to one side, Riaz had appeared irrelevant, dazed even, as Lenin might have been at the Finland Station when the moment to act finally arrived.

"Good afternoon," he said experimentally, and cleared his throat.

Deedee's voice rang out: "What are you going to do with that book?"

Riaz seemed to shake himself before addressing her across the turning heads: "If you will permit me, I shall say something."

"You're going to burn it, aren't you?"

This was helping him. He appealed to everyone. "In one moment I will explain."

"Do you really understand what that means?" she said.

"Pardon me, but is the free speech of an Asian to be muzzled by the authorities?"

"No, no," people murmured.

She said, "But why don't you try reading it first?"

Someone bellowed from a window, "Let the brother speak!"

A voice in the crowd agreed. "His turn on the pot!"

"Say it, brother!"

"Go, man!"

"Yo, speak!"

"You understand?" said Riaz, as the voices rose. "This is democracy!"

"Democracy!" she said.

"May I begin?"

"I think you—"

He interrupted: "Are the white supremacists going to lecture us on democracy this afternoon? Or will they permit us, for once, to practice it?"

Expectantly the gathering turned to Deedee, who was searching the crowd, seeking support. She caught Shahid's eye; for a second she was staring straight at him. He attempted a smile, as if to say, surely we understand one another, but with a dismayed look she had already moved on.

Some students sucked their teeth and began hissing. Others sniggered. Another voice broke through the murmuring uncertainty. "Get off, white bitch!"

"Yeah!" said another voice, and another.

Deedee shook her fist at Riaz and yelled, "Save us from those who will save us!"

She rushed away.

"Thank you," he said. "At last. Now I can start."

Riaz was his usual ironical self, pausing deftly while building his standard argument about the crimes committed by whites against blacks and Asians in the name of freedom. God, like a fair wind, was assisting him. Shahid recalled Brownlow saying he wished he believed in God. He'd assumed at the time that it was a cynical point but now he wasn't so sure. What an advantage in life God could give you—in certain circumstances!

Riaz spoke only briefly before looking at Chad and raising a finger. Chad tilted the book. Its pages quivered in the breeze like birds' wings. Hat thrust a lighter into them. At once Sadiq and Tahira jumped back. Smoke hugged the volume before bulging away into the air.

People hooted and clamored as if they were at a fireworks display. Fists were raised at the flaming bouquet of the book. And the former Trevor Buss and Muhammad Shahabuddin Ali-Shah, alias Brother Chad, who was brandishing it at the sky, laughed triumphantly.

Sadiq began cheering; so did Hat, Tariq, and the others, their pleasure undiluted. Shahid stood among the crowd, neither near the front nor at the back. He was hoping his friends weren't watching him. But how could he evade their eyes? He looked at Hat and Hat saw him. Shahid looked away immediately, with a guilty expression, as if he weren't enjoying it as much as he should. He wanted to appear neutral but knew that wasn't possible. It wasn't as if he felt nothing, like many of the people looking on. If anything, he felt ashamed. He was someone who couldn't join in, couldn't let himself go. Perhaps that was why he'd enjoyed Deedee's drugs so much.

Looking across the crowd at Chad's expression, he was glad of that. He never wanted his face to show such ecstatic rigidity! The stupidity of the demonstration appalled him. How narrow they were, how unintelligent, how . . . embarrassing it all was! But was he better because he lacked their fervor, because he was trying to slink away? No; he was worse, being tepid. He was not simple enough!

"This isn't right," Shahid said to someone beside him. "What's happening to our community?"

The student replied, "What you worried about? It only a book."

A shiver flared through the chapters; scorched pages whirled across the crowd. One paragraph took off toward Kilburn; several passages flew toward Westbourne Park; half the cover went straight up.

Someone cried, "Look, they've called the police!"

The police weren't favored at the college: their presence was more likely than the flambéed literature to ignite a disturbance. At once, jeering, the crowd began to disperse in all directions. Somehow the microphone became disconnected. Sadiq ran about.

Riaz made a megaphone of his hands and shouted garbled exhortations. His posse tried to attend but they were distracted by a commotion at the entrance to the yard, which Shahid moved toward. It was Deedee. She had come out of the building with three policemen. She pointed toward Riaz and Chad. At this Brownlow dashed over and started to speak to them.

Chad charged out of the yard through a side gate and into the street, suspending the charred, reeking book above his head like a ruined umbrella and yelling in incoherent Urdu. Riaz stumbled and fell sideways off his box. He stood there looking about, not knowing what to do.

Hat, Sadiq, and Shahid collected Hat's speakers and humped them back into the building, just as the fire brigade ran in through the other entrance.

They'd burned the book. The event had been a little lame but it was what they'd wanted and it was done. Despite the flames, there had been no catastrophe and no immediate victims. The college principal would have to castigate the book-burners, but Shahid doubted if she'd take further action, for fear of exacerbating the situation. She'd long been suspicious of Riaz's group, but, afraid of accusations of racism, she'd secured them a prayer room and otherwise avoided them, even when their posters were inflammatory.

Students were making their way to the canteen; others went to classes and the library. Normality was rapidly reestablished. British institutions might be rotten, but they still stood, having existed for years; such a minor assault, or even dozens of such impacts, couldn't threaten much, though Shahid disliked hearing himself think it.

It was impossible to sit in the library now. He packed up, knowing he should be with Deedee. Yet he was afraid of her distress and his ability to cope with it, afraid she was angry with him, and afraid all this had been too much, and had finished everything between them.

On the door of her room she'd pinned a notice canceling her classes. He guessed she was discussing the situation with the principal.

A singed page lay in the gutter outside the college. But the buses were running, the kebab houses were open, people pushed prams and walked home from work. On the steps of the subway a priest squatted to read the Bible to a teenage beggar who sat there all day. None of these people knew a book had been burned nearby. Few of them would, perhaps, have been concerned. Nevertheless, that morning there had been another bombing in the City: many roads had checkpoints. He knew it would be wrong to think that everything would remain all right.

He wanted to crawl back to his room, slam the door and sit down with a pen; that was how he would reclaim himself. This destruction of a book—a book which was a question—had embodied an attitude to life which he had to consider.

He was mounting the stairs when, nearing his floor, he heard familiar voices. He cursed. Some of them must have gathered in Riaz's room. He started to turn round. He would get out. He had left the posse. He hadn't made a decision: the alliance terminated the moment Hat soaked the book in petrol. He had been taught much about what he didn't like; now he would embrace uncertainty. Maybe wisdom would come from what one didn't know, rather than from confidence. That's what he hoped.

He hoped, too, that the parting could be straightforward. Or at least without a confrontation. He didn't want to put his case, nor did he want to see any of them for a while. At the same time he didn't want to avoid his former friends as if he were a criminal or outcast. College life would be intolerable. And he wouldn't be driven out of his own building. He could get past Riaz's door without them noticing.

He reached the top of the stairs and realized they hadn't gathered in Riaz's room. Chad, Hat, Tahira, Sadiq, Tariq, and Nina had opened his door, which, since Chili's tenure, lacked a secure lock.

He stood before their unfriendly eyes. They fell silent. There was nowhere to sit. Hat stood beside the computer, fanning himself with a floppy disk. Shahid pointed at the bright screen. "D'you want a hand with that?"

Chad stood up, snatched the disk from Hat and slipped it in his pocket. Hat looked away.

Sadiq resumed the conversation. "Let's go and see her now!"

Hat glanced with a guilty expression at Shahid. "She's not in her office."

"You checked, then?" Chad said.

Hat's reply was almost inaudible: "You told me to."

"Right."

There was a silence before Sadiq said, "I know one thing—she turned the British state on us."

"Without scruple," Chad said. "She is against authority yet tried to have us arrested. Unbelievable hypocrisy."

Sadiq said, "I can tell you something I have researched so that you know it for your information. Osgood is taking lovers among the Afro-Caribbean and Asian students. Definitely." Tahira and Chad glanced at one another. Hat nodded gravely. Sadiq continued, "Evidence has been presented. The college knows she is having it away with two Rastamen. For political reasons she selects only black or Asian lovers now."

Tahira adjusted her scarf. "Our people have always been sexual objects for the whites. No wonder they hate our modesty."

"The pornographic priestess encourages the brothers of color to take drugs," Sadiq continued. "When she is screwed she is heard halfway across London, like a car alarm. And in the end, she is regularly aborted. She has an account with the clinic!"

"Sadiq," Tahira said. "You get carried away with having it away."

"Apologies. Look at the way she dresses, in clothes too tight for her, bulging everywhere like a potato in a sock."

"If only you were here last year," Chad said. "One of our girls was twisted against the truth by the postmodernists. They made her flee her loving parents, who contacted brother Riaz and myself. She had been taken into hiding. These poor people were distraught. The young girl was forced to say the religion treats women as second-class citizens. Riaz personally took up their case. The girl went into a hostel and agreed to meet her parents for discussions. Discussions! You know where she was? Osgood had concealed her at home!"

"The woman stole a child from her parents?" Tahira said.

"Yes! Would I dare to hide a member of Osgood's family in my house and fill her with propaganda? If I did, what accusations? Terrorist! Fanatic! Lunatic! We can never win. The imperialist idea hasn't died."

"What happened to the girl?" Shahid asked.

Chad said, "Good question. Because she was murdered."

"By her parents?"

"Why would you think that, fool? No, by herself in the Thames. That is what happens when somebody doesn't know who they are."

"We can't let this go on," Tahira said. "Let's speak to her."

"Yes!" Sadiq said.

Tahira said, "Brother Riaz has mentioned that at the very least Osgood must be removed from her post for her attacks on minorities. And today she has prevented us from free expression. Isn't that racist censorship, Shahid?"

Shahid dropped his eyes.

"Has she ever debated with us?" said Chad.

"Today," said Shahid. "She tried to."

"Wrong occasion," Chad said. "Trying to show us up in front of everyone. Has she really asked why we will not be insulted? Has she said why our beliefs are always inferior to hers and yet she lectures everyone about equality?"

"She believes in equality, all right, but only if we forget that we are different," said Tahira. "If we assert our individuality, we are inferior, because we believe foolishness."

"And she shopped us to the state!" Hat said.

Chad said, "I would never have done that—not even to my worst enemies!"

"Let's go to her room and have it out," Hat said.

"Yes, yes, let her listen to our free speech!"

Chad looked at Shahid. "What about it?"

Shahid said, "The security will get you before you say a word to Deedee Osgood."

"How do you know?"

"You'll be expelled, too."

Chad went toward him and flicked his hand at Shahid's head as if he had a wasp in his hair.

"I not studying no more! I will expel them! Don't underestimate our power! If we took your advice, we'd never do nothin', 'cept lie down like pussycats with our legs in the air! No, with my usual genius I've thought of what to do. I know where she lives. Tonight we visit her private home."

"What?" said Hat.

"In order to learn, she must be taught a lesson," Tahira said. "Don't you agree, Shahid?"

"I feel like giving her one of these—" Sadiq extended his fist. "To remember us by."

"Who could blame you?" Chad moved to the door. "Riaz is waiting for us at the mosque. We must discuss before the meeting with Mr. Rugman Rudder. He is about to give his decision about the Town Hall."

Shahid wondered if they would ask him to join them. But Chad only tapped his pocket. "Thank you for the disk."

"Which one have you taken?"

"Only the property of brother Riaz."

Shahid reached for it. "Please give it back, Chad."

"Get lost."

"But I'm not ready. I'll let you have it tonight when it's finished."

"It finished."

"No, Chad, it's not!"

Chad's countenance was as hard as frozen earth. "Oh yes. It finished. Completely."

Chad indicated they should leave. As they went Sadiq chanted, "Osgood—no good! Osgood—no good!"

Shahid threw himself on to his bed and listened to the others take up the chant as they disappeared downstairs.

He needed to warn her, but where was she? He rushed back to the college but no one knew where she was. He took the tube and ran from the station to her house, where one of her tenants said she was usually back by now. Today, though, there was no sign of her. Shahid scribbled a note and left it on the hall table, saying he was looking for her and would be back.

Shahid walked for a long time, until he was lost and exhausted. At last he found a phone and rang her several times, thinking she might have returned. Her answering machine was on. Fear possessed every part of him like cold. His chest felt constricted; he couldn't move easily. His body knew he'd done something irrevocable.

He got a bus and ended up in the Morlock, where he sat down with a pint, as forsaken now as everyone else there. Yet still he believed Riaz was compassionate and could listen, that the brother could see one's humanity and acknowledge it. If Shahid could talk with him, Deedee's position and his own might be resolved. But Chad couldn't be there, for he'd stop him being alone with Riaz. What to do?

He considered everything time and again, before having a couple more drinks. Then he got out, having had an idea.

The fluorescent lighting hummed. Hat looked shocked. Shahid's face seemed to cause him pain, so much so that he wouldn't acknowledge him. Yet there was inner movement, as if he were trying to figure out what to do. Shahid continued nodding and smiling, though this was difficult while Hat went on serving customers as if Shahid were invisible.

In the end Shahid was the only person in the restaurant. Hat was rubbing down the glass counter with a rag.

"Don't come near me."

"I've got to ask you something."

"Why?"

"Please, Hat."

"What d'you want?"

"Hat. Hat. We're friends."

Hat appeared to relent. He called his little brother from the back room and installed him behind the counter. But then he went straight up the back stairs to the flat. Shahid stood about, watching the clock on the microwave. He was about to leave, thinking Hat only wanted to get away from him, when he returned. Shahid had never seen Hat like this, looking wary and scared.

"You know what you've done," Hat said, sitting at a table with Shahid opposite him.

"What is it?"

"Why make it worse by lying?"

"You've got to tell me, Hat."

Hat looked as though Shahid were making a malicious joke. "I converted Riaz's poems on my printer."

"Already?"

"Yeah."

"I see." Shahid nodded. "I understand."

"We couldn't believe it!"

"I hadn't finished what I was doing!"

"Finished?"

"The prose poems—"

Hat gave a mirthless laugh. "How d'you think brother Riaz felt, standing there so proud and all, waiting for his rhymes to come out printed and clean so he could hold it in his hands and show his friends? I know he hoping to make a little money from it."

"The original manuscript hasn't been touched."

"I've never see him so excited. After, he hid his feelings well. He a dignified man. But him shattered to pieces. We all were."

Shahid remembered reading:

> *The windswept sand speaks of adultery in this godless land,*
> *Here Lucifer and colonialists are in charge,*
> *The unveiled girls smell of the West and envy the shameless.*

He had begun typing Riaz's work in good faith. But there were certain words, then phrases and verses, he couldn't bring himself to transcribe. Once he'd begun not-transcribing, he'd got carried away. He'd been enjoying himself with Deedee; it seemed natural to express the puzzle of this wonder.

Shahid said, "It was a celebration."

"Of what, yaar?"

"Passion."

Hat looked as if he could strangle Shahid. "I can be a bit dirty-minded myself, but that stuff . . . You're a sewer rat."

"Don't you have sexual fantasies?"

Hat's eyes nearly burst. "Everyone knows I like looking and stuff. But I don't go and put an essay on girls crossing their legs—"

"And on the smell of their hair, and on the skin behind their knees—"

"Yeah! The odors of their body and everything like that—people sniffing one another's, you know, doo-dahs."

"Didn't God give us our doo-dahs?"

"I wouldn't put them into print! I wouldn't mix it up with religious words, would I?"

"You read it, then."

"What?"

"Hat, apart from the negative things you've said, did you like any of what I did? Did you, Hat?"

For a moment Shahid hoped that Hat would yield, and their friendship would resume. Surely what they shared went deeper than this? But Hat was regarding Shahid only with wrathful perplexity. And he kept jerking his head about as if expecting someone to approach him with advice.

"You a raving evil spirit and a double agent working for some other people!"

"Hat, I'm still your friend—if you want that."

"Why rape us, then? How could you do that to brother Riaz? Can I ask—what harm has he done you?"

Shahid knew he couldn't explain, he felt too ashamed; he wanted to stop himself crying. Hat was right. They had burned a book; but what had he done? He'd abused a friend's trust without even considering it. How could he complain now?

"Chad said that brother Riaz saved your life one time. Is it true?"

"Yes."

"What?"

"It's true. He saved me."

"He save you. Is that why you turn on him?"

"Hat, please believe me. I was playing—playing with words and ideas."

"You think you can play with everything, right? I tell you this, some things ain't funny."

"Usually they're the funniest things."

"How can I say this more? Aren't you believing anything at all at the moment?"

"I don't know! But I am in need here, Hat. I must have order and proportion."

"Good. But our religion isn't something you can test out, like trying on a suit to see if it fit! You gotta buy the whole outfit!"

Hat's disgust was getting Shahid heated. He wanted to grasp Hat by the lapels and say, Hat, I'm the same person, I haven't become someone else since you first met me . . .

He leaned forward. "Please, Hat, help me."

"How?"

"I want to speak to Riaz alone. Just for half an hour. I have to explain everything. Will you talk to him for me without letting Chad know?"

But Hat wouldn't even take this in.

"Brother Chad and all of us, we trusted you—apart from Tahira, who say from the beginning you an egotist with an evil smile. And then Riaz put his soulful words in your hands. It would have been a privilege for any of us! But he think you special." The more Hat fed his outrage with examples, the more it increased until he could barely take in the magnitude of Shahid's crimes. "And how can you think to bother Riaz right now? He busy planning."

"Planning what?"

"Other just retributions."

"For instance?"

"I can't tell you. But the book about to be condemned by Rugman Rudder himself. He, the biggest man in the district, say it filth. How can you argue with that?"

"I see."

"Good."

Shahid and Hat stood up together. Shahid put out his hand to say good-bye. Hat reared back, looking at him wildly.

"Where you going?"

"What?" Shahid said in confusion. "Better go. See you again, I hope."

"No! Stay!"

"What for?"

"Don't you want to eat?"

"I haven't got an appetite."

Almost as if he didn't mean to, Hat pushed Shahid. It wasn't a wholehearted shove, but it was sudden, and Shahid, who wanted to slip away, stumbled and backed into the fridge which contained the drinks. The shelf above containing pickles sprang from the wall and the big jars shot across the floor, breaking open and dumping their slimy contents everywhere.

Hat was horrified by his action, particularly when his father ran out of the back room and, without even taking in the scene, swiped at Hat's head, slipped on the pickle—kicking his legs in the air as if attempting the can-can—and landed on his backside. He lay, scrabbling in liquid mango, howling oaths.

Shahid picked himself up, brushed away as much of the smeared pickle as he could, and made for the door. He hurt in several places but he wasn't going to stop and console himself. He would get out before he smashed something or broke down.

Looking up, he saw Chad coming across the road. He appeared to know Shahid was there, and was heading toward him. Hat must have gone upstairs to phone him at the beginning of their conversation. He didn't look in a friendly mood.

Shahid tore out of the door, up the street, across the road and round the corner, pushing past people as he went. Then he stopped and looked back. It was true: Chad was indeed after him. And Chad, although he was large and had big feet, was charging with the ferocity of a wild pig. He ran into the road without looking, fists up, mouth determined, fit to burst.

Shahid ran as fast as he could, but kept falling into a stumbling walk. He wanted to talk to Chad, who appeared to have suffered a slow puncture: he was shuffling, hopping, and looking ready to roll on his back. But whenever Shahid slowed, Chad would find something extra in himself, revive, and continue.

Shahid had more puff than Chad. With open lungs he outran him. He sought an escape by darting into a shopping mall and hurrying past Our Price, Habitat, Dixons, and the Early Learning Centre. At last he reeled out through the back. He gave a little cheer of deliverance when he saw Chad was lost. He tottered and sat down on the pavement, his heart beating heavily, his head spinning.

· · ·

This time, when he rang the bell of Deedee's house, Brownlow answered. Shahid pursued him into the front room and watched him yanking books down from the walls and throwing them into boxes.

"Where's Deedee, then, Dr. Brownlow?" he said hoarsely.

Brownlow, full of booze and agitation, was working rapidly, slamming everything around.

There were books on China and the Soviet Union; travel guides to Eastern Europe—Deedee said that her husband had, for three years, insisted they take their holidays in Albania; as well as books by Marcuse, Miliband, Deutscher, Sartre, Benjamin, E. P. Thompson, Norman O. Brown; books on Marxism and history, Marxism and freedom, Marxism and democracy, and Marxism and Christianity.

There were records which Shahid flipped through, squatting down, appreciative of the lull: Traffic, King Crimson, Nick Drake, Carole King, John Martyn, Iron Stool, the Condemned, Police, Eurythmics.

"Where is she?"

Brownlow said, "I'm getting out of here and never coming back."

"If you know, please tell me."

"Thankfully, I no longer know much about my wife. Maybe she's slipping a few names to the police."

"Shut up. You're a fucker."

This delighted Brownlow. "Why isn't she telling you things?"

Shahid pulled the tab on one of Brownlow's beers and drank half of it off. "It's not like that."

"What a mess, though. If I had your looks, I'd do better than her."

"What are you on about?"

"You're welcome to her, but they expect too much from us, that generation of women. What did all that feminism come down to? A handful of bitter, white, middle-class women taking what they want. Who needs all that argument and aggression?"

"Dr. Brownlow—"

"Shut up! Those women, they'll make you run around like a servant, before stripping you of your money, your pride, every-fucking-thing, as if it were your fault they were put down. Someone like you, who can achieve whatever they want in life, should find some soft, young, blond thing to suckle you—a succession of sweet pushovers. Oh yes. That's what I would do." Brownlow licked his lips.

"Thanks," Shahid said. "Very useful."

He threw himself into a chair. His breathing was ragged; the odor of mango chutney rose from his trousers. Shahid finished the can and dropped it amongst the rubbish on the floor.

Brownlow said, "Who's chasing you?"

"Tell me first why you're taking those books."

"They're mine. Why shouldn't I take them?"

"Maybe we should make a fire, throw them on, and keep warm, eh?"

"Don't take the piss."

Shahid said, "But you're out of it, aren't you? Out of everything."

"How?"

"It's bye-bye. You've been made redundant."

"How d'you know about that? All right, yes. You don't need a weatherman to know which way the wind blows. I'll have plenty of time to read, won't I? History, philosophy, politics, literature. I can't wait."

"Yeah?"

Shahid felt hunted. He couldn't keep still. He went to the window and put his hands on the glass. The room was warm but he could feel the wind seething at the cracks. He strained to sift unusual vibrations from the city clamor. Shahid's fear was of Chad and the others coming round the hedge with machetes, carving knives, hammers.

Brownlow went on, "What is there to teach? How can there be anything when there is no longer any knowledge to transmit?"

Shahid crept through the house to the back door. He checked the garden before jamming a chair under the door handle.

Brownlow was saying, "I will go and live in Italy, even if I'm in a tent. There they know you only have one life and they make the most of it."

Shahid collapsed in the armchair. Uncontrollable tremors ran through him. More than anything, he wanted to go home, lie on his bed, and work out what he might do. But his room, with Riaz next door, was the last place he could go. Unless things improved, he would have to clear out altogether.

Brownlow, with sweat gathering on his forehead, labored noisily, grunting as he pulled gaping holes in the shelves and hauled boxes to the door, muttering to himself, "That's mine. No. It's hers. I'll take it anyway. No, I don't want that one, it's got bad memories . . ." He started throwing books down. "There's no point in taking that one, or that, or that. What will I do with all these useless words?"

Brownlow's relationship with Deedee was over. Maybe they would never see each other again; or if they did, they'd barely say hello.

Shahid thought of what Riaz had once said in the mosque: without a fixed morality, without a framework in which love could flourish—given by God and established in society—love was impossible. Otherwise, people merely rented one another for a period. In this faithless interlude they hoped to obtain pleasure and distraction; they even hoped to discover something which would complete them. And if they didn't soon receive it, they threw the person over and moved on. And on.

In such circumstances what permanence or deep knowing could there be? He and Deedee had plunged into a compelling familiarity. They'd gone out a few times, confessed, and shared the most uninhibited passions people could participate in. Surely, though, their lovemaking was merely an exchange of skills and performances? He did this; she did that. How much did they know about one another? They had been tourists in one another's lives. What prevented her taking other Asian or black lovers? Why shouldn't she? Perhaps she took a different lover each year, using men as Chili had used women, and dismissing them at exam time.

Maybe Deedee would leave him. Perhaps he would stop seeing her. Why not? What was there between them? Perhaps one day, not far in the future, he would be doing what Brownlow was doing now, separating their possessions. And, like him, there'd be another hopeful person waiting in line.

All the same, the thought of Riaz now made Shahid shudder in revulsion. What a dull and unctuous man he was; how limited and encased was his mind, how full of spite and acidity!

"Hey!" said Brownlow, "Give us a hand, will you?"

Not knowing what to do now, and hoping something would occur to him, Shahid began to assist Brownlow. But as he went to move a pile of books, he noticed a shriveled object, like the inside of a cow's ear, perched on a novel.

"Jesus, what's this?" He held the thing up.

Brownlow said, "What d'you think it is?"

"I'm curious to know."

"In fact it's an old aubergine," Brownlow confessed. "Yes. That's it."

"Is it the one?"

"Beg your pardon?"

"Is it something Deedee forgot to marinate? Or is it the miracle?"

Brownlow looked shifty. "Sort of. Well, yes. It is actually—the one."

"What's it doing in your front room?"

"It wasn't bloody deliberate. What would I do with a miracle?"

"You tell me."

"We had to show it to Rudder's colleagues."

"Were they bent over the barrel?"

"You're raving. Are you on drugs? I can guess who gave them to you. You can't say you haven't been getting an education." Brownlow laughed maliciously.

Shahid opened another beer.

Brownlow continued, "The bastards wouldn't exhibit it in the Town Hall without seeing it. And the couple who discovered it were fed up with people tramping through their house. So we took it in and handed it round the other councilmen. When they'd finished smirking, I stuffed it in my pocket without thinking."

"Is he going to exhibit it in the Town Hall beside the Mandela picture?"

"I don't think so."

"How come?"

"Rudder wanted to make concessions. He kept saying he'd support the Islamic school, which is definitely on Riaz's agenda. But with the aubergine he wouldn't go for the full exhibition. 'It isn't the right time,' he kept saying. The book-burning turned them against Riaz. The Nazis and all that."

"How d'you feel about it?"

Brownlow started to stutter. He put his hand over his mouth and bowed forward as if he were going to puke. Eventually he was able to say, "I must admit, the c-c-c-onflagration did stick in my th-th-th-throat."

"But you couldn't resist solidarity?"

"Naturally. What does it matter what I like? I told Rudder that Riaz and his companions are not Nazis. And that your cause has a strange legitimacy."

"Yes. Was Riaz disappointed by Rudder's refusal?"

Brownlow managed to control himself sufficiently to say, "A-after the b-b-burning he knew we were l-l-l-lucky to get into Rudder's office at all. I reckon Rudder won't deal with Riaz for a while. But there was one thing he said."

"What?"

"He's going to say the book's an i-insult and call for it to be withdrawn. Funnily enough, the Conservative leader has agreed to do the same. They both know it'll never happen, of course."

"Why do it, then?"

"Don't be naïve, there's a big Asian community round there. Otherwise Riaz is too r-revolutionary for them—at the moment. To be honest, at the end he seemed a bit sad, as if England would always patronize him. But he isn't going to give up. His work—or time—has barely begun. He's had the right disadvantages, not too many to overwhelm but sufficient to impel him beyond the comfortable people. But he'll have to move into the mainstream and drop the direct action. Did I tell you? He's been invited on television."

"Riaz?"

The producer of a late-night program rang and asked if he'd give his opinion."

"Is he going to do it?"

"He said he'd have to discuss it with the others. But he was flattered."

"Really?"

"His little eyes went all bright. He can't wait. The seduction has begun."

"I'm not certain he'll go that way."

"Aren't you? Why?"

"He'll end up isolated."

"We'll see," said Brownlow. "For those TV people Riaz is a fascinating freak. They've never met anyone like that before. He could end up with his own chat show."

Brownlow went on with his packing but kept stopping to look at Shahid—who was turning the aubergine in his hand—like he wanted to say something. "The thing is, this religion—the superstitions, cults, forms of worship, prayers—some are beautiful, some interesting, all have their purposes. But who'd have imagined they'd survive rationalism? Yet just when you thought God was dead and buried, you realize he was merely awaiting resurrection! Every fucker's discovering some God inside them now. And who am I to challenge this?"

"Exactly. I'd say you're just a weak bastard, Dr. Brownlow."

"Thank you. Are they the fools or am I the fool? Where does that leave me?"

"Where could it leave you?"

"Because, because, you i–idiot, everything I believed has turned into shit. There we were, right up to the end of the seventies, arguing about society after the r–revolution, the nature of the dialectic, the meaning of history. And all the while, as we debated in our journals, it was being taken from us. The British people didn't want e-education, housing, the a-arts, justice, equality . . ."

"Why's that?"

"Because they're a bunch of fucking greedy, myopic c-cunts."

"The working class?"

"Yes!"

"A bunch of cunts?"

"Yes!" Brownlow struggled to contain himself. "No, no, it's more complicated. Very complicated." He was sobbing. "I can't say they've betrayed us—though I think it, I do! It's not true, not true! They've b-b-betrayed themselves!"

He untucked his shirt and wiped it across his drenched face. He threw down his hands, put his head back and, with his lips quivering, angled his thinker's forehead at the ceiling.

"C-c-cut my throat. Please. Lost in more than my fortieth year—no direction home! End me before things get w-w-w-worse!"

Shahid leapt up and rushed to the window. Thinking he'd heard Chad coughing, he concealed himself behind the dusty curtain and peered outside.

"You don't have to plead, Brownlow, the throat-cutters are checking the address right now. They'll be coming up the front path. If you stay in that position, redemption will be on the way!"

Shahid could see no one. But it was dark, and if his enemies did reach him, he'd be trapped here; and Brownlow, gibbering like Gogol's madman awaiting the straitjacket, would hardly provide cover.

"What else is there?" Brownlow moaned, not listening.

"What about love?"

"Love? Why? Have you got love?"

"Me? Oh, I don't know."

"With my wife?"

"Why ask me? I don't know anything either."

"I know. Anyone looking at you during the book protest would have said, that boy is in a pickle."

"Would they?"

"Things are worse for you than for me." Brownlow managed a smirk. "Who are you hiding from? You're fucking petrified. Is it your 'friends'? Do they require you to confess your crimes?"

If Deedee wasn't going to turn up, and Shahid thought this likely, he couldn't stay there any longer. Not that he disliked Brownlow at this moment. He could be intensely irritating, but Shahid was beguiled by his mad honesty.

Shahid checked the street. It seemed all clear. He turned to say good-bye to Brownlow, who was scrabbling through his records.

"Shahid, Shahid, where's 'Hey Jude'? D'you know that record?"

"I've heard it, yes."

"Did you see it when you were poking your nose in? 'His world a little colder,' I want to hear McCartney sing that. I want to hear George and John going 'nah, nah, nah.' I've got to hear it right now!" Brownlow was stooping forward. "That record, not Parlophone, the one with the apple on the label, 'Revolution' B-side, the man in the mac, Paul's face on *Top of the Pops*, everyone singing—" Shahid tiptoed away across the room. "I can see it! Love, freedom, peace, unity! People together—doing their own thing!"

Shahid turned and trotted forward a few steps, as if he were about to take a penalty. He aimed and gave Brownlow a ferocious kick up the arse. Brownlow sprang forward like a diver and sprawled over the books, his head terminating in an empty cardboard box. Thus enclosed, he lay groaning, "But it says everything . . . everything!"

He made no effort to move.

Satisfied, Shahid got his breath back and headed for the door. He stepped out into the raw night but had forgotten something. He returned for the aubergine, stuck it in his pocket, snatched a beer, and got out of there.

J ust in time, my boy."

Chili was standing at the bar. He had shaved, put on his Armani jacket over a white shirt, and composed himself. With a few strokes, he no longer belonged in the Morlock. The barman inquired if he had a funeral to attend. "Our customers frequently drop dead," he said. "If they're not pleasing Her Majesty in jail. Don't tell me another one's gone?"

"Not today, my man. I'm making a visit with my brother here. I think we can deal with it, too." Chili looked at Shahid as if he were his accomplice on a tricky assignment. "Not my first appointment, either. It's been busy, busy, busy."

Two old men had fallen to the floor, pushing over a table. They were wrestling crazily and taking gummy bites at one another's faces like frolicking dogs. In another corner, where a man was trying to barter socks and watches from a suitcase, a dispute had begun.

Strapper considered this indifferently. His eyelids were dropped and weary, but behind them the electric eyes were scatting beyond his control. He was angry and feverishly bored in his soul with a pitiless energy, whereas his mates in the pub were quiescent, almost contented, with many whispering schemes going.

He said, "We ain't going too far, are we?"

"Pal, you ain't going nowhere," Chili replied. "This is business."

"Great—you an' me are in business."

Chili turned to Shahid. "I took Strapper to the rehab this morning. But even they wouldn't take the bastard."

"Why was that?"

"Too stoned. I exploded at them, you fuckers, he's supposed to be stoned, we wouldn't be here otherwise and nor would you! Now cure him!"

"What did they say?"

" 'Fuck off before we call the law.' And what had you had, Strapper?" Chili poked Strapper. "Strapper, what have you ingested, man?"

"Only two Es, a few drinks, a spliff, a crack pipe, and a smack in the mouth in the back of a police van."

"Right," said Chili. He looked Shahid over. "Tuck your shirt in. You been fighting?" Chili finished grooming his hair and dropped the comb. Strapper bent over and handed it to Chili. Getting up, he saw that Shahid had noticed. He reddened and scowled. Chili said, "Got money?"

"Don't keep asking," said Shahid. "I'm looking for Deedee right now. I've got to find her. And I've got a lot of other things to think about."

"She hasn't been in here."

"But she's disappeared!"

"Never chase women. They'll come to you. They're brought up to be romantic and all." Chili turned to the barman, "My man, a pint of lager and a large whiskey on the side. Anything for you?"

"No."

Chili tipped the whiskey into the beer and drank it. While Shahid paid, Chili informed Strapper, "We'll be back."

Strapper hopped down from his stool and planted himself in front of Chili. "No, you won't. It's the big deal you been on about! It's happening now! And you're shoving me out!"

Chili took Strapper's limp hand and attempted to shake it. "I'll be back. Listen, we'll get ourselves together, Strap. This is not talk." He turned to his brother. "Forward!"

Strapper stood at the pub door and howled down the street after them. "It's all a lot of fucking mouth from a dirty druggie!"

"You wait there!" Chili shouted. His car was still "loaned" to the man, so they had to get the bus to Zulma's. "What did he call me?"

"A dirty druggie."

"Fucking Christ." Chili seemed to be waiting for Shahid to say it wasn't true. "That Strapper's becoming a bloody responsibility. But I can't just throw him over." They sat at the front on the top deck, as they'd loved to do when they were kids. "Everyone's done that to him. But he's driving me crazy. That's why I'm trying to install the bastard in the rehab. Get him off my back."

In the lift of Zulma's block Chili combed his hair again, held his palm over his mouth and blew into it. Suddenly he looked at Shahid in panic.

"I'm not slurring my words, am I?"

"What did you say?"

"Am I slurring?"

"Not that much."

"Sure?"

"What?"

On reaching Zulma's floor, instead of walking up the corridor, Chili headed for the stairs and started down them, saying, "I've come over gloomy," as he went.

"Chili, if you don't go in now," Shahid yelled behind him, "I'm leaving. I got a lot to sort out."

He came back. "OK, OK. But you've got to ask her for a few quid."

"You want Zulma to give us money?"

"A few pounds. I can't ask her. Or—maybe I can. No. It's not that I care if she hates me. But she'll start abusing me and I don't want you to be upset. You better be in charge of financial matters."

"Let's see how things go first," Shahid said doubtfully. "She might kick us out on our arses."

"You're fucking right. It could be a terrible experience. I'm telling you, there's no way I'm going in there without being in the mood."

Shahid saw the kind of "mood" he meant. He held the plastic bats and a ball they'd bought on the way while Chili spooned coke up his nose. Though his hand was shaking, he didn't lose a grain. All his life Shahid had known his brother and yet had little idea how Chili could have brought these disasters on himself. He realized, though, watching him, that he was being taught a lesson in how not to live.

They were about to move on when Chili started rubbing his nose and examining his fingers. "Why are you looking at me like that? There're no blood clots, are there?"

"Stop this!"

"Just tell me if I'm going to be bleeding in front of my wife! That would be wonderful, wouldn't it?"

"Oh, God, I think I'm losing my mind!"

Chili rang the bell. Then he propelled his brother into the flat ahead of him. "Everyone's in the same position," he said with replenished confidence. "No one died of self-pity."

Zulma stood there, mocking and exquisite in her lime-green sari, gold bangles, and lustrous lipstick.

Shahid tried to pull himself together. "How you doing, Zulma?"

She gave her husband a brief but keen examination. Her voice tinged with disappointment, she said, "You still look like a ruffian."

Chili plucked a piece of cotton from his jacket and let it fall onto the carpet. He picked up Safire and kissed her fervently. "It's only this princess I've come to see."

Zulma said, "I'm sure."

He took the bats from Shahid and gave them to Safire. "A present."

"Is that all, you blighter?" said Zulma. "Not long ago you were practically burning money."

"Those days every prick went mad."

"Particularly you."

"Zulma, yes! We agree on something!" said Chili heatedly. Shahid had hoped he would curb himself, but seeing Zulma hadn't quelled him. "How we adored money. It was the superiority, too! We loved having what the others didn't. You know what we wanted to do to them?"

"What?" Shahid said, as Zulma wasn't going to encourage him.

"We wanted to crush them! Yes! For laziness, for failure, for poverty! What had they ever done to us? And why were we too mentally stupid to understand how quickly that boom-time would explode into oblivion? Only the exceptionally shrewd came out of it with gold. We couldn't grasp the rhythms."

Zulma looked as though she preferred her husband disordered to Morlock-analytical. She made an amused, relieved smile: how right she'd been to rid herself of him!

"We ignored the certain disaster ahead of us!"

Zulma nodded across at Shahid, who was gripping the table for fear of being sucked into the atmosphere. The room was drifting, its angles unsteady, its distances wayward.

"How are you?"

Everything began to warp and wave like an Escher drawing. All he could hope for was to be standing upright.

"Not too bad, Zulma. A little . . . unsettled by recent events."

He knew the molten floor was about to pull apart like an open wound: cripples, maniacs, torture-victims, and hymn-singing believers, mutated into screaming insects, would foam from the hole and fill everyone's mouths until they suffocated.

"Made new friends?"

"Pardon?"

Zulma turned to Chili. "Is he OK?"

Chili bellowed, "Shahid!"

"I'm worried about him," Zulma said. "He looks about ten minutes from death."

Chili himself was so wired he was almost jogging. Shahid was surprised to see his brother halt at each wall. In every respect Chili lacked ballast; Shahid expected to see a Chili-shaped hole at the end of the room, the lights extinguished, a wall having crumbled, a black wind blowing through, the curtains sucking in and out.

Chili squinted at his brother. "Five minutes from death. But don't worry about that kid, I've taken him into my care, his health is going to improve no end."

"Is that how you take care of your family—by handing them over to religious lunatics?"

"You know, I'll be very candid with you. I don't blame those human beings you call lunatics."

"What tosh, Chili."

"Zulma, they've got something to believe in, to lean on! It gets them through the night. If we believed in something, we would be happier! It is us who have the lack!"

"What nonsense!"

"Why are you going back home, then?" Chili said. "There the lunatics are running the asylum. There is nothing for anyone with a free mind!"

She crouched and looked through a camera at Chili. He covered his face. "I am going to learn photography properly. You know I have always been keen." She continued more quietly: "Some other girlfriends and I, we're going to start a paper, a journal. For women, called *The Woman's World.*"

"Don't be a bloody fool!"

She turned to Shahid, who was attempting an experimental step away from the table but was finding the open spaces too desolate.

"That's the most encouragement he's ever given me." She tapped her forehead. "He could never accept that I've got something up here." She scrutinized Chili. "But there's nothing you can say to smash me up now."

"Zulma, I'm only saying, who will pay for this?"

"Our fathers, brothers, and husbands, of course. They are financing our little indulgence. At the beginning."

Chili wasn't able to disapprove. "Good thinking, as usual, Zulma. What a fabulous woman you are, really! It'll be babies and weddings and fashion and all?"

"You know what we girls are like, we never think about anything else. But there will be other issues, too, discussed."

She had obviously thought about this; there was more to it than she wanted to say.

Chili said, "You don't mean women's concerns—abortion, politics and freedom, the hijab and all?" Zulma bit her lip and gave an indiscernible nod. "Don't be a bloody fool, Zulma. You can't take them on. They'll crucify you in jail and I'll have to come and drag you out. Think what it'll cost me!"

Zulma turned away from her husband. The child, happy and tense at the same time, watched her parents arguing.

Shahid managed to propel himself into the bedroom, where Zulma's cases were half packed. Her passport and tickets lay on the bed. He could hear her and Chili arguing in the next room.

Shahid picked up the receiver and hunted through his pockets for a number. The phone rang in Hyacinth's flat for a long time before a soft voice answered. It had been a good guess. She gave him directions and reminded him of the address. He would meet Deedee there as soon as he could.

When he came out, Safire was giving Chili two of her drawings and an egg carton with pipe cleaners attached to it.

"It's a grasshopper," she explained. "But I'm going to paint it yellow tomorrow. Are you coming with us?"

"Not this time, darling. Your daddy will be waiting for you to come back."

Zulma picked something up off the floor and made a face. "Good Lord, Chili, what is this repulsive thing?"

Chili moved toward it.

Shahid snatched at it. "Safire must have pulled it out of my pocket."

Zulma held on to it. "But what is it?"

"I think it's an old aubergine," Shahid said. "But it could be something else."

"And you want it?"

"If you don't mind."

Zulma handed it to him, turned away and gave a dry laugh. "Your brother thinks he's walking around with an old aubergine in his pocket. What does that say, Chili?"

Chili turned on Shahid. "What you think you carrying, bro? You can't smoke that."

"I'm not going to smoke it."

"Hand it here for safekeeping."

"Leave me alone!"

"Bloody hell." Zulma sighed.

Inexplicably, the brothers struggled over the vegetable. Finally they stood head to head, puffing, ready to throw punches.

"What would your father say?" she said. "I'm out of this family!"

Chili picked up Safire for the last time and kissed her. Safire was rubbing her cheek. There was a stillness in the room. The little girl said, "Let's play hide."

Chili put her down and glanced at Zulma. "I think daddy has got to go. My little naughty. My favorite."

"Just once," Safire said. "And I'm not naughty—you are." She hid behind the sofa.

Shahid realized that Chili was nodding at him encouragingly.

"Zulma," Shahid said. "You haven't got a few pounds, have you?"

"For what, darling?"

"The tube . . . and books. I'm a bit short at the moment."

"I'm only carrying rupees now. But there is a method of obtaining money you could try."

Chili said interestingly, "What's that?"

"Working."

"Oh, Zulma, wife, wife." Chili fell on to his knees and crawled toward her. "I love you, baby, particularly when you hurt me. Give us something. I'll do anything, but don't go away!" As she shuffled backward he grabbed her ankles and licked her toes. Zulma couldn't stop herself; she screamed.

Suddenly Jump was standing in the kitchen doorway, wearing an apron and shaking a wooden spoon.

Chili was saying, "Stay! Let me stay with you forever!"

"I say!" cried Jump. On all fours Chili looked up at him in bafflement. "What is this? Is that him down there?"

"Yes." Zulma picked up Safire and retreated behind the table.

"Back off!" Jump took a hesitant step toward the brothers. "Get back, Mr. Muhammadan! Both of you terrorists! Leave us decent people alone!"

Chili reached into his jacket pocket. Right away Shahid pulled his bewildered brother to his feet, and hustled him to the door.

Chili pointed at Jump. "What is that?"

"Don't think about it," said Shahid.

"Look after him," Zulma said.

"Papa!" cried Safire.

"Who the fuck is that freak?" Chili said.

"Bye, Zulma. We'll be in touch. Nice to see you."

"You OK, Chili? Chili!"

"Holding up."

"Got your knife?"

Chili gave him a quizzical look before slapping his jacket. "Naturally. No one walks round London unarmed, do they?"

He put his hand into his pocket. It reassured Shahid that Chili would comfort him by providing a glimpse of the stabber. Instead, though, Chili pulled out the Marlboro packet which contained his coke envelope, single-edged blade, and rolled dollar bill.

"Don't do that here. This is Knightsbridge!"

"All the better."

Shahid thrust him toward a shop entrance.

"In there—and hurry!"

He scrutinized the foggy, deserted street for passersby and police while Chili crouched, inhaled his grains, stood up with a satisfied sniff and a backhanded swipe of his nose, and flung down the paper envelope. Suddenly the shop alarm, above their heads, erupted into life, vibrating and clanging. Shahid started to drag Chili away. But before he would budge, Chili insisted on groping in the gutter for the screwed-up, discarded wrapper, which he inspected thoroughly, and stuck in his jacket pocket.

At last, to Shahid's relief, they were walking fast.

"Where we going?" asked Chili.

"You're not leaving me tonight."

"Little brother, you're shaking. Who's looking for you? If you tell me, I can sort them out. Unless it's the police."

"What?"

"Thought so," Chili muttered, hurrying forward. "They're after both of us. Keep a lookout for the plainclothes." He put his head back. "The bastards are everywhere, wearing raincoats but not hats."

"Chili, I beg you to stay right by me tonight."

"No problem." Shahid was about to thank his brother when Chili added, looking desperately uneasy, "Thing is, boy, I'm right out of toot here."

"Give up that shit, Chili! What would Papa say if he knew you were addicted to the powder?"

"Addicted?"

"Yes."

"You might be right. Maybe addict's my name now. Tell you what, I'll throw away my drug when you do the same."

"What drug am I using?"

"Zulma named it right. The religion. You got too deep in with those guys. They looking for you now?"

"I s'pose they are."

"And you just started at that college." Chili seized Shahid's arm. "You know, seeing baba Safire today made me want to be free. I could have wept for her." He paused, struggling with his thoughts. "And for myself. And for everything that's gone wrong, to tell you the truth."

"That's something."

"Yeah. Brother, don't worry, I won't desert you. But tonight I'm gonna need Strapper, too." Chili lit a cigarette, ran his jittery fingers over a Mercedes convertible, and observed the street, as if his enemies might appear from any direction. "Is that why Zulma hates me? Did you see that jerk-off in the apron she's got there? I couldn't believe it. But maybe . . . maybe he gives her things I can't."

"Maybe. He's got a stately home."

"Yeah? Did she say when she's coming back?"

"It'll be a few months."

"At least, don't you think? Shahid, I'm desperate. Without the drug I'm confused and can't think about anything else. If I can't think, I can't believe the future holds any peace of mind for me. Five minutes silence in the head is all I want! If only the noises would leave me alone!" He whispered, "Shahid, there's nowhere else I can turn. Strapper's a well-connected boy."

"I had no idea he had so much going for him."

Shahid started down the steps of the Knightsbridge tube.

Chili asked meekly, but persistently, "Are we gonna see Strapper later?"

"Yes, yes. But someone else first."

"Who?"

"You'll see."

Shahid and Chili ran down the steps into the basement. Shahid rapped on the window, softly at first but then harder, until he was slapping the pane with his flat hand. Still no one appeared. He called her name repeatedly.

Chili skipped about, stamping his feet and chewing his lip. "Let's go. Maybe she's at her house. We can check it later."

"I went round and she's not there. Come on, Deedee! Chili, she's got to be somewhere!"

Shahid was about to turn away when Chili pointed. "Look, there!"

A hand tugged at the corner of the curtain. Shahid recognized her rings and almost shouted her name.

Not acknowledging either of them, she opened the gate cautiously. She locked it behind them, and then the door, ensuring both were secure. Shahid had never seen her look so fragile. He brushed her pale cheek with his lips, but she wouldn't touch him.

She had been sitting on the sofa in the basement where she and Shahid had gone to make love for the first time. They had laughed at everything, talked and dressed up until dawn, and in the morning gone out for breakfast. Now the flat was cold, the heating broken. Her coat was around her shoulders. She resumed her place and rocked herself jerkily, grasping her knees. Planted around her were three full shopping bags.

"I've been looking everywhere for you," he said. "Are you OK?"

She shook her head.

They were all in disturbed moods. The atmosphere was quiet but feverish; it inclined Chili to bolt into the kitchen, to "wash his hands and put the kettle on." Deedee bit her nails, sighed, and crossed and recrossed her legs. Shahid sank down at the other end of the sofa, grateful to be alone with her.

He leaned over and stroked her arm. "Why don't we stay here?"

She started in alarm. "When?"

"Just tonight. Chili can sleep out here. You and I—we can talk."

"What for? It's what people do, not what they say, that you better look to. That's what I'm going to be doing."

He hadn't seen her so uneasy; her trust in him was destroyed.

"In the morning we'll feel better," he said. "We could go out for breakfast. What d'you say?"

He reached for her once more. She jumped up and attempted to put her coat on. But immediately she was lunging agitatedly at the cloth as if to tear through it, unable to locate the arms.

"I need to be in my place, and in my own bed. Today has been very bad. What the fuck was my husband doing with that book on a pole? Did you see that arsehole cheering?" Angrily she wrapped the coat around herself again and stood there, securing it with her arms crossed. "Didn't you go out to buy the pole?"

"I did! Let's not think about it now!"

"No? Let's just forget it, particularly when you fucking lied to me about what it was for?"

"Deedee—"

"You lied to my face, didn't you?"

"For now I'm trying to say there's good reason to stay here."

She was shouting huskily, "No, there isn't!"

"There is."

"What is it?"

"Chad and the others know where you live."

"Why? How d'you know?" She gaped at him. "Is that what they said? Have you seen them?"

"Yes. After they burned the book. They don't like either of us."

"How have you upset them? Didn't you help them burn it?"

"No. I did something bad to Riaz."

"What?"

"I . . . rewrote some of his poetry."

"You did? When?"

"While typing it."

"But why?"

"I didn't mean to. I just didn't like it the way it was. I was going to change it back, but didn't have time."

"My God." She gave a sudden laugh. "That's another thing you didn't tell me."

"It was gradual."

"And now they're planning to call on us?"

"Deedee, they could easily work one another up. The group is paranoid, they need constant action to keep together."

"I'll call the police."

"You hate them."

"Who cares?"

"Was it you who called them to the college?"

"Yes." There was a noise from the kitchen. Chili appeared to be talking to himself. Deedee continued, "I'm more concerned about you. Have you broken with your great friends?"

"Yes, yes."

"You said that before. But how can you go back to your room, then?"

"You're right. I know it. I can't go back."

"You'd better stay with me."

The idea sank him. He didn't want his life to change so much; he didn't want to be pushed into her arms.

"You live next door to Riaz. What else can you do?"

"Give me a chance to think."

"Fine."

She went into the kitchen to investigate Chili. Shahid checked the window. He sat down; he walked about the room; he wanted to laugh hysterically; he wanted his father. Then he went into the kitchen.

"Your brother's sniffed out a vodka bottle," Deedee said. "The wretch is welcome to it. But I'll have to pay Hyacinth." Chili was leaning back against the sink with the bottle at his lips. Between gulps he dragged at his cigarette. "He wants to kiss me, too. He wants to put my tits in his mouth."

"You know me," Chili said. "It's always worth trying."

Shahid said, "Only if you want to disgust people."

"What's disgusting? I'm lonely, all right? Tonight I wanted a human touch. To feel the warm skin. Is that too much to ask?"

Shahid smirked.

"Don't think you're better than me, neither. Running away from something, instead of fighting." Chili stuck the bottle under his jacket and checked his knife. "We staying or going?"

"Deedee?"

"We've got to get out of here."

"Good," said Chili. "A bit of fresh air, eh?"

It was sleeting. No one sensible was outside. The city was drenched and slimy, like the inside of an aquarium. They could barely see ten yards ahead. The three of them bumbled and lurched through the haze like ghosts, each carrying a bag of shopping. Deedee was between them, holding Chili's arm now. Despite everything, Shahid and Deedee were reassured by his presence. Shahid still had some odd younger-brother faith in him which Deedee seemed to sense. At last they scrambled on a bus.

Chili pushed at the door of the Morlock and they followed him in. The place was filling up. A snowstorm wouldn't deter the regulars. What else would they do? The boy stood at his decks, boxes of records around him. A couple of girls were dancing in the middle of the floor.

The atmosphere gladdened Chili. He ordered drinks and inquired after Strapper. The barman didn't want to tell them anything, "on principle," he always said.

"The principle of being a bastard, presumably," Deedee remarked.

Chili bought him a drink. He said that some lads had called in for Strapper.

"Which boys?"

"Asians. And the Pakis don't drink, only work. Never seen them before, either."

"Did he go with them?" Shahid asked.

"Yep."

"Willingly?"

The man shrugged.

"And they haven't been back?"

"No."

They finished their drinks quickly and picked up a minicab on the street.

Deedee screamed, "Oh, my God, what's happened?"

"It's OK," Shahid said.

She thought Chad and the others had broken in. The place looked torn apart: the furniture had been shoved out of place; books and records were scattered everywhere, along with empty cans, newspaper clippings and Deedee's things. The sour odor of spilled booze stank in the room. But "Hey Jude" was on repeat. So it was only Brownlow who'd wrecked the place, and he'd flung everything around but left most things behind.

All the same, picking through the jumble, she blazed with anger. Had he been there, she'd have murdered him, murdered her mistake.

"But I married him, didn't I?"

"You left the bastard, too."

"When I'm low, like now, remind me to give myself credit for that."

Chili stood there with the vodka bottle in his hand. He looked spent. "All right if I lie down?"

"Do what you like."

He took his bottle to the bottom of the stairs and started to climb up.

Shahid went to him. "Will you make sure all the doors are locked? Anything could happen, you know."

"Sure," Chili agreed.

"At least Brownlow's fucked off for good," Shahid said, when he'd gone.

He went to the window and pulled the curtains. He listened to the night. He was glad to be alone with her.

She sank down in the debris and tried to pull him down with her, saying, "At least I've got you. Touch me. Hold me all the time."

"Not now."

"What?"

"Deedee, don't pull me."

"All my confidence has gone."

"Everything is fucked for me, too!"

"Let's hold one another. Is that too much?"

"Leave me alone."

"Fine."

She lay apart from him, her lips half open, fretfully passing her hand over her forehead. After a while she forced herself to get up.

She said, "I wanted to eat with you tonight. I think we still should, don't you? Or do you want to go?"

"I want to be here."

She went into the kitchen, put the lights and radio on, and slowly unpacked the shopping. The concentration calmed her and she breathed better. She had a big tin of good olive oil and she poured a little into a saucer for him; he sat tearing up bread and soaking it in the oil. They didn't say much, but she gave him cooking instructions. She prepared grilled mackerel in a tikka sauce with fresh coriander. There were new potatoes, and an avocado and mint salad in a big transparent bowl.

She asked him to clear the table and lay out a clean tablecloth. He put out linen napkins, lit the candles, and turned off the overhead light. He scraped the butter into a dish, set out proper glasses, and opened and poured the wine. By now the kitchen was warm and smelled good. The radio played a song they liked.

She took more bread out of the oven and put it on the table. They were feeling amiable enough to raise a toast.

"Good luck, you know," she said.

"Right!"

They saw, at the same time, the form at the window. Neither of them moved. They stared into the shadows, thinking they were stoned and it was a cat, unable to conceive of this happening now.

Shahid put down his glass and crept out into the hall. He was about to call to Chili. The letter-box rattled. "It's only me, Strapper the strap," a voice yelled through the opening. "Official visit, man."

Shahid immediately regretted opening the door. Strapper strolled through into the living room, putting his feet gingerly in front of him, as if he wasn't sure they'd take his weight. He didn't look good. A cheekbone was grazed; his clothes were messed up. He looked as if he'd been rolled around on the floor somewhere.

Shahid had no choice but to follow him.

"I thought you were with your old pal Trevor," he said, unable to conceal his annoyance.

Strapper turned on him, looking surprised. "How d'you know that? Anyway, he was more friendly to me than most people. Chad's a religious type, he understand the outcasts an' pity the poor people. He see everything from underneath. You just wanna be white and forget your own." He suddenly shouted, "You and your bro just wanna shag the white bitches! That why he don't go for you no more. He gave you a good chance, didn't he?"

"Mind your own business."

"What's made him want to kill you?"

"Does he want that?"

"You gonna get a hard lesson taught you."

"I wish I hadn't let you in."

"How were you gonna keep me out, cunt? Hey, don't touch me, man."

"Get out of here."

"I wouldn't get heavy," Strapper warned, as if he were concealing information which provided him with protection. "Thing is, brown boy, your Chili owes me money. Where's he hiding round here?" He looked at Deedee, who had come in. "Lady, you got my mate?"

"We're about to eat."

Strapper rubbed his stomach. "Feeding the little student boyfriend, eh?" He sneered at Shahid. "Mummy's cooking always tastiest."

She said wearily, "I'll make you a sandwich. You can bugger off and eat it on the street, right?"

Strapper walked everywhere in the room except the doorway. He became self-pitying. "Stick your sandwich up your arse. How d'you think it feels, being rejected all the time?"

She watched him evenly. "Pretty terrible."

"You really liked me the other night in the Morlock. But then you wanted to get high, Miss Teacher. By the way, why are smart people so untidy? Too busy thinkin' about the workers' revolution, or hasn't the cleaning lady been in today?"

"Can't you give us some peace?"

Strapper sank a hand into his hair and started to pull. It took him some time, but he wrested a clump out and threw it down.

He said, "I might still come and live here, though. Plenty of room. Somewhere middle-class 'n' poncy would suit my arse right now."

"You want a place like this? Get a job, then," Shahid said. "Doing a bit of archaeology. Then you can buy your—"

"I've warned you, cunt." Strapper gave him a look of unrestrained hatred. "An' I want you to give me a job—right now."

Deedee said, "Take your hair and the rest of you outside."

"The brothers burned the book, right?"

Neither Deedee nor Shahid said anything.

"An' she didn't like it. Informed the law on them. You an' your books. Funny how you people get into more of a state about a book than about the suffering people."

"You're making me suffer now, Strapper."

"All right, I'm off. But I like to be asked nicely. I'm the sexually abused underprivileged, right? But I'm still a 'person,' aren't I?"

"Yeah, yeah." Deedee said to Shahid, "I'll make the sandwich and take a shower. Then we can eat."

"OK."

Left alone with Shahid, Strapper continued to walk about, picking up objects. He opened a small Indian box which contained some grass. This put him in a better frame of mind—Shahid had noticed how nervous he seemed—and he murmured confidentially, as if what he had just said meant nothing, "I'll fuck off after me draw."

He started rolling the joint. Shahid went into the kitchen to inform Deedee. When he went back out Strapper was holding open the front door, his mouth curled in savage jubilation.

"All here and all clear!" he shouted in a military voice.

Sadiq and Hat were standing there.

"You bastard!" Shahid screamed at Strapper.

Behind the other two Chad ran up the front path and blocked the doorway. What he saw of the situation pleased him.

"Gotcha, and not too late," he said. "There's the scum, as expected—holed up with his bitch. So obvious. Now brothers, hold on to the spy, the infidel!"

Sadiq made a grab at Shahid's arm. Shahid pulled away but Sadiq dug his nails into him.

"Hat—now!" Chad said.

Shahid looked at Hat, who seemed dazed. He knew he'd just received an order and wanted, up to a point, to obey. He grabbed Shahid's hand and held it firmly. Chad pushed further into the hall. Behind him came others, Tariq and Tahira.

Chad took hold of Shahid and threw him back against the wall, winding him and smacking his head. Then he turned him and held him from behind, offering him to Hat.

"Go on." Chad was shaking with anger now. "Go on!"

Hat knew what Chad was asking him to do but he was scared. He blurted out, "But my papa's out looking for me!"

"Your father?" Chad said. "What's he got to do with this?"

"But I can't stay on."

"Beat him!" Chad shouted. "This idiot hates us and he hates God! Give Satan one!"

Sadiq saw Hat's indecision and took a step back and gave Shahid a backhander across the face. "Good!" he shouted as Shahid's mouth bled. Chad jabbed Shahid in the kidneys. "The evil spirit has gone down!"

As Shahid staggered, Chad kicked him. Deedee ran out.

"Leave him!"

With his big arm Chad barred her way. "He belongs to us. Let us take him, bitch, and there'll be no trouble for you!"

Shahid bent over in pain, almost passing out. Sadiq began dragging him toward the door, saying, "We're going to deal with the spy. He has deceived and spat on his own people. He has wallowed in filth."

Deedee pushed past Chad and grabbed Shahid's other arm. He was pulled between them. "Let go of him!"

"Evil has to be returned for evil. Is that so hard to understand?"

"Very religious, Mr. Trevor—" she said.

"Don't use that name on me! That ain't my true identity!"

Chad raised his hand to strike her. She would be easy to hit. But it would be an irrevocable step. She knew it: she flinched but barely moved. He knew it too.

Riaz, accompanied by another brother, hurried in with snow in his hair, carrying his briefcase, as if he were late for a meeting. He looked around in astonishment.

"This is him," Chad said unnecessarily, pointing at the gasping Shahid. "He is sick, sick, sick as you told us."

"And more sick now," said Sadiq, as Shahid retched.

"We've captured both of them!" Chad was clearly pleased to have achieved this for Riaz.

Riaz's companions waited. He looked around at everyone. He was standing rigidly still—petrified; even his eyes didn't blink, afraid that any movement would give him away.

"What now, brother?" Chad asked him with desperate, deferential urging. "Which action to take immediately?" Riaz's teeth, though, seemed to be grinding. "Which step do you want? Shall we take him away?"

"Or finish him here?" Sadiq said.

"Surely we must hurry!"

But Hat was pointing up the stairs with his mouth open as if he'd seen the devil.

"Brothers!"

They looked at him.

"It's that maniac!"

Chili had passed out at the top of the stairs, bottle in hand. But the commotion had disturbed him. He was not only coming round, but he was pulling himself up until he stood there, sturdy legs apart.

He accepted Hat's compliment. "That's right." He smoothed down his hair, flattened his collar, and practiced a few swishing passes with the knife, like a film star preparing for a dueling scene. "Hello, all."

Slowly he came down the stairs, slapping the banister as he proceeded, a leering smile on his lips. The drug of adrenaline was running high in him.

He said, "Robert De Niro's waiting."

"Ha, ha, ha! Right!" Chad brandished himself like a street fighter. He appeared to know—from the old days, presumably—how to do this. "Here we go."

"Yeah?" Chili seemed cheered up by the readiness of his opponents. "Awright."

Chad said to the others, "Ready?"

Sadiq put up his fists. Riaz stood in the same position, saying and doing nothing, eyes darting.

Just then Strapper ran out of the living room and did a furious dance in front of them.

"It's going up, it's going up! Fuck everything! Fuck you all!"

Deedee shouted, "What have you done?"

"It's coming down, you cunts! All right, Chad, that what you wanted?"

"What is this?" said Riaz at last.

Deedee hurled herself into the living room, with the others following her. The bottom of the curtains were licked by flames where Strapper had started a fire.

She ran at the curtains, grabbing them, ripping them from the rail, and stamping on the smoldering fabric. Strapper was yelling, "Burn, burn, ya bastards!"

In the hall Sadiq continued to hold on to Shahid as the others went to see what was going on. Sadiq didn't realize then how close Chili was to him, or how vicious Chili liked to be. He smacked Sadiq down with the side of his hand before seizing him, kneeing him in the balls, and hurling him out into the street. Slamming the door, he wiped his hands on his trousers.

"Who's next?"

In the living room, where Deedee was extinguishing the fire, Chili pulled Riaz to him with one vicious yank. With one arm across his chest, he held the knife at his throat.

"Fuck off," he ordered the others. "Leave my brother, otherwise this brother gets his gullet split."

Riaz had a terrible cringe on his face; his eyes flickered as if everything had inexplicably gone dark and the pain had already begun. Otherwise, with his head snapped back, he kept rigid, for fear Chili would accidentally cut him.

"Go, go," he muttered to the others, barely moving his lips.

"Leave him!" Chad told Chili. "Or you get it!"

Chili laughed. Chad took a brave step forward. Without hesitation Chili touched Riaz with the knife. A crimson thread appeared. Riaz stabbed an ink-spotted finger to himself and stared at the blood. It was unbearable for Chad but he held back.

"And get that fucking shirt off!" Chili instructed Riaz. "I don't know how you got it, man, but I want it back. D'you deny it's mine?"

Riaz looked at Chad. "How . . .?"

Chad mumbled gloomily, "It his."

"Well done, Chad," murmured Hat.

Riaz was forced to undo his jacket and hand it to Hat. Then, looking disbelievingly at the others, he began to unbutton his shirt.

"Hurry!" Chili said.

Finally he removed it; his body was wan and skinny. He had no choice but to put the jacket on over his bare torso.

"Go!"

Chad was reluctant to move.

"Fuck off, fat man!" ordered Chili. "Then I will release this one!"

"There are hundreds like us, hundreds and thousands!" Chad shouted with a wave of his arms, as they all left the room.

"Bring them to me!" roared Chili.

Once the others were outside, Chili pitched Riaz into the front garden and flung his briefcase out behind him.

C H A P T E R

22

C hili and Strapper wanted to get off. They were standing impatiently by the door, sharing Deedee's dope. Strapper's eyes considered the floor, ceiling, and walls with unusual interest; he couldn't look at Shahid. Shahid was about to berate him, but Chili shook his head.

"Wait outside, you," Shahid said.

Strapper was happy to get out. Shahid embraced his brother; Chili held and kissed him.

"Thanks, you know, for saving my balls."

"Impressed? Cool entrance down the stairs, eh? Except who'll believe me? Someone should have videoed it."

"The knife was good."

"Wasn't it? But I should have sliced his nose open or cut my initials on it—there'd be room enough—so he wouldn't forget me. You OK now?"

"Sore all over."

"You will be."

Shahid said, "Going somewhere?"

Chili nodded.

"With Strapper?"

"Yeah."

"After what he did?"
Chili shrugged. "Just tonight. Will you talk to Mum for me?"
"About what?"
"Say I'm OK? Say I'm getting better. You know what to do."
"I'll do it."
"Give me your hand, brother."

Everyone had gone. At last Shahid
and Deedee were alone. They didn't feel like eating now, but
worked in silence, unpacking and picking up the books, before replacing them on the shelves. They cleared, dusted, and vacuumed
the room. It took a couple of hours to recover the semblance of order, but the effort was therapeutic. With glances and encouraging
smiles, they soothed one another.

Before they'd finished, Shahid went into the kitchen to fetch a
bottle of water. He saw Hat at the high window behind the sink,
knocking a coin on the glass. Shahid was about to call to Deedee,
but she was distressed enough. As they cleaned, her eyes would
close even as she stood up, and then would spring open again, staring around in terror.

Shahid pulled a long knife from the kitchen drawer. He clambered on to the draining board and opened the window a little.
Hat was jumping up and down, trying to talk through the crack.

"Will you listen if I say something?"
"What for?"
"Please, Shahid."

Shahid went and shut the kitchen door so Deedee wouldn't
hear him.

He said to Hat, "Why should I trust you?"
"But I'm sorry. I trying to say I sorry about what happened."
"Oh yeah," Shahid was about to shut the window.
"But yes, yes!" Hat shouted. "If only you'd listen! There's no one
else—I alone!" Shahid didn't want to give up on Hat. He opened
the window further but pointed the knife at him. Hat said, "Be-

cause Allah is forgiving and merciful, I will only show love and consideration for others. I ashamed of what they did."

"Why?"

"Whatever you done, it not my place to condemn another person. Only God can do that. I was wrong to put myself in that position, as if I never done wrong things. I hope you don't turn away from God."

"To tell you the truth, Hat—"

"Yes?"

"I'm sick of being bossed around, whether by Riaz or Chad or God himself. I can't be limited when there is everything to learn and read and discover. And you . . ."

"What about me?"

"Your accountancy studies. You'll regret it if you don't pass." Shahid could feel Hat listening in the darkness. "Surely, brother, there must be more to living than swallowing one old book? What men and women do, and the things they make, must be more interesting than anything that God is supposed to do?"

"I disagree," Hat said. "But I get what you say. I said what I have to." He dropped to the ground and stumbled away through the bushes.

Shahid called, "Where are you going?"

"To paradise."

"Tonight?"

"There is other business to be done."

"What business?"

Hat stood there in the garden and shrugged.

"There's something I want to give you," Shahid said. "Will you stay there?"

He fetched the aubergine from his coat pocket, explained how he'd got it, and, wrapping it in a piece of newspaper, dropped it through the window into Hat's hands.

"Can I come to the restaurant? Could we talk?" Shahid asked. "Would that be all right?"

"Any time. And, please, forgive me," said Hat from the street.

"Forgive all of us and may there be mercy!"

"Yes, yes!" shouted Shahid after him, watching him until he disappeared.

Shahid and Deedee sat down to eat some pasta. They drank two bottles of wine and decided to go to bed. Shahid felt relieved and triumphant; despite everything, he had come through and never learned so much before. But Deedee looked troubled and couldn't keep still. She said her body but not her mind felt hysterical; it would be impossible for her to sleep. After watching TV for a while, he suggested they try to walk off their nervous energy. Maybe outside they would be able to talk a little.

It was late. They were muffled against the freezing wind, holding on to one another like a couple of ancient invalids. They were intending to climb into the park and walk through a wooded area, but as they approached they heard sirens. In the distance an ambulance skidded across the street and flashed through red traffic lights. Then there were fire engines and police cars. A pall of smoke rose in the air.

They walked around the outside of the park, looking for a place to get over. But as others came out of their houses and started up the street, they pulled their coats and scarves tighter and, full of foreboding, waded toward the nightmare.

There was a police line. Three fire engines were there. Firemen were spraying water into a smashed shop-window. It was a bookshop they'd visited recently. Some staff members had arrived and were arguing with the police, but they refused to let them near. Shahid heard one policeman saying the forensic department had already started to sort through the debris. Everything had to be left as it was.

Deedee, hugging herself and trembling, asked an old man if he knew what had happened. He said it had been a petrol bomb. The shop had been attacked by fanatics, he reckoned. After all, the attempt hadn't been to steal from the shop—what would anyone do with a load of books?—but to destroy it.

The man said, "I heard some awful screaming."

"How come?" Shahid asked. "Was there someone in the shop?"

The man shook his head. "There was a strong wind. They threw the first petrol bomb and it went through the window. The second one blew up in his face. The others tried to put it out but the boy had his hands and face on fire. What could anyone do? When the police came, they ran away. The kid won't last long, I shouldn't think, with those injuries."

Deedee pulled her scarf over her mouth and nose, so that only her eyes were visible. They stood there a while longer. But there was nothing to see now.

They would go away.

He awoke earlier than they had agreed. It was dark outside. He persuaded himself to vacate the warm bed, and dressed hurriedly. It was as if he were missing something important. This morning there was much he wanted to do.

In the kitchen he made a pot of coffee and thought he might sit at the table until the garden got light. But after a few minutes he returned to her bedroom and snapped on her reading lamp, setting his cup on the desk. If he disturbed her, she could always send him out. Among unmarked essays, letters, and newspaper clippings he found a fountain pen with a decent nib, and began to write with concentrated excitement. He had to find some sense in his recent experiences; he wanted to know and understand. How could anyone confine themselves to one system or creed? Why should they feel they had to? There was no fixed self; surely our several selves melted and mutated daily? There had to be innumerable ways of being in the world. He would spread himself out, in his work and in love, following his curiosity.

She awoke pleased to see him. While she washed her hair and dressed, he ran to the supermarket. For breakfast they had kippers, with grilled mushrooms and tomatoes.

He helped her pack for the weekend. They pulled out books and threw tapes into a bag and quibbled over what to take. When at last they left, she was wearing an ankle-length red overcoat with a black velvet collar, with a short black skirt underneath, and a round tartan cap. They bought three papers at the end of the street, two serious and one tabloid, and took a cab to his place because it wasn't the sort of day to wait for the bus.

They went upstairs apprehensively, but there was no sign of Riaz or the others. Shahid changed and packed some clothes, notepads, and books. He didn't feel safe in the room, he would have to get out, but he wasn't going to think about it now. When they were leaving he put his ear to Riaz's door. There was silence.

The took the tube to Victoria and bought tickets. The train was waiting and they sat opposite one another by the window. Soon they pulled away across the bridge, with the power station to one side, and Battersea Park with its gold peace pagoda on the other. He opened the papers. Two of them reported both the book-burning and the attack on the shop, in which Chad had been badly injured. After this he didn't feel like reading anymore; she put the papers away, and they sat and looked at one another.

He didn't know what would become of any of them; but for himself he'd be with her. He'd take what she offered; he'd give her what he could. He had never relied on anyone before.

They would spend the weekend in the cheap bed-and-breakfasts of a seaside town, walking on the wet beach, lying wrapped up like pensioners in deck chairs on the pier, scoffing crab sandwiches, oysters, and rock candy, and keeping out of the rain in pubs; or they'd waste money in amusement arcades. Any Victorian wax museums they wouldn't miss. The afternoons they'd spend in bed and get up at five for a drink and have another at five-thirty. They would talk everything over until they were sick of it.

On Monday they would take the train to visit Shahid's mother. He could use her car and drive Deedee around the places where he had grown up. He would have to explain that Chili had serious problems and that they'd have to count him out of the business for a while, but that there was a chance he'd return. By Monday night he and Deedee would be back in London.

This was more than sufficient; in fact he could have cheered, particularly when she announced that she'd got tickets for the Monday Prince concert. After, there'd be a private party in a King's Cross warehouse, which someone in the record company had obtained for her.

She pulled a bottle of wine from her bag, opened it and took out two tumblers. She poured the wine, passed it over, and they smiled and touched glasses. She drank hers down and poured another; then he drank his and did the same.

He looked out of the window; the air outside seemed to be clearer. It wouldn't be long before they were walking down to the sea. There was somewhere she fancied for lunch. He didn't have to think about anything. They looked across at one another as if to say, what new adventure is this?

"Until it stops being fun," she said.

"Until then," he said.